Praise for *The Mountain Walks*, the new PEACE COMPANY novel by Roland J. Green

"THE BEST NEW MILITARY SF SERIES SINCE DRAKE'S *HAMMER'S SLAMMERS* . . . Anyone who enjoys good fiction with *real* people between the pages will want to read *The Mountain Walks*."

—John F. Carr,
co-author of *Great Kings' War*

"IT'S A WINNER . . . The finest Peacekeepers book yet. Filled with crackling action!"

—Melinda M. Snodgrass, author of *Circuit, Circuit Breaker* and *Final Circuit*

"FIRST-RATE MILITARY FICTION by a writer who knows his subject matter . . . These are realistic tales of real people living life in wartime."

—John Maddox Roberts,
author of *Conan the Champion*

ROLAND J. GREEN

Roland J. Green is the author of the *Wandor Chronicles*, creator of the *Peace Company*, and co-author of *Jamie the Red*, *Great Kings' War* and *Janissaries III: Storms of Victory.*

"ROLAND GREEN is the only person I know who knows more about the military than I do."

—Jerry Pournelle,
bestselling author of *Footfall*

Ace Books by Roland J. Green

PEACE COMPANY
THESE GREEN FOREIGN HILLS
THE MOUNTAIN WALKS

JAMIE THE RED (with Gordon R. Dickson)
GREAT KINGS' WAR (with John F. Carr)
JANISSARIES: CLAN AND CROWN (with Jerry E. Pournelle)
JANISSARIES III: STORMS OF VICTORY (with Jerry E. Pournelle)

A PEACE COMPANY NOVEL

THE MOUNTAIN WALKS

BY ROLAND J. GREEN

ACE BOOKS, NEW YORK

This book is an Ace original
edition, and has
never been previously published.

THE MOUNTAIN WALKS

An Ace Book/published by arrangement with
the author

PRINTING HISTORY
Ace edition/September 1989

Cover art by Les Edwards.

ISBN:0-441-65742-7
Ace Books are published by The Berkley Publishing Group,
200 Madison Avenue, New York, New York 10016.

PRINTED IN THE UNITED STATES OF AMERICA

10 9 8 7 6 5 4 3 2 1

DRAMATIS PERSONAE

A. The Peace Force

LIEUTENANT COLONEL THOMAS BLAIR—X.O., Peace Force Expeditionary Battalion Fourteen (formerly Company Group 14).

CORPORAL JOHN BREZEK—Supply Company, Battalion Fourteen.

CAPTAIN DANIEL COOPER—C.O., Peace Cruiser *Ark Royal.*

CAPTAIN SONDRA DALLIN—C.O., Transportation Company, Battalion Fourteen.

CORPORAL JOSEPH DIETSCH—Headquarters, Battalion Fourteen.

COMMANDER MARIE DUBIGNON—X.O., Peace Cruiser *Ark Royal.*

MASTER SERGEANT PAUL DUBNICK—C.O., 3 Platoon, Third Company, Battalion Fourteen.

MAJOR GENERAL JEANPIERRE DUCHAMP—C.O., Zauberberg Expeditionary Force, replacing Van Doorn.

FIRST LIEUTENANT KATHERINE FORBES-BRANDON—Naval Liaison Officer, Battalion Fourteen.

ARTHUR GOFF—Mediator, Battalion Fourteen.

SERGEANT FIRST CLASS MICHAEL GUSLENKO—Transportation Company, Battalion Fourteen.

VICE ADMIRAL PAUL KLEIN—Senior Naval Officer, Zauberberg Expeditionary Force.

CAPTAIN VIKTOR KLIN—C.O., Fourth Company, Battalion Fourteen.

BRIGADIER GENERAL SOEMU KUROKI—C.O., 8th Brigade, Peace Force.

MAJOR GEORGE KUZIK—C.O., Support Squadron, Battalion Fourteen.

CAPTAIN MARIAN LAUGHTON—Medical Officer, Battalion Fourteen.

SERGEANT MAJOR MARIA CAMILLA DI LEONE ("Dozer")—Support Squadron First, Battalion Fourteen.

BRIGADIER GENERAL KIRSTEN LINDHOLM—Chief of Staff to Zauberberg Expeditionary Force.

SERGEANT MAJOR LASZLO McKENDRICK—Field Squadron First, Battalion Fourteen.

LIEUTENANT COLONEL DAVID MacLEAN—C.O., Battalion Fourteen.

FIRST LIEUTENANT LARS MAGNUSSON—Supply Company, Battalion Fourteen.

SERGEANT MAJOR JOHN B. PARKES ("Fruit Merchant")—Group First, Battalion Fourteen.

CAPTAIN ANDREAS PODGREBIN—C.O., Third Company, Battalion Fourteen.

MAJOR MARCIA REINHARDT—C.O., Transportation Company, P.F. Expeditionary Battalion Five.

FIRST LIEUTENANT LEONARD SHARPE—X.O., Third Company, Battalion Fourteen.

LIEUTENANT COMMANDER WILLIAM TEGEN—Computer intelligence officer of *Ark Royal*.

ELIZABETH ("Betsy") TYNDALL—Younger sister of Sergeant Patricia Tyndall, K.I.A. on Bayard in PEACE COMPANY.

MAJOR JESUS DESIDERIO VELA—C.O., Field Squadron, Battalion Fourteen.

B. The Zauberbergers, Friend and Foe

CAPTAIN MARIUS ABRAMS—Officer, Triple Federation Security Police.

FRIEDRICH BAHR—Associate Professor of Geology/Vulcanology, University of Nordshaven.

THE VERY REVEREND MONSIGNOR MARIA BIANCHERI—Chancellor of the New Catholic Archdiocese of Zauberberg.

RODOLFO BIANCHERI—Maria's brother, Chairman of the Department of Geology, University of Nordshaven.

BISHOP KARL HEINREID—Bishop of Nordshaven.

HIKO—Senior Team Leader among the Game Master's Teams on Zauberberg.

JAMISHIR SINGH—Member, Hiko's team.

ANGELO CARDINAL PARONA—Cardinal-Archbishop and Primate of Zauberberg.

RUTH SWORN-TO-DO-BATTLE-FOR-THE-LORD—Company Commander in the First Daughters, Protectorate Army.

JUDITH RYAN—Platoon Commander in Ruth's company.

Glossary

AA—Antiaircraft

A.A.C.—Armored Amphibious Carrier

A.D.—Air Defense

A.D.C.—Air Defense Company

A.F.V.—Armored Fighting Vehicle

A.G.—Air Group

A.O.—Area of Operations

A.P.C.—Armored Personnel Carrier

ASAT—Antisatellite

C.O.—Commanding Officer

C.P.—Command Post

C.W.—Chemical Warfare

D.I.—Drill Instructor

D.O.W.—Died of Wounds

D.Z.—Drop Zone

E.C. 6—Explosive Compound 6

E.C.M.—Electronic Countermeasures

E.I.—Electronic Interception

E.T.A.—Estimated Time of Arrival

F.A.C.—Forward Air Controller

F.A.F.—Federal Air Force

F.A.O.—Forward Artillery Observer

F.L.C.—Fuel/Lubricants/Chemicals (three classes of liquid supplies)

H.E.—High explosive

HQ—Headquarters

I.C.—Incendiary Compound

I.F.F.—Identification, Friend/Foe

IR—Infrared

L.A.V.—Light Armored Vehicle

L.M.G.—Light Machine Gun

M.I.—Military Intelligence

M.I.A.—Missing in Action

M.I.R.V.—Multiple Independently Targeted Reentry Vehicle

N.L.—Naval Liaison

N.M.M.—Nuovo Milano Military (the city's principal air base)

O.P.—Observation Post

P.F.C.—Peace Force Command

Q.R.—Quick Reaction

R.H.I.P.—"Rank Hath Its Privileges"

R.P.V.—Remotely Piloted (drone) Vehicle

S.O.P.—Standard Operating Procedure

T.F.—Task Force

T.O.T.—Time on Target (artillery tactic causing all the shells of a unit's salvo to arrive simultaneously)

V.F.—Vertical Flight

V.I.F.—Vectoring in Flight (using vertical lift for maneuvering in combat)

X.O.—Executive Officer

Prologue

"RANGE SIXTEEN HUNDRED meters, Team Leader."

The man so addressed stared into the IR scope. The image of a six-wheeled patrol car was sharp and solid. On the north shore of the Triple Federation, major heat sources stood out even on a summer night.

Zauberberg was listed as "habitable." Anything more would have stretched language unreasonably.

"They're moving at standard cruise," the Team Leader said. He called himself Hiko. He no longer resented being called by the title of his oldest friend and battle comrade, now only organic compounds in the gray seas of Bayard. To many, including the Game Master, what he did here on Zauberberg was more important than who he was.

"Launcher ready," said a voice from behind the next boulder.

"Fire on my command only," Hiko said. He ignored a cough from behind that might have been a comment. He lacked command authority over the local guerrillas. However, if they were free to ignore his orders he was free to ignore their opinions.

The Federal Security Police were much hated, not unjustly. Their day of reckoning would come. Tonight Hiko would not risk discovery of the arms shipment to strike down one car and three men.

The rangefinder showed 1,200 meters when the car slowed. Without stopping, it turned off the seaward side of the road, onto the slope leading to the beach.

The car commander knew his business. The moment he'd grown suspicious, he'd made himself a more difficult target while heading for the beach. The Team and the guerrillas had been careful to erase their tracks as thoroughly as possible. A keen eye would still make out the signs of their passage in the sand.

Now, was the commander good enough to have memorized

the ground here? Halfway to the landing site, the road dipped so that its crest no longer hid a vehicle on the beach. For a stretch of three hundred meters the car would be exposed—and a patch of phosphorescence halfway along the stretch would silhouette it handsomely.

"Shift to IR, Team Leader?" came the gunner's voice.

"No." With a line-of-sight shot, laser guidance was more accurate and allowed a shorter flight time. IR would make sense only if the car stopped before reaching the open stretch of beach, hidden behind the road.

Instead the car rolled steadily out into view, weaving visibly, slow enough for both a visual and an IR scan of the beach. Hiko looked to right and left, and snarled, "Down!" A few guerrillas had risen from cover to get a better view of three hated policemen dying. They'd either forgotten or never learned that a human body had a detectable IR signature. If the car's detectors happened to scan inland—

The men returned to cover with an appalling amount of noise. The car was out of pickup range and the wind was from the sea, anyway, but noise discipline needed improving, too. Hiko decided he could do without command authority over the guerrillas, if he could just put their leaders through a basic infantry course—thirty Standard days could be enough.

The car was approaching the phosphorescence. A few seconds more and the missile's homer wouldn't have two distinct light sources to confuse it—

"Illuminate!"

The car sprang sharply into view.

"Fire!"

The cold-gas cartridge kicked the missile ten meters from the launcher. The rocket motor ignited, its backblast warm on Hiko's cheek even at that distance. The missile dipped, then raced for its target.

At the order to illuminate, the Team's E.C.M. man had started jamming the standard police bands. Even an automatic frequency-switching alarm would take time to work.

The missile gave the car no time. It followed the laser beam straight into the lower hull, in spite of the nonreflective coating. Pieces of run-flat tire sprayed into the air, then the car's power pack began an explosive discharge. The blue-white electrical glow lit the beach from the water's edge to the road.

The orange glare of ammunition going off, one big bang followed by a series of smaller ones. The car rolled over, another heavy explosion hurled the turret into the surf, and a flaming human body followed it. Then silence, except for the last few rounds of ammunition cooking off and the guerrillas rising from cover.

The guerrillas were slapping the launcher crew on the back when Hiko ended the celebration. "Barin," he called to the guerrilla leader. "Best load up and move out fast. I don't think they got through on the radio, but somebody might be close enough to see the fire."

"True. But we ought to escort you to your rendezvous first. It is the least we can do for you."

"We're going to have to stay close to the shore. Our best protection is to stay a small party. Besides, any men you sent with us would have a long walk home, part of it in daylight."

"They are strong. Also, they can find friends."

"I don't doubt they can find friends. But do you want to endanger those friends now, when they can't be protected from the police? As for their strength—better to save it for work that has to be done. Eighty individual infantry kits isn't a light load."

"There is sense in that. Very well. You have our thanks. When a better time comes, you will have more."

"In the Cause, Barin."

"In the Cause, Team Leader."

Hiko hand-signaled his radio operator to transmit a coded change of rendezvous. It was nearly three minutes before they received the acknowledgment. By then the guerrillas were well into slinging the fifty-kilo loads, and some had already moved out. They moved fast, if noisily and in no sort of tactical formation. But then, farming here in the north of the Triple Federation hardened the muscles if it did nothing else.

Hiko's Team formed into its four squads as the last guerrillas vanished into the darkness in the south. In five more minutes, the Team was heading west.

They'd covered six of the nine kilometers to the new rendezvous before Hiko allowed a break. In the shelter of a straggling grove of salt chestnut, he even allowed smoking. They'd been crammed like weedfish aboard the boat for two days; the trip home would probably be longer. The boat not only had to keep its passengers below deck but steer a course that would look natural to enemy observers.

These would probably be airborne, not orbital. The Federal Ministry of the Interior would be hauling in most of the satellites in another week or two, as the Thorshammer Shower climbed toward peak activity. The Federal Air Force would try to compensate, and with a Peace Force Tactical Air Group already landing at Nuovo Milano—

"Team Leader?"

"Yes, Jamshir?"

"Would you have truly let the car go on if it had not become suspicious?"

"Of course."

Hiko could hear a puzzled frown in Jamshir's reply. Either the man was genuinely curious, or he was a fine actor. He seemed rather old to be asking such naive questions, but old in years did not mean old in military experience.

"Did we not need to encourage our allies?" Jamshir added.

"We did. It would not have encouraged them, to bring the police down on them by an unnecessary fight. As it was, we had to buy time, by destroying the car before it could send a message. Now it will have to be missed before anyone comes searching. Even then, they may suspect a large force and move cautiously."

"Time is a great gift."

"Yes, to those who use it wisely." Uncertain of Jamshir's discretion, Hiko said nothing about the guerrillas' poor combat-readiness. If Protectorate M.I. or the Master's Representative didn't know enough about that already, he could hardly influence them. More likely, they would see him as lacking confidence in their allies—who were important enough to the Cause to be worth handling delicately.

Jamshir began softly chanting the prayer to Kali, that she might consider herself honored by tonight's deaths. Hiko unwrapped a piece of hard candy and sucked on it. It might be consoling to believe that the hand of some Higher Power was over you, sixty-five light-years from Earth, to judge and protect, reward and punish.

Hiko had no such consolation. He had abandoned the gods of Shinto with his youth, and never turned to Kali or Allah. What remained was a faith in the wisdom of *ninjitsu*, perhaps younger but surely more real than any gods.

More recently, he'd developed a faith in the wisdom of fighting in the company of allies. That came after Bayard, when the Game Master sent his men beyond the solar system for the first time, to play a lone hand against the Peace Force on Bayard. Seven Team men of the thirty who reached Bayard left it alive.

1

IN THE EAST, the sky still held the green of sunset. Toward the zenith the green faded into the purple blackness of the Zauberberg night. Silver-gold against the dark, a trail of fire arced downward, to vanish in the sunset.

Angelo Cardinal Parona stared at the fading fire trail. Meteor, cargo pod (and if so, Peace Force or civilian?), perhaps even a satellite knocked from orbit by a meteor strike? He would learn nothing useful staring into the darkening sky.

A tap on the control plate, and the window irised shut. He turned back into the library, watched the dance of light on the fireplace's copper reflector, then adjusted gas flow and humidity.

When Parona found himself adjusting the dust precipitators, he disciplined himself. He did not want to face the two people standing with their backs to the shelf of bound volumes, or the crisis that had brought them to him. Duty demanded otherwise. Duty as a cardinal of the Church, duty as a citizen of the planet of Zauberberg.

"Sit down," he said. "We may be here for a while."

"Thank you, Your Eminence," Bishop Heinreid said. The chancellor of the archdiocese, Maria Biancheri, merely smiled. As she sat down, light played on the brandy in her glass. The brandy was nearly the same color as her hair.

Parona clasped his hands behind his back and looked at a space between the chancellor and the bishop. "The Ministry of the Interior has decided to proceed as usual. They will begin withdrawing the planet-watch satellites next week. They expect that any lost surveillance capacity can be made up by the Peace Force satellites."

"How many of those will there be, and how soon?" the chancellor asked. Her voice betrayed nothing; the long fingers tightening on the stem of her glass were eloquent.

"The minister either would not tell me or did not know himself. They will be armored, of course, and the battle stations will be capable of self-defense."

"No doubt. They also say that the Thorshammer Shower will be at a two-hundred-year peak this time. I would expect that the two systems combined would be just barely enough."

"Enough for what, Chancellor?" said Parona.

"Enough to watch for a Brotherhood invasion!" she snapped, as if speaking to a slow-witted child.

The bishop raised a hand in protest. The chancellor turned to him. "Don't keep me from bringing it into the open, please. If the wolves are on the prowl, your flock is the first they'll fall on!"

If an invasion was coming across the Great North Bay, it certainly would strike Heinreid's See of Nordshaven first. *If.* Was Maria trying to shock her audience, or had she learned something they had not? Parona remembered that her nickname of *La Strega*—the Witch—came as much from her uncanny insight as from her sharp tongue.

"What makes you expect an invasion? More guerrilla action, certainly. But in the face of a Peace Force expedition . . . ?"

"The Peace Force is sending the Air Group, an air-defense battalion, and two—what were Company Groups until early this year. Now they're 'Expeditionary Battalions.' That's all."

"How did you learn that, if I might ask?"

The cardinal's tone would have discouraged withholding information, if his reputation had not. Clerical intriguers had for many years found that Parona's wrath might not last as long as God's but struck considerably faster.

"The advocate-chief of the Ministry of Defense was a law school classmate of mine. We've kept in touch. We had dinner together two nights ago. He was complaining about how little help he would have from the Ministry of Justice, if Peace Force and Security Police legal codes clashed. I lent a sympathetic ear, and he filled it."

The old classmate had a right to complain. The Ministry of Justice was notoriously under the thumb of the Ministry of the Interior. Otherwise the Security Police could never have been allowed to become so nearly a law unto themselves. They had not begun that way, but after a few dozen cases of excessive force and unauthorized arrest or confiscation had gone unpunished, the scum rose quickly to the surface.

"Two battalions are still enough to repel any invasion the Brotherhood could launch, I should think."

"Perhaps. Kept together and supported by a partial mobilization, probably. But I don't think they're going to be used that way, at least not until it's too late. I never did think so, and now I'm almost sure."

"Why?"

"The satellites! Interior wouldn't be pulling them down if they didn't think matters would remain quiet."

"Or at least at a level where the Security Police are expected to handle them," put in Heinreid. The chancellor seemed torn between indignation at the interruption and surprise at the bishop's support. Parona sensed no gratitude in her.

"A mobilization, of course, would serve notice that the situation is far from normal," Parona said, by way of prompting.

"Exactly. As it is, the two battalions are supposed to be split up into task forces, to support the Security Police. The Security Police will move onto the north shore in force and eradicate the guerrillas. They'll search every hill and valley, then start on the houses. They'll be as clumsy and cruel as usual.

"Then the Brotherhood will have to act. They'll lose all credibility with their friends in the Triple Federation if they don't. If they act fast enough, they'll find both the Peace Force and the Security Police exposed to defeat in detail. The Army won't be mobilized, and the Air Force will have to rely on the Peace Force satellite system!"

It made a nightmarish picture. Not an implausible one, either. The great barrier to a Brotherhood invasion had always been the futility of grabbing territory from the Federation. Now they might see a chance to win everything they needed without the encumbering inconvenience of conquered territory to administer.

Parona cleared his throat. "You have described a danger. Very convincingly, I might add. What do you suggest we do about it?"

"Lay the matter before the Chamber of Delegates. The government is letting Interior define the whole crisis. That is leaving the flock to the care of a dog who may refuse to bark because he thinks he can fight all the wolves himself! Nothing could be more stupid!"

"The fact that we believe it is stupid will not make it so in the eyes of the Anti-Clericals," Heinreid said briskly. "If the government does listen to us, they will withdraw their support.

That is at least thirteen votes in the Chamber, and the government's majority is only seven. Throw in the five or six votes of Brotherhood sympathizers, and the government would fall the day after it granted us a hearing."

"Then at least we'd save the satellites!"

"Would you rather have us with satellites and no government than with a government and no satellites?"

"Are you that lacking in compassion for your flock, Your Grace?"

Parona cleared his throat again, this time as a warning. He had to try three times before he produced more than a wheeze. By then the chancellor and the bishop were glaring at each other, very much like the dog and wolf of the chancellor's image.

Parona nodded to Heinreid. "I am not lacking in compassion for my flock," the bishop said. "I merely remind you that the satellites cannot mobilize the Army or feed and house refugees. If we kill the government trying to cure it, the Ministry of the Interior will be among the least affected. The Ministry of Social Services, on the other hand, will be unable to carry on more than routine business.

"Meanwhile, the refugees will be flooding into Nordshaven. I know that five hundred have already come, in the ten days since the bombing at Livo and the church burnings at Krakenheim and Ropi. They are only the first, mostly children and old folk sent in to stay with relatives.

"What happens when those who have lost everything but their faith and the clothes on their backs come to us? Will we be able to answer to God and our consciences if we have crippled the very machinery intended to stand between them and beggary?"

Heinreid was now speaking as passionately as the chancellor. He had learned eloquence in urban missions, she in the courts before she found her vocation. Both had learned it well.

Parona held up a hand for silence. Tragedy, he'd heard it said, was the conflict of good and good. He had that here, for both the chancellor's boldness and the bishop's caution made sense.

Heinreid made more, Parona decided. He had to admit that he was also being influenced by his housekeeper's request for leave, the first since her father died and only the third in her twenty-eight years of service. Her brother was sending his wife, wife's mother, and three children into Nordshaven. They would need help; could she go north for a few days?

"For the next few days, at least, we shall hold our tongues

and open our hands,'' Parona said. ''Karl, draw up a plan for handling as many refugees as you think we can expect. Maria, help him in every way you can. I'm sure that together you can find a solution that will neither bankrupt the archdiocese nor starve the refugees.''

The use of first names said that this was a favor he asked of friends as well as an order he gave subordinates. They were both, and Maria might have been more if they'd met while she was still a lawyer and he had not yet sworn his final vows of celibacy.

They both knelt and kissed his ring, an unasked gesture he knew was a peace offering as well as a sign of respect. The bishop rose first. The chancellor remained kneeling as the door closed behind her colleague. Parona saw that she was trying not to weep.

''Maria, I know as well as you what might come of this. But perhaps the government is not wholly composed of men too foolish to know it also.''

''Is there anything we can do except pray that is so?''

''Not for a few days. But if neither of us believes in the power of prayer, then perhaps we wear these collars and robes under false pretenses.''

She rose. ''I think we also believe in not leaving too much to God. But I will obey.''

''Thank you, Maria.''

Alone, Parona turned back to the window. It irised open on a sky grown completely dark. In spite of the double-glazing, the window now exuded a chill that made him draw back.

''Let God's will be done.''

An easy thing to say, if one was presumptuous enough to believe that one knew God's will. All Parona presumed was to believe that it was God's will for humanity to use His gift of intelligence to get out of the troubles that same gift often got them into.

Fortunately both bishop and chancellor agreed with him there. He would not have to discipline Biancheri, and risk losing her invaluable administrative skills and political insight. Nor would he have to submit a disciplining of Heinreid to the Standing Conclave on Freiheim, a body notoriously uncharitable toward archbishops who couldn't keep order in their own houses.

Of course, chancellor and bishop would need to make a more enduring peace before their archbishop retired. That could not be delayed indefinitely; at sixty-nine Standard/fifty-two Zauberberg, old age was staring Parona in the face. So far he'd been able to stare it down, but that could not last forever. A time would come when he had to ask the Conclave to either ratify Heinreid as his successor or appoint one themselves.

He'd prayed often to have more than those two choices, but that prayer hadn't been answered. Zauberberg hadn't thrown up anyone he could reasonably nominate over Heinreid's head. It also hadn't resolved enough of its religious, political, or economic problems to make it safe to bring in someone from outside.

Parona added a prayer for his own continued good health, and decided it was time to end this long day. A small glass of brandy, half an hour with one of the bound volumes—*Moby Dick* in English, he decided—and then a warm bed.

2

THE LOUDSPEAKER OVER the control tower door crackled and spat like bacon fat in a campfire.

"*Ark* Three to N.M.M. Tower, we have a problem."

Lieutenant Katherine Forbes-Brandon saw Captain Sondra Dallin's head jerk and swivel.

"Here." She handed Dallin her binoculars. Dallin had just started to focus them when the loudspeaker began a rapid exchange.

"Tower to *Ark* Three, repeat your last."

"Tower, I said we have a problem. Fire warning in number two jet engine."

"*Ark* Three, we'll give you a visual scan. It may be a faulty—no, sorry. We've got you, and there's definitely smoke. We'll enhance and try to locate it more precisely."

"Thanks, Tower, but we've already got it located. It's by the fuel feed. We're purging the line and turning on the extinguisher."

More bacon fat, conversation too low to reveal words, and an unmistakable expletive. Dallin scanned the horizon with the binoculars.

"Who's on board?" Forbes-Brandon asked.

"Just Thanh and a co-pilot. They're loaded to the limit."

More low conversation, then:

"The fire isn't going out." Thanh's voice remained cool, like a surgeon recording the results of a biopsy. "I think we must have taken a meteoritic impact during reentry. At max stress it might not have registered, but the heat and buffeting could have finished the job."

"*Ark* Three, we recommend that you jettison your cargo. We are clearing all runways and scrambling the crash crews."

"We appreciate that, Tower, but negative on the jettison. Our load is ammunition. We're already over the coast."

"What the—!" said the loudspeaker and the two officers together. Ammunition and fuel were transported in manned shuttles only in emergencies. If there was such an emergency, why hadn't Expeditionary Battalion Fourteen's Naval Liaison and Transportation officers been told about it?

"Ah, Tower." Thanh sounded more disturbed by the prospect of an argument than by the emergency. "I don't have time to go into details. I'm going to turn onto a heading of 260. That should stretch the glide at least into the Sangerwald, maybe out to sea again. Then I can jettison—that's an order, Lieutenant Killian!—and use the rockets to set up for a deadstick to the field. *Ark* Three, out."

"Doesn't sound like Killian wants to jump," Forbes-Brandon said. She knew she was talking in order not to break into a cold sweat. Dallin's back might have been carved in marble. Only her white knuckles and a tic in her left cheek betrayed her.

"There," Dallin said. "Under that patch of cloud." Squinting, Forbes-Brandon made out the flash of sunlight on metal.

The next few minutes would be critical. With only one jet operating, a fully loaded shuttle couldn't go around for a second pass if it missed the first time. Thanh would also be reluctant to fire up even the undamaged engine; the extra vibration could worsen marginal damage.

With a load of construction material or rations, Thanh could still have come in. He wouldn't be risking anything except the shuttle and its two pilots. Thirty tons of ammunition could wipe out a good chunk of Nuovo Milano Military Field.

If he could turn and stretch his glide far enough, he could dump the cargo where it would hurt nothing except trees and fish. If the shuttle was still in the air then, it would be light enough to handle on one jet. Even if he still didn't want to risk the jets, he could use the last of the rocket fuel to turn back toward the field, then make a deadstick landing.

"Come on," Dallin said. Her jaw muscles jerked and her forehead developed a crone's wrinkles. "Come on. Come on." She sounded as if the words could conjure up a giant hand to ease the shuttle safely down.

"There. He's coming up on his turning point. He's—"

"Damn," said the loudspeaker and Dallin together.

What else they might have said was drowned out by the deafening roar coming over the loudspeaker. It cut off, and the two officers stared in silence at the expanding fireball where Shuttle Three had been.

The crash alarm began to wail. The rescue verti lifted off, fire-fighting ball slung under its fuselage. The crash crew wouldn't find anything, of course. At least for Thanh and Killian, it had been quick. Not like Hugo Opperman's long, slow dying, as his rock-crushed internal organs gave up the struggle one by one . . .

Forbes-Brandon swallowed. "Let's get something hot, and a bite to eat. What do they drink here, tea or coffee?"

"Coffee or some local weed that tastes—that tastes—sorry." Dallin pressed both hands to her eyes and shook for a moment.

"I am going to have somebody's *cojones* barbecued for that load of ammunition! If there was an emergency and I wasn't told—"

"If it was an emergency, the *cojones* may belong to somebody fairly senior," Forbes-Brandon said.

"Is this a time to go by rank and rule book, damn it?"

"No. I just wanted to remind you—"

"Don't remind me! Either help me or shut the hell up!"

"I'm on your side, Sonny. The order must have gone straight up to *Ark Royal* just before they started loading. Somebody up there may be willing to answer a few questions."

"Sorry, Kat. I—well, Thanh was an old friend. He's got a wife and three kids and a handful of relatives back on New Frontier. He was all set to go on driving shuttles there until his term was up, but I painted a really sexy picture of ship duty. He volunteered, and now . . ."

Forbes-Brandon put an arm around her shoulders. "He might have volunteered, anyway. Or he might have been transferred. They're doing a lot of that these days."

She didn't add that "they"—Peace Force Command—were probably only just beginning the process of adding muscle to the ships and field units. Olympus Machinery, the family firm, was a major defense contractor. Their sources of intelligence were well ahead of what P.F.C. had so far chosen to tell the combat swine.

Everyone knew that fifty thousand uniformed personnel were to be added to the Peace Force over the next four years. It was known but not discussed that most of these and a good many people already on the strength were going into the field.

What even Forbes-Brandon didn't know was what all this muscle was going to *do*. She suspected that she had a lot of company, including most of Peace Force Command. Was somebody afraid of a situation like the one on Terra that led to the Collapse War of 2084? It couldn't be that bad now; humanity was spread across seventy-five planets instead of one homeworld and a score of colonies. Also, statesmen had learned *something* from the death of two-thirds of Earth's population.

Hadn't they?

Forbes-Brandon had always hoped so. It was one of the reasons she'd joined the Navy, or at least the most important reason she was willing to discuss.

She hadn't lost those youthful hopes. What she had lost was any belief that racial survival took the sting out of personal death.

A second verti droned overhead, one of Fourteen's lights with podded guns. Cover for the rescue crew, but against whom? Surely the guerrillas hadn't been reported here, thirty kilometers from the largest city on Zauberberg?

If they had, that was another thing she and Dallin hadn't been told. Forbes-Brandon decided that she was going to be rather bloody-minded if the higher-ups continued to treat her like a mushroom—kept in the dark, fed on manure, and cut off if she got too big.

Maybe she and Dallin could collaborate on the *cojones*-barbecuing. Meanwhile, it was only an hour to the Command Group briefing, which she was not going to face on an empty stomach.

"Come on, Sonny. I've got some tea in my gear, and maybe we can bribe the cooks at the A.G. Officers' Mess to open early."

"You're on."

By the scale of the A.O. map display behind him, Mediator Arthur Goff's shoulders were 250 kilometers wide. They covered half the 500 kilometers of the north shore, from Nordshaven to the foot of the Great North Gulf. The 100 kilometers between the coast and the Serpent Mountains stretched from Goff's Adam's apple to the middle of his chest.

That 500-by-100 rectangle was where the Brotherhood guerrillas were operating. It was where the Federal Security Police were going after them, with Peace Force Expeditionary Battalions Fourteen and Seven holding their coats. Everything else on Zauberberg was theoretically irrelevant.

Theoretically. Sergeant Major John Parkes hadn't become a Battalion First by leaning too heavily on theory. There was no regulation against it, just the iron law of battlefield survival.

So he gave half his attention to parts of the map outside the A.O. and half of it to Arthur Goff's briefing on the internal politics of Zauberberg's armed forces. Either might tell him something he needed to know.

Northwest from Nordshaven stretched the 70 kilometers of the Teuffelberg Range—actually no more than the 6,000-meter Teuffelberg itself and its foothills. Parkes decided that territory really was of limited interest, since he was neither a rock climber nor a vulcanologist.

The southern edge of the map cut across the foot of Dietrich's Bay. In the ten years since Parkes's last assignment on Zauberberg, they'd finished the all-weather road around the inner shore of the bay. Now the road that crossed the mouth of the bay on the railroad bridge was no longer the only north-south route between Nordshaven and Nuovo Milano.

Farther west, the map cut just below the knuckle of the Kevo River, where it swerved sharply westward. The railroad now crossed the knuckle on a bridge, and the land between the Kevo and the Serpent Range had sprouted a few towns in the last ten years. Parkes wondered who the homesteaders were. If he'd been the government of Zauberberg, he'd have made very sure they were people who could safely be enrolled in the militia, to support the Army in holding the passes of the Serpent Range . . .

Goff flipped another page of notes onto the lectern. "Another factor reinforcing the barriers between the Army and the Security Police is their base of recruitment. The Army has been heavily recruited among the Italian-descended population. The Security Police are predominantly German and Finnish. The two latter groups appear to be influenced by the venerable stereotypes of the Italians as bumbling, if not cowardly, fighters."

A disgusting truth, but at least Goff was telling it. The mediator was no fool, even if he was a former professor of sociology. When he stumbled over a fact, he picked it up and looked at it, and hang the theories.

"I also suspect there's another division within the Security Police itself. They've expanded rapidly in the last eight years. Many of the new recruits and junior officers seem substantially less professional than the older cadre. I will defer to expert opinion as to how much trouble this may cause us, or what we can do to cure it while operating on Zauberberg."

Another fact! That was something that stuck out a kilometer when Parkes walked into the White Swan two nights ago. Once it had been a student hangout, where he and Denise had spent several agreeable evenings. Now it was unofficial HQ for the security types watching the university community. The old cadre and the younger toughs kept more strictly apart than faculty and students ever had.

Goff was looking a challenge at Major Vela, the Field Squadron C.O. He knew he was up at the lectern talking politics because Vela wanted to fill the time until Colonel MacLean appeared. No one knew what was holding up MacLean, which wasn't easing the tension that Parkes could practically smell.

Since Greenhouse, Company Group/Expeditionary Battalion Fourteen had spent ten Standard months in training and garrison and one month on alert for a return to Bayard that never materialized. The voyage to Zauberberg had been flawless, and the first twelve days on-planet freer of incident than any deployment Parkes could recall.

Then two good people died in a senseless accident. The Command Group were professionals; death didn't shock them. It did make them want an enemy to fight, or at least a bungler to blame.

Instead they were getting a political lecture.

Parkes was about to volunteer his own observations, to take Goff off the hook, when the door slid open.

"Attention!" Vela was rising before the word was halfway out of his mouth. Parkes and Lieutenant Forbes-Brandon were the first to join him.

"Thank you, people." Colonel MacLean stepped up to the lectern, returned the salutes, and motioned everybody back to their seats. Goff took his with the look of a man with dysentery who's sighted a vacant bathroom.

MacLean shrugged off his overcoat and hung it and his hat over the lectern. Above the sand-shot-with-gray beard, his cheeks were red from the chill breeze.

"I'm sorry to be so late. But every time I thought I'd finished my business, something new came in. I'm glad I waited, because it adds up to mostly good news.

"First, the order to land ammunition by manned shuttle came from General Van Doorn, under protest. He was under pressure from the Ministry of Defense, because they claimed the security of unmanned landings could not be guaranteed. I don't want this discussed outside the room, but I believe Defense is playing games. They want to discredit the Security Police or pressure the government to order a partial mobilization or both.

"The Defense representative seemed to be really shocked by the crash. Van Doorn and the battalion C.O.'s have proposed that in return for our following the order, the Feds accelerate our deployment. In the west, we can set up a secure area for unmanned drops south of the Serpents. In the east, we'll be using the Ponte d'Oro field, which has several safe approaches for jettisoning. If we get Fed cooperation, the worst that will happen is slowing down our ammunition buildup."

That could be bad enough, if something happened to make them need that ammunition in a hurry, and the loads had to be sent down from orbit through a meteor-ridden sky. *Leave it be, Parkes. Sergeant Majors don't get paid to take on lieutenant colonels' worries.*

"The rest is good news. Light cruiser *Robert the Bruce* will be joining us in ten days." That meant manned orbital support from a ship more expendable than *Ark Royal* or *Lexington*. Not that the big peace cruisers couldn't be expended in a major crisis, but a minor crisis could still kill good people without fire support from on high.

"Aboard *Bruce* is Major General Jeanpierre Duchamp, to assume the post of ComExFor." MacLean managed to stop at a grin. Several of the Command Group cheered out loud. "General Van Doorn will assume the post of Commander, Field Brigade.

"We're also getting two more Expeditionary Battalions, within thirty days. Two full brigades, one Peace Force and one Union planetary, have been put on deployment alert. The current estimate of the situation is that the Brotherhood won't move in force against the suppression of guerrillas in Triple Federation territory. Peace Force Command still wants to be in a position to retaliate against any harassment or terrorism.

"Finally, to aid us in our relations with the local forces, every officer on the ground and selected officers aboard ship are getting a one-step acting promotion. I'm sure you can all live with that prospect."

No cheers this time, but smiles all around. "Captain—excuse me, Major—Katsouros has complete intelligence and logistic updates in all media. I want everyone to study the updates and have their preliminary inputs to the deployment plan by 1030 tomorrow. Assume we want to be moving within eighty-one hours, and cut that if you can.

"Dismissed."

"Attention!" Vela snapped again. He led the salutes, holding his until MacLean was gone. Then he picked up the folder Katsouros handed him and led the exodus.

Parkes brought up the rear. He knew there was no point in talking with Dozer di Leone until she'd settled things with (now) Lieutenant Colonel Kuzik, Support Squadron C.O. His own personal responsibility, Battalion X.O. Lieutenant Colonel Tom Blair, was still aboard *Ark Royal*.

So how he was going to avoid looking lazy or stupid tomorrow morning was an interesting—

"Sergeant Major."

Parkes whirled as if he'd been on a battlefield, then saluted. "Sorry, sir. You startled me."

"I'm about to startle you some more," MacLean said. The sober face didn't match his light words. The C.O. went to the door and punched it shut, then turned back to Parkes.

"Sergeant Major, there's no provision for field promotions to Warrant rank. However, I am authorized to offer you a field commission as first lieutenant, effective as soon as you sign on the right line."

Indignation surged in Parkes. He wasn't even going to get to wait until tomorrow morning to look like an idiot!

Then the indignation passed. He had reasons for refusing. Now, if they just sounded like reasons instead of excuses to both MacLean and his conscience . . .

"Sir, I appreciate the offer. I've really been thinking the matter over, since we got home from Greenhouse. If it had come six months ago, I'd have probably said yes."

The words were out of his mouth before he realized that they were close to the truth. *Better not drop any hints to Dozer, or she'd start spending the winnings off her bet that he'd accept the next time they offered him a commission.*

MacLean said nothing. Natural tact, no doubt; he had that in spades. Also, he'd been private and N.C.O. for ten years before he took his own commission. He probably knew more than most field grades about the reasons for taking or not taking a commission—and how few of them might be the sort of thing you wanted to talk about.

"Right now, though—well, the X.O.'s new and so's the Field First. Blair's good, but most of his experience is staff."

Also, he didn't like Hrothmi or officers who'd served on Hrothma and got on well with the raccoon-like aliens. He wasn't going to remedy his lack of field experience by sitting down with Vela. The Field Squadron C.O. had done fifteen of his twenty-five years of soldiering with Hrothmi and thought they were the next thing to Grand Galactics.

The truth—but one of those truths too plain for an N.C.O. to lay before a field grade. Not to mention that MacLean probably already knew it.

"The thing is, sir, if I stay on as Battalion First, you've got more redundancy in the T.O."

"We already have that, with the extra rifle company and the air defense and scout components."

"Yes, sir. But you can't go robbing them of their senior N.C.O.'s."

"Tell me something that I don't know, or that I didn't know you knew, Parkes. You're saying what's right for the battalion. I don't want to ignore what's right for you."

"Sir, I may not know what's right for me. But with all due respect, I think you're even less likely to know it."

"Very well. I stand corrected. Any other reasons?"

"Yes, sir. It has to do with what Mediator Goff said about the split in the police ranks, the old cadres versus the new political appointees. I got to know some of the old guard fairly well when I was here ten years ago. Some of them have retired, but I can drop in on them even more easily than the ones still serving."

"Will they care if you're a sergeant major or a lieutenant?"

"They won't, probably. But the officers—don't they smell a little rank-happy to *you*, sir?"

MacLean frowned, as if the smell of rank-happiness resembled a field latrine's. Then he nodded.

"I thought so. Now, the officers can't really do anything to me. But they might make trouble for their people, even the retired ones. Then they'd shut up, not trust the P.F., and feel I'd betrayed friends to suck up to my own superiors.

"But if I'm just one more over-the-hill N.C.O. hoisting steins with a few of his own breed—well, what do you think?"

"I think that the day you're over the hill, I will be promoted to Peace Force C-in-C. However, I take your point. You can stay a sergeant major for the time being. I'll ask only one thing in return."

"Sir?"

"If Intelligence blows a fuse at your breaking their monopoly of covert work, don't expect me to save your ass single-handed!"

"Yes, sir."

3

HIKO ENDED HIS run along the shore while he still felt sure-footed. A bit of additional exercise wasn't worth the risk of a muscle-twisting or even bone-breaking fall on a patch of shingle.

While he did his cooling-down exercises, he scanned the area for a tidal pool for his final dip. The Great North Gulf lay ready a hundred meters away, but he knew its undertows too well. (Not as well as the Team rifleman whose drowning had taught his comrades, but what good was knowledge that could not be communicated? No scout ever sent back word from beyond Yasukuni, or wherever Dobu now found himself.)

The tidal pools were also warmer than the gulf itself. Ten years ago, Hiko would have thought it weak to consider this. But ten years ago, he could have endured the icy embrace of the gulf with no aftereffects. The passing years had made him more ready to accept the wisdom of the *sensei* who told him:

"The purpose of *ninjitsu* is not to strengthen your body until it will meet any demand you may place upon it. Its purposes are to strengthen your body to whatever limit it may have, and to teach you what those limits are so that you do not ask of your body more than it will give."

Hiko saw only one pool, too shallow for swimming. Continuing his exercises, he trotted slowly inland, toward a dune that should extend his vision half a kilometer in all directions.

He was at the foot of the dune before he realized that there was someone standing on top of it. He identified the figure in the same moment as he drew his pistol. It slipped back into its shoulder holster as he called.

"Hoaa, Sister Ruth! What brings you here?"

The tall woman on the ridge of the dune cupped her hands and shouted, "The Lord's will and my own strength. What else could there be?"

After that aggressively orthodox opening, Ruth strode down the face of the dune toward Hiko. He shifted to firmer ground and waited until she was close enough for normal conversation.

Ruth almost smiled as she stopped. "I awoke with the belief that it was the Lord's will I follow you today."

"I didn't make myself easy to follow."

"I knew that. It was also the Lord's will that I have the strength to do so. It became good training in tracking. To know more is to teach better."

"Blessed be the Teachers," Hiko said, with a piety for once not entirely assumed. "May they increase in numbers and wisdom." No fighting force ever had enough; the Army of the Protectorate of the Brotherhood of the Cause of the Lord was no exception.

"Indeed, I am sure you are greatly blessed even among Teachers," Ruth said. "Is there nothing you have learned lately, that you might teach me?"

"I doubt that I have much to teach one who commands a Company of the Daughters of the Lord Mighty in Battle."

"Not even what you learned in your most recent exercise with live ammunition?"

Hiko kept both face and voice expressionless. Was this a transparently clumsy effort to draw him out, about arms-landing mission? The Proctors cast their spy net far and wide, and where willing agents were lacking, coerced ones went into action.

Or was Ruth really trying to learn something that would help her be a better leader of her Company of Daughters when the Protectorate invaded the Triple Federation? That would be out of character for anyone presumably the soul of orthodoxy, but Hiko had known the demands of combat leadership to outweigh orthodoxy in less likely candidates than Ruth Sworn-to-Do-Battle-for-the Lord.

So assume that Ruth recognized him as a seasoned combat leader, suspected the raid, and wanted to hear him talk about it. Should he?

If he did, and the Proctors or any superior discovered it, both would suffer. Ruth would have been guilty of violating security, unholy curiosity, and unseemly consorting with a male. She would surely lose her company, and probably have to serve as a common soldier if she escaped a penal battalion.

Hiko might get off lightly if the Master's Representative intervened. The man might also value good relations with the Protectorate's religious hierarchy more than he did a Team Leader. Hiko would certainly have less freedom in training his Team, with the invasion day approaching as relentlessly as an avalanche.

It was not worth it—unless he could learn something from Ruth. She was, after all, the first opportunity the Master's Teams had to study the Daughters of the Lord at first hand. Not a small matter, when rumor said that two battalions of the Daughters would be part of the invasion force.

"Our exercises taught us something about the tactics of the Federal Security Police," Hiko said. "Whether it was something you don't already know, I can't be sure. Also, who can say whether we'll be opposing the police or the Federal Army?"

"Did you—exercise—on level ground? Not in the hills or the—shadow of the mountain?"

"On level ground."

"The Daughters have done the same."

The exchange of veiled hints went on until Hiko was satisfied that the Daughters weren't being trained to go ashore near the Teuffelberg, perhaps to surprise Nordshaven. He wasn't surprised, but he was relieved. Committing two battalions of first-line troops to even the most effective suicide mission was always a gamble. A direct attack over the rugged mountain country on the garrisoned Catholic city could be nothing else unless the Federation stood by with folded hands. It was good to know that the Protectorate's War Council wasn't stupid enough to expect that.

"You came prepared to teach, even though you did not know you would have a pupil," Ruth said finally. "The Lord's blessing is truly upon you. Would—would you be willing to teach more, after this pupil has meditated on what she most needs to learn?"

"How long were you thinking of meditating?" This might be the only chance they would have to talk freely; it would certainly be one of the best.

"An hour."

"Very well. I am going to go swimming, and meditate afterward. Perhaps we should meet back here in an hour?"

"With the Lord's favor, we shall."

Ruth vanished over the dune as if she was fleeing from a burning building. Hiko remembered too late the rigorous nudity taboos imposed on the Daughters—"to neither expose nor witness the exposure of sinful flesh."

As he headed toward the nearest deep pool, he wondered briefly how the Daughters would fare in combat without a concept of field modesty. From latrines to death itself, very little on the battlefield respected fear of being seen as nature made you.

No doubt those Daughters with their wits about them had worked out their own compromises. The whole Regiment of the Lord's Daughters was a compromise, between those who saw war as a sacred male monopoly and those who refused to let thousands of able-bodied young women go to waste in an underpopulated country. Forty years ago that compromise had brought the Daughters into existence, disciplined and effective in spite of the host of quaint and curious restrictions surrounding them.

Twenty years ago, a conservative reaction hadn't abolished the Daughters, but it had created the Proctors. They were the enforcers of the quaint and curious restrictions, on the Daughters and everyone else. How they and their charges would work together in the field was a question to be answered—not, Hiko hoped, at the cost of too many lives.

Less briefly, Hiko wondered if Ruth was only seeking tactical instruction. Was she reaching out as one human being to another—tentatively, clumsily, not fully knowing what she was doing but too much in need to draw back?

If so, was she the only one reaching out? If she was not, was that another weak point on Zauberberg, where judiciously applied pressure might serve the Game Master's cause?

By the time he had stripped and plunged into the icy pool, Hiko knew the matter deserved more than meditation. Thorough analysis, at least—not to mention a serious attempt to arrange another meeting with Ruth.

The anomalous status of the Daughters of the Lord under the Protectorate was only one of Zauberberg's potential weak spots. Added together, the planet's weak spots seemed to virtually guarantee effectiveness for the Master's Teams and an expensive commitment of Planetary Union resources.

The Representative had summed up matters at the last prelanding briefing:

"This isn't a stone so delicately balanced that we're enough to start it rolling. This is a stone that's already on the way downhill. We just have to jump aboard, hang on, and help it smash whatever's in its path."

The history of Zauberberg's weak points was as long as that of most planets Hiko had studied for possible Team intervention. Like them, Zauberberg had been handicapped from the first, when humanity rode the Yariv Drive to the stars without reaching peace and unity on Terra first.

Hiko had heard of twentieth-century philosophers who believed that the challenge of space would unite humanity, out of sheer awe at the majesty of Creation or something similar. He'd also read the 22nd-century philosopher Motal Singh, the Great Cynic, and his most famous aphorism:

''God made Man intelligent. Then Man used that intelligence to invent stupidity.''

Zauberberg was settled in the 2070's by a German-Italian-Finnish consortium. They needed a planetary base to help exploit the rich mineral resources of the nearby asteroid belt. Belters could live in their ships or depots nine months out of ten, as long as they had someplace to stretch their legs, eat fresh food, and look at a horizon during the odd month.

Within a generation of Zauberberg's settlement, Germans, Italians, and Finns in flight from a ravaged Earth were swarming over its rugged hills and rocky fields. They were soon joined by the Brotherhood of the Cause of the Lord, sixty thousand fanatics who made a convoluted claim of descent from the Renaissance Anabaptists, through a motley sequence of Protestant Christian sects.

For nearly a century after the Collapse, its aftermath caused Zauberberg less trouble than many worlds. The planet was cold and harsh, but its air and gravity made no unreasonable demands on human lungs or bones. It was rich in hydrocarbons, and local plants and animals plus DNA-tailored Earth grains solved the food problem. The asteroid mines were the cheapest source of metals for more than a dozen worlds settled even more hastily than Zauberberg, and too poor in capital or technology to develop resources closer to home.

By the end of that century, Zauberberg's markets began to close, one by one. The other planets either developed their own mines and asteroid belts or collapsed completely. What Hiko called Zauberberg's Century of the Full Rice Bowl came to an end. All the divisions papered over during that century came into the open.

German vs. Italian (and Finn vs. both). Protestant vs. Catholic. Old (Roman) vs. New Catholic. The hypertrophied cities vs.

the undercapitalized farming areas. Above all, the Brotherhood vs. everybody not of the Brotherhood.

It was that last division that broke into open warfare fifty years before. Two years and five thousand dead later, the Brotherhood was ceded the territory now called the Protectorate—700,000 square kilometers (as far as the borders were defined at all) north of the Great North Gulf.

Most of the Brotherhood's followers moved, along with their portable wealth, their survival skills, and their fanatical commitment to hard work. In their new home they prospered in the modest fashion they found appropriate; they might have prospered more if they hadn't put so much effort into an armaments industry. Within a generation the Protectorate was exporting light-infantry weapons, in trade for heavy equipment matching anything in the hands of the Triple Federation.

Meanwhile, the Peace Force presence in the Triple Federation shrank from a brigade to a battalion, and from a battalion to a Security Company for the stockpiled vehicles and supplies plus a few advisers. The Federal Army's standing forces didn't shrink, but they didn't grow, either. The readiness of the reserves and militia behind them shrank as more money went to the Federal Security Police.

With more money, the confidence of the police grew. Their professionalism did not, and neither did their care in handling the minority of Brotherhood believers who'd remained on the north shore.

When Hiko and his Team reached Zauberberg, he began by wondering if any number of men the Game Master could send would make any difference. They weren't even the only mercenaries; the Protectorate's War Council had assembled a battalion of off-planet odds and ends, mostly from worlds that had supplied heavy equipment.

It didn't take Hiko long to realize his mistake. The mercenary battalion (the "Chosen") was kept in almost the same purdah as the Daughters; some of the Chosen were women and few were Brotherhood believers. The two Teams were all male and apparently devout in the faith of their employers.

This made more of a difference than Hiko was happy to see, even if it did make the Teams rank with the Angels and other elite units. If Hiko worshipped anything, it was treating soldiers on the basis of their military skill and loyalty to their comrades.

The Brotherhood made free with the name of the Lord Mighty in Battle, but what they did or left undone in His name . . .

Still, Hiko remembered stranger employers and worse causes, entirely apart from his oath to the Master. With freedom to move to where their skills might be most effective, the men of the five Teams could do a great deal—even in a war that might see fifty thousand soldiers under arms, apart from what the Peace Force might send.

Hiko returned to the rendezvous a few minutes early. He watched Ruth stride up the inland side of the dune, with her hood down around her shoulders as she toweled her dark brown hair dry.

Some extra sense told her that she was being watched. Without breaking stride she turned her back and pulled her hood over her hair, then tied it into place while she finished the turn.

It somewhat spoiled her act, that she hadn't finished blushing when she reached Hiko. Carefully stopping two meters away, she said in a level voice, "Only the Lord saw me bathing, and it is not in Him to lust or desire."

That was probably just as well for Ruth. Zauberberg clothing tended to be shapeless enough, just for warmth. The Daughters' uniforms were almost tentlike, for the sake of modesty. Ruth's fatigues hid her figure, but not the long-limbed height, the athletic grace of movement, or the austerely beautiful face. If the invisible matched the visible . . .

And he had best keep even such *thoughts* invisible. To offer a sexual threat to Ruth would not only eliminate her as a source of intelligence. It would be senseless cruelty to whatever humanity lay beneath the dedicated servant of a contorted notion of the Divine.

"It is not in me to lust or desire, save at a time and in a place blessed by the Lord," Hiko said.

"You are not married?" Ruth asked.

"Being sworn to the Brotherhood offends many women among the Godless. Being a mercenary soldier offends most of the rest. If one wishes a woman fit to raise one's sons in the way of the Lord, one must contain oneself."

"Blessed be your wish, and may the Lord grant you its fulfillment," Ruth said. "Now. I have meditated at length about what I wish to learn. The Lord sent me, first of all, the desire to know about our brethren in the south. Has your training taught you how to deal with them?''

She wanted to know more about the guerrillas than she'd been told, in case her Daughters had to operate with them. ''I rejoice that I may help increase your knowledge,'' Hiko said. ''I have learned much about our brethren, and the first thing is that they themselves need much teaching . . .''

By the time they'd talked for an hour, they'd exchanged practically everything they'd learned in the past sixty days. In the end they were talking mostly as two military professionals, with few religious circumlocutions. Hiko even gained Ruth's permission to pass on to his Brother Team Leaders anything that would not expose her as its source.

This was only partly military sense. The rest was political calculation. If the Representative wanted to keep the peace with the Brotherhood by making an example of one Team Leader, he might risk it. He could hardly risk disciplining more than one on the eve of the invasion. Weakening his command structure would please neither the Brotherhood nor the Master.

Unless more Teams were on the way? It was quite possible that they were, and if so quite in order for Hiko not to know about it. He would be gambling, taking other Team Leaders into his confidence—but war always had an element of chance, and at least the stakes were worth something.

4

Whump, whump, whump.

THE LAST THREE rounds smacked the rocky ground, bracketing the "enemy" trench. The practice rounds left only drifting white smoke and bits of gravel pattering down the slope.

Sergeant Dubnick still hesitated. Captain Podgrebin jumped up and shouted:

"Dubnick, move your assault out *now*! Who told you to wait for the return of the Azteca Expedition?"

Parkes winced. The two squads sprinted across the open ground and dove into the trench with bloodcurdling yells. Paul Dubnick ran with the leading squad, though not quite at its head.

Podgrebin stood by the boulder that had concealed the squads during the preparatory fires. Feet apart, arms crossed on chest, and helmeted head thrown back, he looked like a recruiting poster and probably knew it. Maybe this fondness for striking poses came from too many manuals about command presence and not enough actually commanding soldiers. A few more months running Third Company might cure him.

And maybe it wouldn't, and maybe none of them would have the time, anyway.

Parkes stayed concealed until Dubnick led the two squads of his 3 Platoon back downhill. Podgrebin watched them with the eye of a prison guard counting the returning work gang. Reluctantly Parkes rose to stand beside Podgrebin. He saw no safe way to disassociate himself from what his guts told him was coming.

"Dubnick, preparatory fire isn't laid on to provide a pretty show. It's to kill or confuse the other side while you're getting in close. If you don't push your people up fast and close, you get them killed. The only thing I saw done right was setting up the L.M.G. Otherwise you might do a good job running a Labor Company for the Fourth Empire. What you're doing in the Peace Force, God only knows.

"Since He hasn't told me, I suppose there's some reason you've got a platoon. Let's go through the basics again, and maybe you'll still have one after your first firefight."

Dubnick looked at Parkes with the mute appeal of an animal in a hold trap. The look lasted a moment too long; Podgrebin saw it and his own face promised volumes, or at least essays. His tone to Dubnick didn't change as he shifted from general roasting to specific tactical instruction.

Parkes had to admit that the tactical instruction was sound. He also had to admit that Dubnick *had* been slow off the mark. That still didn't make dressing him down in front of half his platoon smart or even acceptable.

The launcher team had used up their quota of rounds for the training exercise, so Dubnick got a partial reprieve. Instead of another assault against an enemy position, he was ordered to lay an ambush for an enemy patrol consisting of another squad from 3 Platoon, led by Parkes.

Parkes welcomed the job. It helped him fill out his mental dossier on both Dubnick and Podgrebin, and got him out from under Podgrebin's eyes for nearly an hour.

By the end of the hour, it had also reminded him that he was going to have to work harder at staying in shape for the field. Forty-two was barely decent middle age for some standards, but not for doing basic infantry work. The spectacle of the Group First pulling up lame wouldn't help anything or anybody.

The exercise ended with Parkes's patrol "annihilated," after inflicting "medium casualties" on Dubnick's ambushers. Parkes wondered if Podgrebin thought that kind of vagueness would help Dubnick's mangled self-confidence, or if his staff background made it a natural turn of speech.

Dubnick took all three squads off for weapons inspection and a smoke. Parkes resurrected himself and was reloading his rifle with live rounds when Podgrebin marched up. That was another irritating thing about the man; he never just *walked*. Didn't he know how much extra energy he was using up, or didn't he care?

"Sergeant Major, let's walk."

Parkes decided not to insult Podgrebin by saluting him in the field and nodded. "Fine, Captain. But I'd rather jog a bit."

"Very well. Know any level ground? Or do you have goat ancestry?"

"There's a stretch back behind the trench, if you don't mind running in circles."

"Isn't that what we're all doing, anyway, Sergeant Major?"

Parkes managed a polite smile, then slung his rifle and began his warming-up exercises.

The level ground ran about three hundred meters from east to west. Footing wasn't too good, with boulders, imported scrub pine, and native crown-of-thorns vine that covered most of the boulders and sprawled aggressively over the ground around them as well.

One of the problems of fighting on Zauberberg was going to be a shortage of both cover and concealment, not to mention a rocky soil that made digging your own a slow job. Parkes made a mental note to check the supply of E.C. 6 and everybody's training in setting it; if either was short, somebody was going to get killed unnecessarily.

Podgrebin moved out fast and smoothly. He was at least ten years younger than Parkes and in top shape, so it didn't really matter if he was trying to run Parkes into the ground or not. It was a couple of minutes before Parkes was sure he had enough breath to talk while they ran.

"Parkes, what did Dubnick expect from you?"

"I don't know, Captain. I haven't asked him."

"Meaning you really don't know, or that it's one of those things between N.C.O.'s that officers aren't supposed to discuss?"

"Meaning that anything I said before I talked to Dubnick would be a guess. Do you want me to guess?"

"If this was a tactical situation, you'd have to. The enemy wouldn't wait for you to get all the facts. Treat me as the enemy and guess."

Podgrebin probably didn't have enough sense of humor to appreciate his own double meaning. Parkes took another two hundred meters to sort his thoughts, then said:

"I think he wants me to tell him how he really did, in private."

"He doesn't trust my judgment?"

"Captain, it's not a question of judgment. At least not your tactical judgment. Dubnick has no way of evaluating that."

"I thought any sergeant fit to have a platoon of his own could size up a captain well enough."

"In six weeks, two-thirds of it aboard ship? Sir, Dubnick's good. What you're asking for is either a miracle or telepathy. All he's got to go on is how you treated him in front of his subordinates."

"I see. That old business."

"Old doesn't mean it's no longer important, Captain."

"Did I say I thought that? Never mind, maybe you don't have an open mind on the subject. All I'll do is ask you two questions. Don't you think we're likely to be facing combat before long? And don't you think Third Company is a weak spot that has to be strengthened before we do?"

"Yes to both, Captain."

"Then I don't see what we're arguing about. It's like field surgery—better leave a scar than let the patient die."

That was an analogy that Parkes might have accepted from somebody who hadn't spent eight of his ten years in the Peace Force in staff and support assignments. Besides, there really wasn't any argument good enough to justify humiliating somebody in front of his own people. If he was likely to have to lead them in battle within a few weeks, there was even less reason.

Podgrebin was in the position of somebody trying to justify incest by describing the sibling's physical attractions. He was going to be deaf to anything Parkes could safely say. Parkes could only hope that the outcome would be no worse than embarrassing to anybody, or if fatal, only to Captain Andreas Podgrebin.

Dubnick's platoon had policed up the training area and vanished by the time Parkes returned. Two vertis were unloading a platoon from the Air-Defense Company, spraying dust and pebbles that rattled off the launcher pods and radar and laser cases.

Dubnick himself had stayed behind; he was pretending to swap war stories with the A.D.C. platoon sergeant when Parkes came up. The A.D.C. sergeant took one look at Parkes, gathered her loader, and got out of hearing.

"Dubnick, this isn't too bright. There's nothing we have to say that couldn't have waited. Besides, Handy Andy's bound to notice. Who's running 3?"

"Gunnison. I'm bringing her along so she can take over if I

get chopped. It'll be better if there's an officer running the platoon before then, but—"

"She's not up to platoon command, or does she need somebody between her and—?"

"Damn it, Napoleon would need somebody between him and Podgrebin! Just because he's a chiphead, he thinks he's got three balls and six decorations!"

"A chiphead?"

"You didn't know, First?"

Parkes knew he should have, but—

"No, I didn't. How did you find out?"

"Handy Andy told us."

"Oh."

For a Peace Force officer to have a biochip implant in his brain meant one of two things. Either he had money and the intention of staying on staff duty much of his career, or he'd had a major head injury that left him needing help to restore adequate brain function. The first always smelled bad to Parkes. Of course, Podgrebin could be like Doug Petersen, who'd scrambled his brain trying to run up a down escalator after the fifth drink . . .

"All right, he's a chiphead. You could use a little augmentation yourself, all things considered. Podgrebin was saying the right things in the wrong place."

"Yes, sir—First."

"Like I said, try to tighten up on getting your people to move out. Also noise discipline. I'll help as much as I can. If you can't reach me, try Sergeant Major McKendrick." The Field First would give good advice; he had combat experience to burn even if he was a little new to the rest of his job. Being asked would also boost his self-confidence.

"Bring Gunnison along as fast as you can, both for C.O. and for platoon sergeant. We really have to take seriously the rule about everybody being ready to jump two levels.

"I'll also see what I can do to get 3 Platoon the first spare lieutenant who's worth the trouble." That might mean using up some of his credit with Vela; he didn't have any to speak of with Lieutenant Colonel Blair. He hoped he wouldn't have to use too much; there were more important jobs for lieutenants than protecting Paul Dubnick from Captain Podgrebin while the sergeant finished learning a job he should have already known. However, if the job turned out to be protecting the thirty-eight men and women of 3 Platoon . . .

"Oh, and one thing more. Anything happens to Podgrebin, it had damned well better be the enemy who does it."

"Sargeant, I wasn't thinking—"

"That's all you were doing, and as long as you stop there—'can't be court-martialed for thinking.' Beyond that, you could get somebody worse. After your six rounds with Podgrebin, anything happens to him, your ass is grass whether he's alive to play lawn mower or not.

"Finally, I outrank you. If Podgrebin really drops one, I won't be too busy to help."

"Thanks." Dubnick swallowed. "That—that helps a lot. If we're really going to be doing some serious shooting—"

"When, not if. The way things are shaping up, the Brotherless would have to be very stupid not to move. Go around assuming the other side's that stupid, and you might as well climb straight into the bodybag and seal yourself up. Save everybody else some work."

Dubnick swallowed again. He seemed to be fighting to hold on to some of the reassurance Parkes had given him. Parkes turned away and headed for the nearest verti. Dubnick would have to fight that battle himself.

The I.F.F. gave an interrogative chirp. The onboard computer returned the correct signal; the I.F.F. telltale turned from red to green.

"We're clear for overflying the bridge," Major Dallin said. "Where do you want to go after that?"

"Let's head over to the Teuffelberg Peninsula," Forbes-Brandon said. "We're not planning to operate there, that I've heard. But I'd like to eyeball a couple of D.Z.'s."

"On the south side, this time around, if you don't mind."

"The F.A.F. being trigger-happy again? Or still?"

"Let's say it helps to give them more notice than we could do today, without landing for a couple of hours."

"I'm supposed to be on the train to Nordshaven at 1300, with my mess dress and civilian fancies. Some sort of combined high tea and orgy the city parents are laying on for Duchamp."

"Rain check?"

"Maybe—no, forget it. The north coast is either too rugged

or it's the lower slopes of the Teuffelberg itself. We don't need a D.Z. for blue scramblers or goats."

The eight kilometers of bridge and causeway across the mouth of Dietrich's Bay spread across the front window, then flashed below. The verti was low enough for Forbes-Brandon to see the A.D. crews waving.

Dallin made one of her usual stomach-straining hard turns, to slow down and fly parallel with the bridge. Forbes-Brandon saw the copilot-gunner looking at her, clearly alert for any sign of queasiness.

Every so often, Forbes-Brandon felt like kicking Dallin's people for their fanatical loyalty to her. Just as often, she envied the Transportation Officer. Most of the time, she was just glad of it. A well-run Transportation Company made her own job so much easier that it was worth putting up with Dallin's hot piloting and much more besides.

Not to mention that her people's loyalty and a few hairy missions had helped Dallin bounce back from Thanh's death. Guilt was something that some people (better not even *think* "Sergeant Major Parkes") wore like a skin, others sloughed off like a sweaty track suit after a good run. In between lay the people who could do either, depending on what kind of help they had—hers from Hugo Opperman (*Greenhouse, make something bloom from his ashes*) or Dallin's from her hours in the cockpit.

Another turn, pulling as many G's as the verti could handle with three people and overload tanks. As they climbed, Dallin saw a silver-green freight train sliding across the bridge. The IR sensor *wnnngged* at the heat pulse from the turboelectric locomotive until Dallin switched it off. In silence, they flew out to sea.

For ten minutes and sixty kilometers, there was nothing to see but slate-gray water below and amorphous blue-gray hills growing larger ahead. Visibility was less than twenty kilometers; the Teuffelberg itself was only a dim triangular hint of itself on the northern horizon.

Forbes-Brandon lifted her head from the map display. "Let's check out the meadow above the Troll's Bath. It looks like the biggest piece of level ground with reasonable access to both the coast and the inland hills."

"I can't imagine our going into Trollsheim unless everything can be done by air," the copilot said.

"Maybe," Dallin said. "Maybe not, too, if we're still here when the autumn gales start blowing off the High Seas."

"Yeccchhh," the copilot said.

"Nervous in the service?" Dallin asked.

"No, ma'am—well, maybe. If they'd consulted me, I'd have said leave the Feds and the Brothers to fight it out."

"But they didn't consult you. Or me, either. So here we are. Any more objections?"

"No, ma'am." The copilot sketched a rigid salute. *"Befehl ist befehl."*

"Gesundheit," Dallin said, slapping control switches. The verti banked. "Coming up on the Troll's Bath in—what the hell?"

From photographs, Forbes-Brandon recognized the hot sulphur lake known as the Troll's Bath. Normally it steamed gently, with occasional small geysers. Now it was throwing plumes of boiling yellow-brown water fifteen meters in the air. Smoke and steam streamed off downwind, completely hiding the ground for half a kilometer.

"It does look a bit like hell, doesn't it?" Forbes-Brandon said. "Mind dropping me for a quick scout on foot?"

"I do mind, but will that stop you?"

"What do you think?"

Dallin shrugged. "An officer and a lady after my own liver. All right. Josie, give her the mask and portable air bottle."

"Ah—"

"Did you empty it completely, curing that last hangover?"

"Only half."

"How much time is that?" Forbes-Brandon asked.

"Twenty minutes."

"I shouldn't need more than ten in close. I don't see our using this except for emergencies."

"I read you. All right. We'll drop you upwind, then make a pass or two downwind with all the sensors turned up full."

"Let's time it for between those geysers," the copilot said. "I don't mind the smoke, but one of those rocks could ruin our day."

"No quarrel with that," Dallin said. The verti tipped over from horizontal flight into a steep descent toward the northern end of the meadow. Forbes-Brandon tried to simultaneously adjust her boots, her jacket, and her mask. She'd managed a fix for all three by the time the verti landed.

• • •

Forbes-Brandon was on the ground barely twenty minutes altogether, and on the mask less than ten. That was enough to tell her that the heat and fumes were nearly as vicious as they'd looked from the air. The Troll's Bath meadow could be used as a D.Z. for orbital supplies, but they'd have to be retrieved by air. Stationing anybody here permanently made sense only if they had a sealed-environment shelter.

She walked to within a hundred meters of the lake's edge before the heat drove her back. A backhanded gift, as it turned out—she'd just started her retreat when the biggest geyser of all spewed up from the lake. Thirty meters up, the wind turned the water into a plume of spray, but didn't touch the flying rocks. One the size of a plum pudding came smoking down less than five meters away.

Clear of the heat and fumes, Forbes-Brandon took off her mask and unslung her carbine. She drew a bead on the verti swinging low in circles around the lake, then on successively more distant rocks. Finally she picked one about two hundred meters up the hollow-faced hill to the north and squeezed off two bursts. Dust and rock chips flew, then the rock itself lurched and rolled a few meters to the next patch of rough ground.

Her shooting eye hadn't deserted her. A pity they weren't going to stage a marksmanship contest to welcome Duchamp; that would have been a lot more fun than this upcoming bunfight. Not that she could have reasonably expected the locals to ignore the arrival of an authentic Peace Force hero, when each and every faction of them was trying to woo the Peace Force, but still . . .

She shoved a fresh magazine into her carbine, sat down on the flattest rock she could find, and pulled the polishing cloth out of the sling. With the steady motions of polishing, her frustration ebbed.

It would be back again, of course. She hadn't done anything about the underlying causes. Somewhere in the last year, she'd ceased to be a naval officer doing a tour of duty with the groundpounders. She'd become a new kind of "giddy harumphrodite," half star sailor and half infantry, with neither half quite ready to let the other take over completely.

Seeing the stars come out as a shuttle climbed toward orbit could still bring her heart into her throat. So could watching a rifle company deploying into unknown country, seemingly so casual, in fact so alert and deadly. A sleeping bag and a tent with a view of some distant horizon seemed as much home as her cabin with its screen view of the planet rolling below.

You're at home everywhere, and that means nowhere—

"Hey, Kat!" came Dallin's voice in her earphones. "Ready for pickup? You've been staring at the sky for the last five minutes."

Forbes-Brandon swallowed resentment at the interruption. "Affirmative."

In silence, they climbed back to two thousand meters. Dallin set the autopilot and punched up a readout from the sensors, then whistled.

"Just like I thought. Anybody working less than five hundred meters downwind of that lake, they'd better work in C.W. gear. Or a buttoned-up tank."

"It's not the only hot spot that seems to be working overtime, either," the copilot said. She was adjusting the gun sight as she spoke. "We followed a flock of drachenkopf sheep and chivvied them along to test the gun. Some of them ran right into a mud flow, hot enough to be steaming. Anybody want roast drachenkopf?"

"It'll probably be better than the plastic fish tonight," Forbes-Brandon said, in an emphatically neutral tone. She leaned back in her seat as the verti crossed the coast.

She needed help to decide what to do about her harumphroditic status. Only—where to find it?

Her father? A sick joke. Her mother? A sicker joke. Captain Cooper? Nobody better for professional problems, but for one with so many personal elements . . . ? Colonel MacLean? She didn't know him well enough to impose that sort of an obligation on him.

The only person who'd gladly put on gloves and juggle this hot potato was Vice-Admiral Newton. Or at least, he'd gladly juggle it until he learned exactly what it was. After that—*quién sabe?* He'd taken a few chances with his own career to grease her path toward two stars. What would he say to the thought of her turning her back on the stars, in every sense of the word?

Come on, Kat. give the admiral credit for being a big man. Don't talk yourself into believing you're all alone when you probably aren't.

"Probably" isn't "certainly." And Newton's a long ways off. Forty-two light-years to Helvetia, isn't it?

This is the real world, so "probably" is the best you get. Besides, the question can wait long enough to get a secure letter to Helvetia and back.

Can't it?

It had bloody well better!

5

FROM A FAR corner of the prefecture's reception room, an indignant male voice rose. Other heads besides Cardinal Parona's turned.

Parona wondered if the indignation or the volume was drawing attention. In the hour since his arrival, this was the first voice he'd heard rise above a conversational level.

With his glass and stomach full and no one demanding his attention, Parona allowed himself to wonder about this muting. Reverses in the campaign against the guerrillas? Unlikely, or Chancellor Biancheri would have heard. Resentment against the Peace Force, whose presence implied that Zauberberg couldn't settle its own problems? Possibly. (The opposite opinion, that it was time somebody showed the Security Police their limitations, was widespread but unlikely to be expressed here.) Fear of a wider war? Again, Biancheri would probably have heard, but it might be worth the cardinal's time—

The voice of indignation solidified into words. "There's no need to bring in Union mercenaries! The Brotherhood's not supporting the guerrillas. We'd have them on our hands regardless, as long as the Security Police—"

The rest was lost in a gabble of voices, as people tried to drown the man out or perhaps disassociate themselves from his views. Parona couldn't see the speaker, but guessed that he was addressing a short dark Peace Force lieutenant colonel, with what looked like Hrothmi script on some of his ribbons. Parona suspected that the speaker had chosen the handiest victim, rather than the most receptive audience.

The gabble died away into the previous buzz and rumble. The voice of indignation made itself heard again. "Look at the five subbarges. The Protectorate is salvaging and refitting them at its own expense. That will save at least one shipping firm from bankruptcy. Is this a gesture of hostility? I should call it one of conciliation."

"Many things are possible," the Peace Forcer said, in what was clearly intended as a placating tone. "One is that the Protectorate is being conciliatory because they know they'll have to deal with us if they aren't."

"Do you think everyone worships force the way you do?"

The reply forming on the Peace Forcer's lips would be neither placating nor even polite, the cardinal suspected. Before his suspicions could be confirmed, an immensely tall figure in an immaculate Peace Force uniform with stars on the shoulder boards loomed up behind the lieutenant colonel.

"I doubt if Colonel Vela worships Kali any more than you do," the tall general said precisely, almost primly. "He merely speaks from an extensive body of experience. Also, we are under orders to be prepared for the worst, even those of us who have no experience to teach us." The Francone accent was quite pronounced.

Duchamp's intervention set the crowd into motion, giving Parona a view of the indignant speaker. He immediately signaled a passing waiter (even the best restaurants in Nordshaven were using robots tonight).

"Cardinal Parona would like to speak with Chancellor Biancheri."

"Ja."

A moment later he saw the chancellor emerging from behind Duchamp and approaching the speaker. Parona smiled. Maria must have recognized Professor Bahr's voice and been on her way to deal with him since the first outburst. The cardinal remembered a concise description of Bahr, when the Chancellor and her brother, Professor Biancheri, entertained him at the University of Nordshaven.

"He's a brilliant geologist, if he would just admit it and stick to his work," Professor Biancheri said. "But he thinks he needs political allies to rise. Then he compounds the error by putting all his money on the Opposition. He ends by spouting their whole line, both the sense and the nonsense."

Parona remembered asking, "The Security Police haven't started investigating political matters, have they?"

"Not yet," Professor Biancheri said, with an eloquent shrug.

That was still true, as far as Parona knew. The fact that he'd threatened excommunication against any Catholic of the *polizia* who thought it would be amusing to play Gestapo had probably done its share. Would it be enough?

That had to depend on the length and seriousness of the present crisis. If the Security Police were able to clean up the guerrillas' arms caches and make it impossible for them to assemble and move, malice might not have time to work. Folly would, but when was that not true?

The best source of an accurate measurement of the crisis was now standing beside Colonel Vela.

Parona moved forward, slowly until people saw that he was on the move, then more swiftly as they cleared a path. Duchamp waited until the chancellor had drawn Bahr safely out of Vela's range, then stepped forward.

"I join my voice to all the others in saying welcome to Zauberberg," Parona said. He noticed and appreciated that Duchamp stopped close enough so that the cardinal didn't have to raise his voice, but far enough that he could meet Duchamp's eyes without having to crane his neck.

"I repeat my thanks. I will be even more grateful if I could have something to eat before we talk. I only just escaped from the reception line."

"I'll arrange something, sir," Vela said. "Where do you want it?"

Parona's eyes indicated a half-curtained alcove in the middle of the opposite wall. Duchamp nodded and pointed. "Over there." Then he fell in beside the cardinal, allowing the shorter man to set the pace.

Parona appreciated the politeness. He also savored the frustration on a number of Very Important Faces in the crowd. *That is fate, my friends; Duchamp may be the guest of honor but in all eyes but the Anti-Clericals'*, I *am the highest-ranking person in the room.*

Duchamp sighed audibly when they stepped behind the curtain. "Forgive me if I seem a trifle preoccupied, Your Eminence. Nothing is causing it that need give you concern for your flock. It is only that I was virtually kidnapped for this reception before I had time to set up my headquarters. I had to leave my whole staff at their labors and improvise aides for this reception.

"Colonel Vela. He is Battalion Fourteen's Field Squadron Commander. Also Lieutenant Commander Forbes-Brandon, their Naval Liaison Officer. I gained a good opinion of them on—a previous mission—and they were both going to be in Nordshaven in the normal line of duty, anyway."

"Indeed." Parona sipped wine. "General, you know that I have questions to ask. Doubtless you have some of your own. I will answer any that do not violate the secrets of the Confessional or the Conclave, if you will answer only one of mine."

"I could almost agree to that at once. But I am an old gray wolf. I am as skeptical of the motives of cardinals as of any man's."

"The question is simple. Will I end my years of service to God and my fellow humans trying to heal the wounds of a major war?"

"I can easily give you an honest answer to that one. Do you mind that it is not a simple one?"

"I hardly expected it would be."

"Very well. There is a significant possibility."

"Not a probability?"

"No, and still less a certainty."

"The older I grow, the less I believe in certainties. God has them, but they are usually denied to human beings."

"Soldiering has taught me the same. Oh, there are some things that by normal standards are certainties. Avoid frontal assaults—"

"One worked against you."

"I wasn't prepared to hold my position. Avoid frontal assaults, give everyone a hot meal and dry socks once a day—a hundred little things. Some people have worn stars through nothing more than remembering more of these than their rivals."

"Not you, if the stories are to be believed."

"Half the stories may have some truth in them. One more certainty is that in a situation like this much depends on your enemy."

Duchamp clasped his hands behind his back. "If I were the Protectorate War Council, I would be seeking four conditions. Surprise, superiority in men and firepower at certain crucial points, enough air cover to protect my own supply lines, and Peace Force deployments that left most of the on-planet forces vulnerable."

"Those are the four conditions you are trying to prevent?"

"Precisely. What degree of success I will have over the next sixty days remains to be seen. That degree of success will determine—"

A polite cough interrupted Duchamp. Then the curtain was twitched aside, and a tall female officer in Navy full dress stood there with a loaded plate in her free hand.

"Excuse me, sir, Your Eminence. There's a meteorite Yellow Alert. Colonel Vela sent me to warn you ahead of the official announcement. They don't expect it to become Red for this quadrant, but they're going to have a go with the lasers. That could divert it from its present course."

"Thank you. Make sure you have something to eat and drink yourself, in case they close the buffet."

"Yes, sir."

Parona followed the retreating officer with an appreciative eye. She was close to a meter eighty, with heavy blond hair and a strangely attractive face. By themselves, the big beaked nose and the strong jaw could have been ugly, but as part of a harmonious ensemble they were striking.

Duchamp's laugh made Parona realize that his appreciation had been noticed. "Is it true that on some planets the Peace Force shows off its most attractive female officers, to prove that being a soldier doesn't make a woman ugly?"

"I've heard rumors that it's done on planets settled by Arabs and the like. Surely you don't believe we think Zauberberg's that uncivilized?"

Duchamp started emptying his plate in large but decorous mouthfuls. Parona peered out from behind the curtain. The chancellor was gone, but Bishop Heinreid was deep in conversation with a Peace Force Medical Corps officer, a major, judging from the insignia on her—well, it was neither uniform nor civilian dress. Call it a multiform, and—

"Your attention, please," the prefect boomed. His voice was as round as he was. He also wore a self-satisfied look at being able to impose himself on everyone. "Your attention, please."

Duchamp muttered something in Francone that Parona judged unwise to have translated.

"Your attention, please. A meteorite has entered the Yellow Alert zone. It is being engaged by Skyguard Stations Two and Three as I speak. No major impact effects in this quadrant are expected, but we shall be shuttering the windows and closing the buffet in two minutes."

Quick work by the waiters staved off a stampede for last-minute refuelings. Duchamp emptied his plate and glass, then set them down as the window in the alcove vanished behind its shutters.

Parona led the way out of the alcove, noticing that Heinreid was still absorbed with the Peace Force doctor. The bishop's years in urban missions and as a hospital chaplain had made the poor and doctors his favorite kinds of people.

Surreptitiously Parona looked at his watch. From entry into the Yellow Zone to impact was never more than eight minutes. A few people were already sweating. Parona couldn't help a sense of relief that he'd confessed this morning.

He would have gladly traded that relief to bring the low-orbit satellite network back on line. Perhaps something could be done with the Skyguard satellite's radar, reprogramming it to make an occasional surface scan.

This was a technical question he'd have to lay before an expert. Discreetly, and that meant the Peace Force. If anyone on Zauberberg learned that the cardinal archbishop was even discussing such an infringement of the Code of Limitations on the Skyguard system—well, the Conclave would certainly hear the howl and might have to take action on it.

God knew that the Code of Limitations had its value! Without its ban on military uses of the Skyguard satellites, they might never have been built. Zauberberg might have been left to be hammered at will every time the Thorshammer descended. This time, with the shower at a two-century high, the Skyguards might be at full stretch, anyway.

Parona knew he'd have to consult with Heinreid and Biancheri before he approached the Peace Force. Maria would doubtless be gratified at the prospect of drastic action; Heinreid would be dismayed. Neither reaction would last long. They would know that they were once again a team with their cardinal, very necessary to face a time like this.

Parona became so absorbed in rehearsing his remarks to the bishop and the chancellor that he completely missed hearing the "All Clear." Only the rush at the reopened buffet brought him back to reality.

As Hiko's foot touched the stone quay, he felt a faint impact on his soles. Looking around, he saw that the other men on the quay and the turtleback of the subbarge must have felt it, too.

An Elder thrust his head out of the control booth carved in the rock wall. "Be at peace in the Lord's favor. His Grace has caused yet another meteorite to pass by without harming His children."

One day an Elder would convey a message in plain language. Then everyone within hearing would drop dead of surprise. On the whole, Hiko preferred that death to the boredom that might otherwise claim him if he had to spend much more time in the company of the Brotherhood.

Jamshir Singh climbed out of the barge's forward hatch and hurried across the gangplank with questions almost dripping from his mouth. He waited until his Team Leader had taken him a hundred meters up the tunnel toward the surface before letting the questions overflow.

"Will we cross the gulf in one of *those*?"

"What bothers you, Jamshir? Claustrophobia?"

The Sikh started to look indignant before he realized that his Leader was joking. "I am no more and no less content in the belly of a whale than you, Team Leader. If I have no need to know . . ."

"You probably do not. But if I knew that we were crossing in one of those, I would inform you and the rest of the Team at once. I swear by the Six Shrines." Mollified, Jamshir fell into step behind his leader. "They did look like they were being modified for L.A.V.'s and A.P.C.'s. About twenty apiece, I should say."

"That would be eighteen, allowing for the weight of basic loads of fuel and ammunition."

"True. I forgot."

"Best you learn to remember things like that before you become a Team Leader. Pardon, I joke too often. You do well. May you live long enough to do better."

"As God wills," Jamshir said. They covered another hundred meters in silence before Hiko saw someone coming down the tunnel. Another twenty meters and he recognized Ruth.

"Greetings, Commander," Hiko said. "It is my turn to crave instruction, by the Lord's favor and yours."

"If it is proper for a Daughter to give it, I shall," Ruth replied.

During the exchange of formalities Jamshir had prudently concluded three was a crowd and kept on going. When he'd disappeared around a bend, Hiko smiled.

"What service of the Lord brings you here, Commander?" He could ask her a fairly direct question now, as long as he couched it in properly devout language. His simulation of an earnest convert to the Brotherhood of the Cause of the Lord had been more profitable than he'd expected.

"I wish to examine this tunnel, to learn how it might burden the Daughters if it is the Lord's will that we use it. I come by the order of the Elder Sister of the Daughters," she added hastily.

In other words, she was studying how long it would take to move the Daughters through the tunnel. Interesting. Were the Daughters going to ride the barges?

"That is well, if the service of the Lord demands that the Daughters embark here."

"The service of the Lord may demand many things. It is my duty as a faithful Daughter to be prepared for all of them, so that those in my charge may serve better."

In other words, she didn't know whether the Daughters were going across in barges, hovercraft, fishing boats, ferries, vertis, fixed-wings, or swimming. Probably not swimming; the bathing suits the Brotherhood required for women would sink half the battalion before they got five hundred meters offshore.

Hiko searched for a reply that would convey devoutness without also conveying the reproach for curiosity that devoutness demanded. "You are zealous in the Lord's service, and for the welfare of your company. I also suspect you are wise. The barges will surely be loaded here, but other craft can also be hidden from hostile eyes by the Lord's gift of that overhang."

"Indeed," Ruth said. "Unless the enemy flies a low-altitude mission with a multisensor pack along the coast."

Hiko wanted to smile and bow to Ruth, to honor her talking like the professional soldier the real Lord had made her instead of the religious zealot the Lord's self-anointed spokesmen had produced. Instead he nodded. "They would learn little, without violating Protectorate territory. By the Lord's favor, they seem too weak to risk that."

"Have you finished your work here?" Ruth asked. The translation was unmistakable: *I would enjoy your company if you have not.*

Hiko nodded again. "Go with the Lord's favor, and pray we speak together again before we set out on His Service."

"Indeed I shall."

As he hurried to catch up with Jamshir Singh, Hiko considered what he would have asked for if he'd really believed in the efficacy of prayer. He finally decided in favor of a clear picture of the Protectorate's strategy.

Not that the Teams hadn't pieced together much of the puzzle. Among them they had been nearly everywhere the Protectorate's ground troops were to be found. They'd also made friends among the mercenaries of the Chosen. What one Team learned, the others knew.

This might change, now that the Representative had called the Team Leaders together to discourage that sort of private intelligence network. Now it would have to go underground, becoming a good deal less efficient.

Hiko wondered if the Master's Representative had been under pressure from the War Council, or if he was simply being carried away by a sense of his own self-importance. At least matters hadn't reached the point where it would be desirable for the Representative to have an accident.

What was known? Little about the air support, not too much more about the airlift, and almost nothing about antisatellite plans. The Protectorate had the skills and resources to do a good job in all these areas. The enemy could do even better.

If the Protectorate could at least keep the enemy from using the third dimension at will, what would happen? Use the sub-barges to land an armored battalion on the north shore and team it up with the guerrillas and maybe two battalions of air or sea-lifted infantry. Put another armored battalion at the foot of the gulf, also brigaded with enough infantry to push through the Federal Army units there.

If the amphibious landing took place close to Eggerstadt, it would strike the strongest enemy forces on the north shore with surprise, superior firepower, and concentration. A Federal Army brigade (one battalion active, two in militia form), a police HQ, and Peace Force detachments could all be wrecked.

Then the amphibious force could join hands with the force coming overland and build up an air-defense zone. Reinforced, the two brigades could strike west at Nordshaven or south into the heartland of the Federation. Failing that, they could do much by simply occupying the north shore, turning the guerrillas into a government of liberation, and defying the police, the Army, and the Peace Force to drive them out.

Hiko would have liked a clearer vision, but what he saw still told him enough. Used as pathfinders or any other kind of elite infantry, the Teams would have ample opportunities to use their skills and make a favorable impression.

Meanwhile, the Protectorate's strategy could hardly fail to produce a war large enough to cripple Zauberberg for generations. The Union could try to repair the damage, but that would drain even more of its resources.

The Master and his Teams would both have a victory.

6

THE SMALLER RESTAURANT at the Eggerstadt Airport would have been fairly secure even if it hadn't been reserved for the military. The tables were set in small alcoves in meter-thick stone walls. The window in the outer wall was floor to ceiling, but double-paned, both panes laced with microfilament, and equipped with blast shutters.

The window showed Parkes nothing except airport lights, clouds creeping toward the greenish crescent of Wotan, and two attackers on pad alert. As he finished marking up the roster printout, a commercial verti drifted in for a landing. Parkes watched it taxi up to the terminal, scanned the roster again, then pushed it across the table to Dozer di Leone.

She took a swig of her coffee, then a look at the marked printout, then frowned as if the coffee had been cold. "Is that the best you can do, Fruit Merchant?"

"I'm a Group First, not a billeting officer. You expect a miracle on this kind of notice?"

"If I expected miracles, I wouldn't have asked you to hitch north and work things out privately. The Lord's hand would be over us, no matter how far we stuck our chins out toward the Brotherjammers. Since I don't believe in miracles—anyway, I didn't have much notice myself. Maybe Kuzik had more, and was trying to get the orders changed."

"When did he tell you about the pullback?"

"Yesterday."

"Then he didn't get much notice himself," Parkes said. "At least, that's assuming it was the pullback that put a flare up Blair's tail. He was complaining about not maintaining an aggressive posture. He was also trying to get Dallin on his side, over the wear and tear on the air assets."

"That smells like Hotrock, all right. I might even agree with him, if we had another battalion on-planet. But Five's ten days out and Eleven's not even in-system. I think two rifle companies and supporting detachments up front is aggressive enough."

Of Fourteen's two "up front" companies, the First was deployed farther west, about halfway between Eggerstadt and Nordshaven, backing up the Security Police with a visible P.F. presence. The Fourth was based out of Eggerstadt.

At the moment, Eggerstadt also held nearly half of Fourteen's Support Squadron, finishing their job of building a base capable of supporting two P.F. battalions. The original plan had been for the support people to stay until the other two battalions reached Zauberberg. Now orders (probably Duchamp's) were to pull everything except Fourth Company and basic supporting detachments out of Eggerstadt.

Dozer called Parkes as soon as she got the word, asking his help in smoothing out the lift and the billeting. Neither of them wanted any unit caught with half its people at one end and half at the other, with no place to sleep either place. Neither of them had much faith in the ability of mere officers to do the job right.

A light verti was leaving in an hour, to bring back two prisoners-at-large from Logistics Company, people best pulled out of Eggerstadt with its large population of Brotherhood sympathizers. With five minutes to spare and no baggage except his weapons and a change of socks, Parkes was aboard the verti.

"Never mind," Dozer said. "I can live with this. Where were you billeting me?"

"Dozer, you're the three-hundred-kilo strangler. You can tent anywhere you want."

"Well, I don't want to intrude on you. McKendrick might get twisted out of shape. Besides, I might cramp your style with the Amazon."

Parkes looked at the ceiling and decided that only a computer could count high enough fast enough. *Scratch that option.*

"Laszlo McKendrick isn't Chuck Voorhis. He knows you and I are tight and doesn't care as long as he can get his own job done. So far, he's earning that torch. He may need some help if Podgrebin really starts riding Dubnick, but—"

"You mean you aren't going to take that commission and Forty-six the—" Parkes's face must have told Dozer her joke had gone over the line. "Sorry."

Parkes reached under the table and made motions of pressing

his left leg back into its socket. "Dozer, the next time you pull that hard, I'll grab my leg back and beat you to death with it."

"Okay. But—what's the truth on that commission?"

"MacLean offered. I refused." Dozer's wide dark eyes showed polite reproach at that brief answer. "For the first time, I thought I needed explanations, not excuses." He quoted himself on redundancy.

"What did MacLean think?"

"He thought it was my business." *For the time being.* "Anyway, the Amazon's billeted with Dallin."

Dozer made hand gestures—an interrogative and the sign for a sexual relationship. Parkes made a negative.

"Good. That didn't strike me as what either of them needed, Dallin especially. I think she made enough grief for herself, not transferring to an attack squadron after Greenhouse. She doesn't need any more."

"She won't get any from the Amazon, Dozer. I think she might get the kind of help she needs."

Dozer's eyes this time showed skepticism. Parkes didn't blame her. He'd told the truth as far as he knew it, but how to explain his knowledge?

A P.F. private gave Parkes time to deploy his explanation. With another private and a corporal, he came into the restaurant and took a booth opposite the two N.C.O.'s. He unslung his rifle and put it down, not only out of reach but out of his line of vision when he was talking to his friends.

Dozer's head swiveled like a turret tracking. She cleared her throat, a noise that had been known to make veteran corporals start sweating. It made this corporal lean across the table and tap the private on the shoulder. The rifle returned to a secure place on the private's lap.

"It'd be a lot easier if they could prove Darrow's death wasn't an accident," Dozer said. "That might spice people up a bit." Corporal Darrow had been run over in the streets of Eggerstadt three days ago, by a skidding truck with a Brotherhood lay reader at the wheel. "Natural selection's all very well, but let's not rely on it completely."

Parkes nodded, thinking of Captain Podgrebin and hoping Dozer had forgotten about Forbes-Brandon and Dallin.

"Now, you were about to say, about our two officers and ladies . . . ?"

"The Amazon's slowed down this past year. Quite a lot."

"I seem to remember she doubled the Company Commander's and Commmunications courses. If that's your idea of slowing down—"

"Okay, maybe not a lot. But some. She's got a bit left over from that push for two stars. Something that Dallin could draw on, if she wanted to."

"You're hot for defending the Amazon, all of a sudden."

"So? Has she given you some grief I haven't heard about?"

"Not at all. I was wondering what had happened to her, besides Hugo Opperman. The thing is, Fruit Merchant, I was more worried about you than I was about Dallin. After this campaign there's not going to be so much redundancy in Fourteen's senior N.C.O.'s."

It was Parkes's turn to look skeptical. "You're pulling the plug?"

"Why not? Twenty-six years means a pretty good pension and bonus. I could buy a nice piece of land or maybe buy into Papa's construction business. He always thought I was wasted on the Peace Force when there were houses and roads to build on New Frontier.

"Or maybe I'll just spend a couple of years on the warmest planet I can find, soaking up the sun. This damned icebox brings out the Mediterranean or maybe the lizard blood in me."

Dozer's light tone rang oddly on Parkes's ears. Maybe he didn't have the right to push, considering how he'd snapped at her, but—

Dozer sensed Parkes's thoughts. "Okay, Fruit Merchant. We've been together long enough. That's the half of it. The rest—well, let's say Auntie Maria's heard the banshee."

"I didn't know there was any Irish in you, Dozer."

"Well, when I was a corporal this ex-seminary student named Fitzgerald and I bedded down a few times. He must have been making up for the two years he—"

"Dozer."

"Yeah?"

"It won't be the same outfit without you."

"I hope to God not! I'd hate to think I wasn't indispensable." She blinked and gripped his hands under the table. "Let's have another round, then go herd those clowns onto your verti."

Corporal MacBride turned from his console toward Forbes-Brandon.

"More interference?" she asked.

"Sounds like it. Estimated direction is from Skyguard Two. It's like their com gear was broadcasting randomly on our tactical wavelengths. It's been off and on now for about twenty minutes."

"Probably a malfunction the Feds don't want to admit. Their own people would give them holy Hades for it, this close to the Thorshammer."

"Likely enough." He sounded polite rather than convinced. Forbes-Brandon wanted to ask what MacBride thought, but he was turning back to his console with an obvious air of wanting to be let alone.

Forbes-Brandon stood up, wished briefly she'd picked up Dallin's vice of smoking, then turned to the tactical display on the opposite wall, across from the three consoles and their operators. Her eyes fell on Nuovo Milano, and memory brought up a conversation there with Lieutenant Commander Tegen.

Ark Royal's computer intelligence expert had been talking with his opposite numbers in the Federal Army and, less officially, in the Security Police. She remembered him tugging his thinning red beard as he looked at her over the rim of a coffee cup. Outside was the uproar of the main P.F. airfield on Zauberberg, so they hadn't feared being overheard.

"I think they're more afraid of the Brotherhood's cracking the Skyguard control codes than they admit," Tegen said. "Their own security's only adequate against what they know the Brotherbuggers have. If the Protectorate has some high-priced off-planet help . . ."

"No margin for error?"

"Damned little," Tegen said. "The Security Police have some good people. Better than I expected. But they can't really go through the whole Skyguard staff without being noticed. Then the howls would be heard on Clovis, and we might not be here. If the Security Police really were the Gestapoids they're supposed to be, we probably wouldn't be needed."

Set aside Tegen's political opinions, with their usual flavor of "Stomp first and ask questions later." Suppose the Skyguard system did start interfering with the Peace Force's communications system on a large scale? Suppose twenty minutes of *continuous* interference, or the lasers opening up on the communications satellites and battlestations?

Her fingers danced. Numbers flew into the display's controls and radii appeared on the map.

Curiouser and curiouser, to quote Alice. In twenty minutes, the Avia 169's of the Protectorate's Saint Michael Wing could move from ground-based detection range to striking distance of every P.F. and Fed base on the north shore. Another ten minutes would take them south to Dietrich's Bay or Fourteen's HQ—five minutes, if they sent pilots like Dallin, who could take an attacker low and fast through the passes in the Serpents.

The incoming strikes might still be detected by airborne or orbital radar. But detection isn't much use without the ability to tell the AA weapons what you've detected. No radar operator, human or computer, is an island—not if he wants to do his job.

Forbes-Brandon looked at the map again, remembering other places farther away in time and space than Nuovo Milano. Pearl Harbor, 1941. Egypt, 1967. Singapore, 2026. Nagoya, 2084. Half a dozen Peace Force campaigns over the past fifty years, on as many planets.

She turned back to the consoles. "MacBride."

"Yes, ma'am?" He sounded irritable to just this side of insubordination, but that wasn't important now.

"I'll take over your console. Go warn your reliefs to come on duty with weapons and armor."

Irritability turned to sobriety. "Yes, ma'am. Should we put our own kit handy, before we turn in?"

"Yes. On your way out—my respects to the duty officer and I'd appreciate it if he could come to the Communications Center."

"Yes, ma'am."

Hiko trotted uphill, pumping his arms to stretch muscles tightened by standing in the chill. The spot inspections weren't really necessary, not for anyone worthy of a place on a Game Team. All they did was keep it from being too obvious that the Team Leader was bored, waiting for the war to start.

At the top of the hill, Hiko stopped and looked back into the shadows at the foot. His Team waited there. Thirty-two men, each with a rifle, helmet, radio, body armor, first-aid pack, parachute. Twenty-four grenade launchers, four rocket launchers. Sixty-four hundred rifle rounds, a hundred forty-four grenades, twenty rockets.

Hiko hoped there was also the favor of whatever Powers guided the destiny of fighting men. Nothing to be done about it, of course, if those Powers were hostile or nonexistent. Some of the more devout were praying to Kali, Allah, or the gods of Shinto; one man prayed to the Wise One.

Hiko sat on the base of the hold-down stand, as close to the lotus position as he could manage with full equipment. The stand's balloon had long since climbed into the sky, carrying its ASAT missiles and decoys to their launching altitude. The transparent balloon had vanished in minutes; its nonmetallic loads would be almost equally hard to detect on radar.

How many balloons, how many missiles and decoys with each? Certainly all that the Protectorate possessed. Their strategy for denying air and space to the enemy was still only partly clear to Hiko, but one thing was obvious. Every air-space weapon the Protectorate had was to be used at once.

A line of shadows crept across the field toward Hiko. Their noise discipline was good; without Wotan's light and his own night sights, Hiko would have barely seen them. He wouldn't have recognized them as Daughters at all.

A familiar voice softly ordered a break, no drinking, no conversation. Then a long-legged form almost as familiar loped up the hill toward Hiko.

"In the name of the Lord, greetings, Team Leader."

"Greetings, Sister Commander. Are your Daughters ready for their testing?"

"As ready as the Lord has allowed them to be."

"I have seen them. His favor has been great. They will do well."

"I pray you see clearly. Some of them were not happy with the crowding aboard the ship. The Elder Sister saw fit to speak harshly to these."

Hiko didn't blame either side. The Daughters who were sharing the hold of a fish-processing ship with a load of R.P.V.'s and miniature cruise missiles must be sleeping three to a bed if they had beds. But the flank attack from the sea against Dietrich's Bay was vital. More evidence of that was the two Game Teams and two companies of Angels committed to preparing the way for the Second Battalion of Daughters.

Personally, Hiko was not unhappy that Ruth's company was in the First Daughters, the battalion crossing the Great North Gulf to Eggerstadt. He was thoroughly relieved that the War Council seemed to have avoided drastic last-minute changes in plans and deployments. Such changes had ruined stronger armies faced by weaker opponents.

"We must all bear our burdens. Soon they will be lighter, for the Lord will deliver His enemies into our hands."

As if he'd ordered her, Ruth raised both hands. Hiko gripped them before either quite knew what was happening. For a moment he felt and savored her warmth, although he knew it had to be mostly his imagination, through two sets of gloves.

"The Lord—" she began, then stopped. He saw her swallow. "Be careful, my friend," she blurted out. Then she was almost running back down the hill to her company.

As she reached them, golden fire lanced across the sky. The first ASAT missile had fired its rocket and was climbing toward its target.

The duty officer was Lieutenant Colonel Blair. He came bouncing into the Communications Center as Forbes-Brandon was belting on her sidearm.

"Expecting trouble, Katherine?"

"I hope to be disappointed, Colonel. But I don't like what we've been hearing."

She drew her pistol and checked the rounds as she told her story. The futility of the gesture kept it from being very soothing. Pistols weren't much good for serious fighting; Forbes-Brandon knew hers was even less useful than most. Anything with a long barrel, she could use effectively—carbines, assault rifles, and especially L.M.G.'s. With a pistol she was more of a menace to her own people than to the enemy.

"I see," Blair said when she finished. "Good work, MacBride. And a good thing you called me, Katherine."

She would have swapped all his compliments since he joined Fourteen for the privilege of telling him where to put his informality. If he ever called her "Kathy" she would do it for free.

Somehow, politely or otherwise, she was going to have to make it clear she wasn't prepared to shut out regulations and the rest of the battalion for his sake. She'd rather do it politely; Blair probably didn't think he was very attractive to women, thin as he was and with that big nose. Although it was probably his manner rather than his matter; John Parkes clearly didn't suffer from *that* kind of insecurity, and his nose was half again as big—

"Katherine, what about a Yellow Alert?"

"Sir, I still wouldn't recommend it except at the C.P. It's

going to be a long day tomorrow, when the supporters come back from Eggerstadt. A C.P. alert will extend our warning time if anything's going to happen, and let everyone sleep if nothing does.''

Blair looked around the room, obviously memorizing the names of the console operators in case they were needed as witnesses. Then he nodded. ''Let's go outside.''

The summer night would have been midautumn on her family's estate on New Frontier. Forbes-Brandon holstered her pistol and fastened up her coat. Once clear of the Com Center door, she walked rapidly away into the darkness.

Zauberberg's night skies made up for much of the chill. The stars seemed almost as bright as they were from orbit. The Thorshammer was beginning to lace the darkness with meteor trails, so far none of them large enough to draw the scarlet and green flame of the Skyguard lasers—

Blair slipped out of the darkness, to stand uncomfortably close to her. She stiffened, ready to move away.

A grid of golden fire streaks seared across the sky to the north. Scarlet and green laser trails joined them. From inside came a half shout, half scream, barely recognizable as MacBride's.

''Bloody hell! They're jamming us, all tac frequencies. And we just lost four comsats!''

''Red Alert!'' Blair and Forbes-Brandon shouted together as they ran for the Com Center door.

7

THE LIGHT VERTI darted over the crest of the Hoehnlicht Pass a hundred meters above the rocks. Automatically Dallin noted the southern slope of the Serpents falling away below, the moonlight reflected from the snowcap of the Adlersheim, the beacons of the Federal air base twenty kilometers to the southeast. More consciously, she made a 360-degree visual scan for unidentified aircraft. Then she tipped the verti's nose into the steepest descent possible without shifting into V.F. mode.

From the rear seat, Vela coughed. "Sonny, I'm not trying to tell you your business, but do we need to hedgehop all the way home?"

"No, and we aren't going to. I just want to stay low enough so we won't be casually picked up on A.D. radars. I don't think the Brotherless are jamming the tac frequencies to give themselves a thrill. Neither will the A.D. people. They're going to have their thumbs on the buttons and maybe not be too careful about listening to I.F.F."

By "not hedgehopping," Dallin meant staying above fifty meters. Even at economical cruising speed, trees and farmsteads and small snow-fed lakes whipped past at dizzying speed. Dallin heard what sounded like a stifled groan from the rear seat.

Maybe she did like excuses to show off her piloting, but this wasn't showing off. It was even money there'd be shooting before they landed. If this had been a Tollhouse verti, equipped for air-to-air combat, she might have been willing to stay up. In this clunker, she couldn't shoot and she'd be damned if she was going to be shot at.

The bearing of the air base shifted steadily aft as they swept south at three hundred kilometers an hour. Dallin made a new position check, using the beacon at the southern end of the Pfeiffer Tunnel, where the railroad began an eleven-kilometer burrow through the hills toward Nordshaven.

The check showed the beacon only seven kilometers away, bearing 50 true. She'd wandered a little far west, it seemed. Her hands danced, the verti began a slow bank—

—and flame mushroomed from the air base.

The flame seemed a kilometer wide. For a paralyzing moment Dallin thought it was a nuclear burst. Then she recognized the orange-white flare of an F.L.C. explosion. With recognition came reaction, a shallow dive to take the verti to treetop level.

Except for one *"Nombre de Dios!"* Vela was silent, even when they passed a barn *below* the level of the ridgepole. From the uproar in her earphones, Dallin knew Vela was trying to find an unjammed frequency.

Finally he said a number of things much less polite than *"Nombre de Dios!"* "The goat-raping Brothers must be using an orbital jammer. All I can get is bits and pieces."

"Can you make anything out of them?"

"A ground attack near Livo. That's at the foot of the gulf. Air attacks in a couple of places I couldn't identify. Lots of fragments that indicate somebody is unhappy about something, but not who about what."

"Damn," Dallin said. This time it was a bathhouse they passed. Their propwash churned a wake across the pond behind it.

A large-scale Brotherhood attack, and here she was a hundred kilometers from the nearest P.F.'ers in a verti that couldn't fight *or* run away from anything the Saint Michael Wing was likely to send over—

"Sonny! Unidentified aircraft, ten o'clock high!"

Dallin turned into the contact without bothering to look. Seconds counted now. They'd be making a head-on approach, but unless the other also came down on the deck they wouldn't collide. Wouldn't even be easy targets for each other, if the contact wasn't a Federal plane burned out of its base.

White flame flared in the darkness ahead. It assaulted Dallin's night vision, even through her self-polarizing face shield. At this altitude she didn't dare close her eyes. The flame lit up the launch aircraft in the moment before the missile accelerated. It was an Avia 169.

"Brotherhood!" Vela shouted.

Flame again, this time overhead. Dallin started jinking as hard as she could without losing altitude. Vela played spotter, tracking the two missiles as they raced for the mouth of the Pfeiffer Tunnel.

The missiles sailed straight into the mouth. The explosions lit up the hillside, but any fire they started died at once under tons of rock.

"We're clear of the first two," Vela called. "They're heading for home. We—"

Dallin was too busy with the controls to stifle a yelp of dismay. Almost dead ahead and only a little higher came a third Avia, a fire in its starboard engine lighting up the flaming-sword insignia on the fuselage. A missile hung from a centerline rack. As Dallin watched, the plane swept past, the missile fell away, and its engine flared briefly.

Then the flare died and the missile arced down to the ground. Sparks flew as it struck hard ground, then Dallin's brief hope that it wasn't fused vanished in a blue-white explosion.

Telltales for the port engine screamed and blinked, painting a picture of impending failure. Dallin fed power to the starboard engine and started to climb. She had to gain enough altitude for a shift to vertical flight. It would still be a controlled crash, but better than slamming into rocky ground at three hundred kilometers an hour.

At two hundred meters Dallin cross-connected the propellers so that the starboard engine now drove both. With sweat in her eyes, she transitioned to vertical flight. A hundred fifty, a hundred, fifty—

At forty meters the cross-shafting snapped. The port propeller flew off, sending a chunk into the control panel. Dallin swore, slapped at sparks, felt something sting her cheek, then stopped feeling anything at all as the verti slammed into a hillside like a falling footlocker.

Parkes saw a tall armed figure silhouetted against the sky. A moment later he recognized it.

"You going to be out here long, ma'am?"

"Just for a breath of air," Forbes-Brandon said. "HQ's between crises."

"Better hop down here, anyway," Parkes said. "With everything they're throwing at us, they might have guerrillas with rockets just outside the perimeter."

The Amazon nodded and slid down into the breast-high slit

trench. Parkes looked to right and left along it. Nobody but experienced people were in hearing. He'd freely robbed the squadrons of cadre to make his job of HQ defense easier. He'd had qualms of conscience about that, but they'd faded away tonight, when every part of Fourteen looked about to come under attack at once.

"Do we have a tac net again?" he asked.

Forbes-Brandon nodded, waving crossed fingers. "Bits and pieces of one, anyway," she amplified. "We're concentrating on—"

Two Shrike 5's took off with a double-barreled scream that suppressed conversation. By the time the night was silent again, another figure was standing on the lip of the trench.

"Hello, First, ma'am. Want some coffee?"

"Well—"

"It's local, not ration," Dietsch said. Everybody on Zauberberg except Brotherhood types agreed on at least one thing: a supply of good coffee was worth any amount of foreign exchange. Parkes had tasted worse on planets where it grew in people's backyards.

"Thanks, but I'm awake enough and I don't want to get any more nervous."

"Okay. Make that two, Dietsch."

"Coming up."

This was Parkes's third cup since the alert routed him out, an hour after turning the two prisoners-at-large over to Blair. He'd never managed to be a quick waker, a problem that sometimes made him wonder why he was still alive. Right now his brain wasn't exactly screaming for sleep; more like muttering darkly—

"Sergeant Major. Does the waiting ever get to you?"

Being honest wasn't a decision; Parkes couldn't recall realizing there was any other choice until he'd already spoken.

"Most of the time. It's the opposite of sex—the more you do it, the worse it gets."

That's the kind of thing I wouldn't normally say to anybody except Dozer, who already knows it.

"Nice to know I'm not the only one."

"Lieutenant, the people who don't have that problem are either liars or damned fools. I think we're evolved to either fight or run away, not wait until somebody tells us which to do."

Another look around, for eavesdroppers. Then:

"Not that I think we're going to have much more waiting. If this goes high-intensity—"

"You think it will?" She sounded as if she wanted reassurance—that it wouldn't? No, the Amazon was a professional. If she wanted reassurance, it was that somebody she could talk to knew more than she did.

"I don't think the Brotherless are laying on air and A.S.A.T strikes just to set up a bigger and better guerrilla movement. I think they're after the north shore, and anybody who might get in their way.

"Of course, it might not be so bad if we had the other two battalions on-planet—"

"Didn't I once overhear an experienced N.C.O.—a field first, he was—saying that 'if' is a dirty word once the shooting starts?" It sounded as if she was smiling.

"Guilty."

"So we have to do the best we can with what we have. Who was it, who said that originally?"

"John Paul Jones, except I also read that it was apocryphal. Maybe he wasn't talking about tactics, anyway. He was quite a chaser."

"How many did he catch?"

"Enough for three—"

The air-raid alarm squealed, then howled. Forbes-Brandon slapped her hands on the lip of the trench, vaulted out, bounced to her feet, and ran for HQ.

"Heads up, people!" Parkes shouted. The squad leaders on both sides acknowledged. Parkes chambered a round, checked the telltales on his mask, and turned to watch the Amazon's dash for safety.

An ugly image knocked on his memory—Laurie Sugg, who'd looked a lot like the Amazon, caught in midstride by a Confederate cluster bomb. Tall blond Laurie, hurled onto blood-spattered ground with half her chest and most of her guts scooped out . . .

Bile rose in Parkes's mouth. He'd just swallowed it when the alarm died. Half a breath later, every A.D. weapon in sight opened fire.

From first to last, Parkes estimated the raid took two minutes. The Brotherhood strike rode in on the deck behind a screen of jammer and bomblet-laden drones. These soaked up a good share of lasers, shells, and warheads. The sky turned into a light show, spraying hot fragments onto everything below.

In the middle of the uproar, the four (as far as anybody could tell) Brotherhood Avias reached their launch positions, salvoed their loads, V.I.F.-turned well clear of the close-range weapons, and cranked on speed to evade and exit. More missiles raced after them; ten kilometers away the Federal 8th Artillery salvoed boosted AA rounds to add to the gauntlet and the falling debris.

That was as much as Parkes cared to watch. He didn't know where the bombs were aimed or where the jamming would drop them. If they were heavy-case penetrators their lethal radius might be small, but if they were light-case frag or cluster loads—

"Hit the dirt!" Parkes shouted, and followed his own order. He felt the trench wall vibrate against his face as explosions ripped across the base. *Penetrators, and at least one secondary explosion.*

When the vibration and the explosions both stopped, Parkes half straightened. A quick look showed one of the hardened fuel dumps spewing flame, a gaping crater where a hardstand and two medium vertis had been, and several sprawled shapes.

"Away, fire and rescue squad!" Parkes called.

Dietsch led the F.&R. squad out of cover. They'd gone just far enough to be silhouetted against the burning fuel dump when a delayed-action bomblet popped off. All eight went down. Seven got up again, two carrying the eighth.

"Away, clearance party!" Parkes shouted. Eight more people scrambled out of cover, dividing into four pairs to scan the area around HQ for more bomblets. A blue-white explosion flared in the sky, high and far away, then the night was quiet except for the rumble of flames and the cries of the wounded.

First round to the Brotherhood, and they weren't fighting by the rules. But then, very few people ever did—including the Peace Force, when they were pushed this hard.

The four grenades soared through the shattered windows of the Eggerstadt Airport control building. The explosions blew the last fragments of plex out of the frames and scoured the ground floor clean of enemies.

Live ones, anyway. Two dead P.F.'ers lay against the wall when Hiko vaulted in through an empty window frame. A third had dragged herself halfway up the first flight of stairs before collapsing. Her blood made the stairs slick. Hiko's first squad still took them at a run, without waiting for orders. They already knew what to do—clear the building, find and disarm all demolitions, suppress any enemy fire within range that threatened the air-landing troops.

Hiko watched a second squad checking the bodies for booby traps, again without waiting for orders. It was no surprise to him, what fifty-seven veterans could do. It was still a pleasure to watch it. He'd inherited Team 3 in addition to his own 4 when their Leader and Second both went down, but after some initial shakiness they were blending with his own men and doing just as well.

The building shook and flame belched down the stairs. The first squad came back down much faster than they'd gone up, not all of them landing on their feet. All but one bounced up, cursing in four languages and five religions as they slapped at burning fragments on their armor.

"What in the—?"

"An I.C. round, Leader."

"Masks on!" Hiko shouted, hurrying across the room. Had Intelligence guessed wrong, putting no enemy launchers in the area? Or were friendlies in range and letting fly in an unfriendly way?

He took the stairs at a run, head up and rifle at the hip, pulling and throwing a hand grenade as he reached the bend. The explosion cut through the crackle of flames and drew screams. Hiko followed the grenade up the stairs, two at a time.

He sprayed the control room without bothering to aim, half a magazine in one burst. Two Team riflemen did the same. Already-burning consoles quivered and spewed sparks and fragments, already-dead P.F.'ers jerked and twisted, and another set of window frames emptied themselves.

"Squad search. Salvage weapons, take names, then clear out." If any demolition controls had been up here, they were unlikely to have survived the I.C. round.

Hiko was turning toward the stairs when the ground beyond the runway spewed flames, fifty meters long and thirty high. The fuel-tank charges at least had been properly placed and properly detonated.

The glare and the shock wave made Hiko stumble over a body lying beside the door, one hand burrowed into a console already twisted from blast and heat. Bullets, grenade fragments, and flames had made the man a good deal less than human.

Hiko drew the man's hand out of the flames and turned him over. One shoulder showed a lieutenant colonel's silver leaves; his name tape read "Kuzik."

Did you die destroying the fuel we'd hoped to capture? Or were you only doing something less heroic but just as much your duty? Well, you are dead but not nameless. That is as much as a warrior can hope for.

"Anyone in Jericho Four. This is Salamander Green Five. Jericho Four, are you in the control tower?"

"Salmander Green Five, this is Jericho Four Leader. Affirmative, and was that your I.C. round?" Silence. "Answer, you demon-spawned Lordless fool!"

"A-a-ff-firmative."

Hiko couldn't think of anything else adequate to the occasion. He led the way toward the stairs, followed by his men with the captured weapons.

As they left the control building, the first of the air-landing fixed-wings slid out of the sky to a short landing. Shorter than intended—two tires blew on hot debris from the fuel tanks and the plane nearly ground-looped off the runway. Reversed props, pilots jumping on the brakes, and perhaps some real Lord's favor kept the plane from running into the fire. It stopped with its nosewheel jammed hard against a runway light.

Two more fixed-wings landed, taxiing around the first one. It was already disgorging its 110 mercenaries of the Chosen Battalion. From beyond the runway fence, tracer looped toward them; about a squad went down. A grenade followed. By then the rest were lying down or dispersing, and mostly shooting back. The plane's turret gun, a platoon's worth of riflemen, and an L.M.G. all sprayed the source of the tracer until it stopped.

Hiko saw five tanks of Salamander Battalion rolling out of the darkness, their 76-mm guns swiveling to keep all directions covered at once. Hiko ordered his Teams into a perimeter around the control building, then trotted toward the tanks.

He wanted to see their C.O., and not just about the trigger-happy Green Five, who'd hopelessly wrecked the control tower. The plan for H+30 called for two Jericho Teams and Green Company of the Salamanders to move to a blocking position between the airport and the city. They were to cover all the land approaches to the airport while the Chosen and the engineers of the Samson Battalion cleared the airport and put it back into service.

Without a control tower or fuel, was the airport going to be back in service anytime soon? Instead of a defensive stance, would fifty-odd crack infantry and fourteen tanks be better employed pushing toward Eggerstadt? They could brush aside any small Federal or P.F. detachments, capture civilian vehicles, support Brotherhood guerrillas . . .

Was this thinking beyond his level of responsibility, even by less rigid standards than the Brotherhood's? Hiko didn't see that he had any choice. The Brotherhood was trying to combine blitzkrieg speed and rigid planning and control. They had too few combat veterans among their leaders to know how incompatible these were. Did they at least have officers sensible enough to know when to listen to the Lord and when to listen to experience?

Hiko didn't know of any, apart from Ruth and some of the Chosen. For the sake of his own men and the Master's victory, he had to find others.

8

CONSCIOUSNESS RETURNED TO Dallin in the brusque assault of a stim shot. She flailed at the arms holding her. For a grisly moment she thought she was being raped.

The world snapped back into focus. She saw Vela's bearded face close to hers, dark eyes wide with concern. He smiled.

"My apologies, Sleeping Beauty. We have to move."

"Where to?"

"Away from here. Our plane burned, and a better beacon—"

"Are we in enemy territory?"

"Not that I know. But I have heard small-arms fire. We can pray that it's only nervous Federal sentries, but I would rather not rely too much on prayer."

"You're on."

Dallin put a hand on Vela's nearer shoulder and lurched to her feet. She felt as if a puff of wind would send her soaring away like a balloon, her usual reaction to a stim shot. It was a moment before she noticed that Vela was wincing under her grip, and holding her with only one hand.

"Something wrong with your shoulder?"

"Dislocated. I was in something of a hurry to get us out of the plane, so I didn't notice until I'd done a good deal of work with it."

Dallin winced in turn. Vela's "good deal of work" had probably kept her from being burned alive.

"Sorry about the bad landing."

" 'Any landing you can walk away from—' "

"I didn't walk."

"Somebody could. That was enough."

"Do you want me to pop the shoulder back in?"

"I'd rather put a kilometer or two between us and the wreck.

If there's no sign of either enemy infiltrators or friendly forces, I'll take a painkiller and you can do your worst."

Dallin touched Vela's face, to be sure they were both still alive. She felt beaded sweat, in spite of the cold.

"Colonel—"

"Sonny, it doesn't hurt that much. Well, perhaps it does. It is still not just *macho* for us to be away from here without worrying about my shoulder. It is good sense. One of us also has to be clear-headed. Now, if you can shift my pistol so I can draw with my left hand—"

"This Command Group meeting is now convened," Colonel MacLean said. With one hand he switched on the map display and with the other stubbed out his third cigar since the air raid. "Major Katsouros, you have the floor."

Fourteen's long-awaited Adjutant was a good deal less decorative than usual tonight. Her ivory complexion looked like a poor grade of soap, her dark eyes were red, she kept licking her full lips, and battledress did nothing for even her generous Mediterranean figure. She looked, in fact, rather like Parkes felt.

I am definitely beyond the ideal age for this sort of thing. I wonder if Dozer was trying to drop a hint, when she talked about pulling the plug? I'll ask her, if she gets clear of Eggerstadt. No, when. *The banshee may wail for a lot of people, but not for Dozer.*

"Thank you, Colonel. You all have printouts of the Estimate of the Situation. This is only going to be a short update. We'll have complete new printouts before you move out."

A few of the gaps in the printed Estimate had been filled in the last two hours, by partly restored communications, educated guesses, and the deaths of good people. How many, Parkes didn't want to think.

From west to east, the Federal 6th Brigade was still holding against a major enemy ground thrust in the Livo area. The enemy had limited tactical air and no airmobile assets. The brigade's second militia battalion was both mobilizing and deploying.

"Or trying to and making a hash of it," Blair said. "The Federals are full of good intentions, but except for the Jaegers—"

MacLean fixed him with a "we've heard that song before" look that produced a welcome silence. The adjutant went on.

Along the north shore, the enemy had effective control of the Eggerstadt area. Nothing but fragmentary communication from any P.F. or Federal units in the area. A recon flight by one of *Ark Royal*'s fighters showed major IR signatures—some combination of fuel and ammunition explosions, sabotage, and collateral damage.

Between Eggerstadt and Nordshaven, Fourteen's First Company and Security Police units had reported heavy guerrilla attacks, one with tactical air support. They were withdrawing toward Nordshaven.

Norshaven itself was filling up with refugees but otherwise seemed to be a zone of calm. Farther south, around Dietrich's Bay, the railroad had been cut by attacks on both the Pfeiffer Tunnel and the bridge. Some of these attacks had been carried out and all had been supported by cruise missiles and drones apparently launched from somewhere out to sea. Two fighters were making a low-altitude search for suspicious vessels, but under the Rules of Engagement they had to make positive identification as hostile before they attacked.

Parkes hoped that Brotherless fire discipline was poor. Short of that, positive identification of a ship from the air was a tedious and difficult job.

Air- and sea-landed infiltrators were reported in the Dietrich's Bay area. Air attacks had also been launched on several Federal and Peace Force installations south of the Serpents.

"These attacks have destroyed an estimated 52 percent of our F.L.C. supplies, thirty aircraft, and more than sixty A.F.V.'s. P.F. personnel casualties have been light, Federal casualties medium, so far as we have any reports."

"Thank you, Elena," MacLean said. "Lieutenant Commander, the space situation?"

Nobody could look elegant in battledress, but the Amazon came as close as humanly possible. "The space situation is a bloody mess. I'd call it a bloody balls-up, except that we don't know if anybody dropped a real clanger. For now, I'll assume we were good and the Brotherbuggers were both good and lucky.

"The Skyguard system is down until further notice. The lasers of Skyguard One were turned against Skyguard Three. One and Two were then shut down manually and garrisoned. The Federal Navy is deploying to provide as much substitute coverage as possible. They don't want to ignore the Thorshammer Shower, even with a war going on."

Parkes hoped that the ersatz Skyguard would do the job. Otherwise they'd have to fight with one eye on the sky, ready to get out from under large flying rocks. It would be a new sensation, but Parkes found he was losing his fondness for new sensations.

"*Ark* is ready to deliver either supporting fires or supply drops. Most of the fighting is under conditions where the Rules of Engagement prohibit orbital fire without ground direction.

Robert the Bruce is acting as primary tactical communications link. *Hipper* is protecting the Federal Navy's efforts to redeploy the satellite network. *Ivanhoe* and *Siegfried* have moved to a high orbit, out of range of any known Brotherhood ASAT weapon."

"What about the shuttles?"

"Two of them are docked with *Ark*, one with *Hipper*. The rest are ferrying supplies from the transports to *Ark*. Oh, yes, Admiral Klein and General Duchamp have jointly requested Special Weapons Release."

Parkes could have reached out and gathered the silence up in handfuls. A message was on the way to the dispatch vessel, at the Yariv Radius; she would jump back to the Union system, relay the message, wait for the reply, then return to the Zauberberg system and squirt it back to *Ark*. If the reply was affirmative, Klein and Duchamp could use any of the fifty-odd thermonuclear weapons aboard the squadron's three warships at their discretion.

The stakes in stopping the Brotherhood's attack as soon as possible had just gone immensely higher.

MacLean broke the silence with the flare of his lighter as he lit another cigar. "Any comments or questions?" The silence continued. "Very well."

He cleared his throat. "In this situation, the battalion commanders are using full discretion to execute standing orders. Battalion Seven will secure the Dietrich's Bay area, restore the railroad, clear up local infiltrators, and reinforce Nordshaven. If they have anything left over, they may be able to send us some help.

"However, we are closer to what seems to be the main enemy attack. Once they've secured corridors across the north shore, I expect them to come south, over the Salla Pass in the east and the Kocher Pass farther west. This is assuming they'll want their mechanized units sooner rather than later, and won't be able to use their airmobile assets freely. We can't do much about their airmobility with what we have; the Air Group and the Federals will have to tackle that one.

"We're going to have to split the Command Group *and* the Battalion even further. I'll be staying here, with Second Company and all available Support Squadron units except what's needed to support one rifle company in the field. So will Major Katsouros, Field First McKendrick, and Colonel Vela and Major Dallin when they return."

MacLean's cigar traced a smoky line from the Kocher Pass northward. "Colonel Blair, you are to form a task force with Third Company, all our organic light vertis, the scout platoon, and necessary support units. There's a Federal battalion deployed in the area, with heavy-weapons support. They are supposed to be under orders to cooperate with any Peace Force units, and probably will do so even without orders. At your discretion, add one of their rifle companies and as much transport as you can beg, borrow, or steal to your task force.

"Your orders are to execute a reconnaissance in force, cover the withdrawal of Peace Force and Federal units from the Eggerstadt area, and if possible link up with the Federal 6th Brigade. You are *not* to engage the enemy except as necessary to carry out those three tasks, and not at all if it will endanger your whole force."

Blair looked moderately unhappy at that. Parkes suspected Captain Podgrebin would look even more so, but the Wise One be praised, he was *not* going to be the senior officer of the task force.

"Your Command Group will include the Group First and our primary Naval Liaison team. Where you'll be operating, I suspect you'll be the best candidates for orbital fire support and resupply." The Amazon nodded.

"All right. Full orders will be cut along with the updated Estimate, about 0400. Be ready to move out by 0500. Any questions?"

The silence this time rang like a bell. They were all professionals; they all knew that a halfway decent plan executed at once could do more than a perfect plan executed a day late.

"Thank you. I plan to throw a hell of a party when this is over, and I don't plan it to be in Valhalla! The Brotherhood is good, maybe better than we expected. But their plan obviously depends on keeping to schedule, and if we can throw off that schedule—well, that's how we'll earn our pay this year.

"Thank you. Dismissed."

• • •

The stim shot was wearing off. Dallin was now aware of bruises, cuts, minor burns, and what felt like fragments of plas sticking in her skin. Compared to what Vela must be feeling, none of it was worth complaining about.

She was still glad when the time came for their second breather. As they sat down with their backs to a hammernut tree, they felt the ground quiver.

"That's the third time since we started moving," Vela said. "The explosion must be underground. Otherwise anything that big should be visible."

Dallin wondered what was underground here to explode. Maybe Fed engineers were already trying to clear the Pfeiffer Tunnel? Just as likely, Brotherhood saboteurs were trying to finish the job their Air Force had begun.

She knew she had to be feeling better; she wanted a cigarette. She ignored the impulse. A lighted cigarette could be seen a lot farther than she could see the sniper who'd kill her for lighting up. *If* there were any snipers about. She was used to the functional paranoia that came with being in enemy territory. It was frustrating to have to be paranoid just as a precaution!

"How's the shoulder?" she asked.

Vela managed a one-shouldered shrug without wincing. He was no longer sweating, but the wind was up. "Try to control the impulse to lay your hands on me a little while longer. The civilians in this area should be friendly, when we find—"

He broke off as a medium verti droned overhead, less than five hundred meters up, a ghostly dark shape passing by without lights and impossible to identify. A medium verti at that altitude around here was probably friendly, but a lot of good soldiers had died of "probably's."

"Upsy-daisy?" she said, making it a question only out of politeness. She had to keep moving, before either the shakes or stiffening wounds hit her. Vela nodded, and almost managed not to gasp as she helped him to his feet.

The tree they'd rested against turned out to be an outrider of a small forest. They'd skirted the edge of the forest for about two hundred meters before a shout came from the darkness ahead.

"Halte! Wo ist dar?" Then, in accented Anglic, "Halt! Who is there?"

Dallin and Vela stepped behind a tree before she replied. "Lieutenant Colonel Vela and Major Dallin, Peace Force Expeditionary Battalion Fourteen."

What must have been seconds but felt like half an hour went by, then a low-voiced exchange ended it:

"Advance and be recognized."

They holstered their sidearms but left the holster flaps unbuttoned, on the "you can always take one with you" principle. Then they stepped out into the open, hands spread and away from their sides.

This time the sentries talked out loud, in German. Dallin knew that someone was saying the newcomers looked all right and that someone else was saying they'd better check ID's. Then a heavyset man in Jaeger battledress stepped into view.

"Your identification, *bitte*." The "please" didn't make it any less an order.

Their ID cards slipped into the scanner on the Jaeger's belt; the scanner *peeped* four times; the Jaeger smiled and handed the cards back. "I am *Unteroffizier* Kunz of the Second Jaegers. You seem to be in order."

"We'll be more in order if you can rout out a medic," Dallin said. "We were shot down by the raid that hit the Pfeiffer Tunnel. Colonel Vela has a dislocated shoulder, and—"

"Immediately, *Frau* Major," Kunz said. His shout brought out three more Jaegers, one with a Red Cross armband, another pushing a sniper's night-vision gear up from his face, and the third a lieutenant.

"Lieutenant Liebermann," said the last. He was thin, blond, and clearly new enough to take everything very seriously, including the duty not to appear frightened in his first battle.

"How soon can we get back to our battalion?" Dallin asked as the medic carried Vela off.

"I—I do not know," Liebermann said. He obviously disliked admitting this to Peace Force officers. Dallin was tempted to spare his pride, but she needed information more than he needed pride.

"Why the hell not?"

"*Frau* Major," Liebermann said stiffly. "Enemy infiltrators have entered the area, in company strength or more, by both air and sea. The principal concern of the Jaegers must be to hunt them down."

"Of course, but you can always put us on a verti—"

"By the time we reach the nearest secure L.Z., it will be dawn. The—the standing orders now are no airmobile operations by day, until—"

"Until when?"

"Until further notice."

"Crap." Liebermann winced as if she'd slapped him. "Sorry. It's not your fault." It was damnably inconvenient, nonetheless. Unless Fourteen had finished regrouping a couple of days early, they were going to be caught not just with their pants down but with all their washing on the line. She and Vela were going to be *needed*, damn it.

"All right," she said. "We've heard small-arms fire twice since we came down, so I don't blame you for being cautious. Are they also doing demolitions?"

"Was?"

She explained about the explosions. Liebermann looked even blanker for a moment, then nodded. "*Ach*. Those were not explosions. They were earthquakes—little ones."

"Earthquakes?"

"Yes. We are not so far from the Teuffelberg here. If he turns over in his sleep, the ground shakes."

"Earthquakes," Dallin said, shaking her head.

"Are you wounded, *Frau* Major?" Liebermann asked earnestly.

"I can wait until the medic's done with Colonel Vela," she said. "But I'd kill for a cigarette." She'd just discovered that her last pack had fallen out of her breast pocket, probably when Vela dragged her out of the verti. Not being a smoker, he hadn't bothered to pick them up. For a moment she entertained thoughts of dislocating Vela's other shoulder. Then she held out a hand for Liebermann's cigarette and lighter.

"Thanks."

"That's the last charge, First," Sergeant Guslenko said.

"Okay, Mike. Let me check." Dozer di Leone knelt briefly, then straightened up. "Good work."

"Thanks."

She hadn't expected too much trouble; Guslenko was a lot more squared away now than before he'd lost a hand on Greenhouse. Half a year in a regen ward and the other half in therapy could do that to you. He still wasn't a trained demolitions expert. She wasn't, either, but she was closer to it than he was.

Dozer, Guslenko, and the two escorting privates headed for the door of the sprawling vehicle-repair shop. Dozer stopped to post a warning sign on the door. That should keep any civilians clear in the gap between the P.F. pulling out and the charges going off. It would have been nice to use booby traps, but there were going to be too damned many civilians swanning around!

Dozer pulled her jacket tighter and blinked as the wind swirled dust around her. Then she knelt and crawled through the hole in the fence, into the ice-pear orchard running down to the banks of Maurki Creek.

Lieutenant Douglas, the senior medic still on his feet, met her by the bank. "Lieutenant Markey's down. I think she had internal injuries."

"Holy Mary."

That left only Douglas and Lieutenant Magnusson of Supply Company on their feet, and Magnusson was a newlie who might make good if he lived long enough. Captain Klin was dying of a head wound, and Markey had been the only other combat officer able to join this ragged detachment who were probably the only free, live P.F.'ers within fifty kilometers of Eggerstadt.

"Go report to Magnusson. It won't help him if he thinks you're turning to me."

Douglas nearly saluted before he caught himself. Doctor Laughton never bothered about teaching her medics the military courtesies she barely knew herself, but Dozer would have liked to have her here now. She was a damned good doctor; please God she'd joined up with First Company to trek out with them.

Three hovertrucks sat on the gravel beach of the creek, invisible from any direction except directly above. A line of battle-dressed figures was moving toward them, each standing pair carrying a limp form or helping a stumbling one. The detachment was seventy able-bodied P.F.'ers and forty-odd wounded. That was P.F. tradition—get your wounded out, if you possibly could. It was also Captain Klin's last conscious order.

Two minutes later, Magnusson himself appeared.

"How's it going, sir?"

The lieutenant frowned. "We're going to be packed. I'm thinking that we might be wise to leave a rear guard. If Lieutenant Markey's not fit—"

"I'm not sure we need to leave a rear guard when we've broken contact with the enemy."

"We hope."

God deliver me from the orders of glorified clerks. " I think we'd have had snipers, or guerrillas at least, if they knew where we were. Besides—sir, do you know how to fight off ghosts?"

"Ghosts?"

"If you don't, let's do what Captain Klin wanted, and get *everybody* out. Otherwise he'll haunt you, and I don't wish that on anybody."

"Oh."

Magnusson obviously couldn't tell if she was joking. She wasn't. Klin would be a bad ghost to have haunting you; he'd been a lonely man, who'd given everything to the Peace Force and got little enough back. It was typical of him to give up his old Second Company, to take on the thankless but essential job of organizing the newly added Fourth. In spite of all his hard work, he'd have been lucky to make major. Now all he could hope for was a posthumous citation.

He'd have a lot of company, too. Everybody in and around the airport must have gone in half an hour. In Eggerstadt things might have been better if those crazies hadn't come storming down the road with their tanker friends, shooting up everything that moved. They'd been only half a company at most, but they'd sucked some good mercs after them and then a regular battalion, the Avengers . . .

It got so mixed up that you didn't know who was on your flank or in your rear—or under your feet, because one Federal company trying to deploy was blocked by guerrillas coming out of the storm drains. There wasn't much to do after a while except stand and fight anybody who was fighting you, wherever you met them.

That made sense, too. The Brotherless were clearly on a tight schedule; speed and surprise were a big part of what they had on their side. A tight schedule could be loosened up a lot if it ran into enough people willing to die where they stood.

That was one thing the Peace Force was good at, even the clerks-in-disguise like Magnusson.

The Feds hadn't been too bad, either. Not always smart, but gutsy, like that squad that teamed up with the P.F. on the outskirts of the city just before Klin got it. They'd insisted on trying to rejoin their comrades to the west, even if it meant a twelve-kilometer hike around the perimeter of a hostile and enemy-held city. Dozer had let them go, and added them to the people she'd burn a candle for, if she ever got to church again. (The banshee wasn't just screaming now; she could hear the flapping of his wings.)

"All right. No rear guard."

"Thank you, sir."

Dozer pulled out the transmitter, whose signal would start the timers on the charges laid in the repair shop, two fuel stations, and the heaviest road bridge in the area. Ten minutes later, there'd be the loveliest lot of bangs you wanted to be a long way from, and fewer usable installations.

The Federal government would probably be pissed, but that wasn't a sergeant major's headache. Her job was to give the headaches to the Brother—

A sonic boom crashed down over the orchard. Branches swayed and overripe pears thudded to the ground. One bounced off Dozer's helmet. She stared at the sky, the transmitter forgotten, then shut her eyes as a dozen high-intensity flares blazed over the city.

The cheers of the P.F.'ers around the hovertrucks didn't drown out the whine of a fast recon drone low overhead. Even half dazzled, Dozer saw the flare of its jets. It would be transmitting a sight picture to *Ark* or some other orbital relay, and that picture would be going back down to the guidance systems of missiles, already airborne or racked under Shrike wings—

"Let's get moving," Dozer said. "Sir."

"We don't have any I.F.F.," Magnusson said.

Glory be, he's heard of I.F.F.. Aloud, Dozer said, "Those missiles won't be targeted for anything this far outside Eggerstadt. If we're spotted visually by a strike, we have smoke and lights." Her fingers itched to signal the demo-charge timers.

"All right. The strike will certainly be better than a rear guard, for keeping the Brotherhood busy."

You'll make a leader yet, Lieutenant Magnusson.

"Yes, sir." She turned on the transmitter and was setting the frequency as Magnusson shouted:

"All hands—load up and prepare to move out on my command."

9

BROILED SMOKED FISH and fried potatoes weren't Parkes's idea of the perfect breakfast. It still beat rations.

"Thank you," he said to the wife. She grinned, and gently pushed a twelve-year-old girl forward.

"It was Kari's cooking. When she is as old as I am, the angels' mouths will water for a taste of what she serves."

"Thank you, Kari," Parkes said. He swigged the last of his coffee.

"My sister Viktoria is in the Air Force," Kari said breathlessly. "And my brother Mauno has been called up with the 2nd Brigade."

"The 2nd is coming up behind us," Parkes said. Too far behind Task Force Blair for his peace of mind, but no point in disturbing these hospitable people. "Maybe Mauno will be able to stop by, on his way to driving the Brotherhood into the sea."

A distant explosion jarred Parkes into turning. On the northern horizon a column of smoke curled up into a sky patched with dirty white clouds. Kari stared, her proud smile slipping.

"Trouble, Sergeant?" the mother said.

"Not for us, I suspect," Parkes said, mentally crossing his fingers.

The line of P.F.'ers waiting to use the house's bathroom went into reverse. The Amazon came out, still hitching up her trousers, and loped across the road toward her command vehicle.

"Kari, go clean up the bathroom," the mother said. When the girl was out of hearing she looked at Parkes. "Who will be here first, the 2nd or the Brotherhood?"

"We'll try our best to keep the Brotherhood away," Parkes said. "You won't do any harm by keeping a couple days' food and clean clothing packed."

"Thank you, Sergeant Major. God keep you."

Parkes's similar prayer to the Wise One was silent; nobody on Zauberberg seemed to have heard of the Lodge. A few locals had given him strange looks.

"Hey, First."

"Yeah, Dietsch?"

"Trouble. That smoke's the X.O.'s verti."

"Hot L.Z. ?"

"Sniper with a missile. Hit the gunpod and set off the ammo. One survivor, and it's not Blair."

"Damn." That left Captain Podgrebin in command of the task force. A hardcharger who knew less about pacing himself than the Amazon ever had, and nothing about pacing his men. From what Parkes had seen of Third Company, they weren't just trained, they were taut as a twelve-kilo line holding a hundred-kilo fish.

Dietsch was looking over Parkes's shoulder at the Amazon climbing back out of her command vehicle. "First, does she wiggle it deliberately or—sorry."

Parkes realized he'd nearly slipped into karate stance. He tried to grin. "Dietsch, you've got a one-groove mind."

"I've never stuck with one groove, First. Pretty soon they want to make it permanent. Of course, if the groove's good enough—sorry again."

"Dietsch, you may have a one-groove mind. You'll have a multipiece skull if you don't cut the power to your mouth and feed it to your brain."

"Okay, First."

"Now let's get ready for Handy Andy's Council of War."

"Sure. Maybe he'll surprise us."

"That's what I'm afraid of."

Podgrebin neither surprised nor pleased Parkes. He did look as if he'd been going on stims and coffee for a lot more than thirty-six hours.

"Colonel Blair's dead. We continue our advance, to execute the battalion commander's orders." He looked at his watch. "We move out at 0830."

That just *might* allow everyone a hot breakfast and a few minutes off their feet. Maybe Podgrebin could be persuaded to do the same.

And maybe vulture pigs would turn vegetarian.

"Captain, I have a suggestion," the Amazon said.

"Yes, Lieutenant?" The emphasis on her permanent rank had to be deliberate. Technically, of course, their permanent ranks were equal; the Amazon might even be Handy Andy's senior. And she had taken that Command Course—

No safe way to discuss that. Best not even *think* too loudly. Besides, an infantry officer would *look* more qualified to the locals, unless and until he really mucked his job . . .

"I was thinking that we might have the launcher sections in both columns fall back, then leapfrog. We may need to call fire *fast* if that sniper's brought up all his friends."

"Negative on that, Lieutenant. We'd need to leave a security platoon with each section. Or don't you trust our crews to be able to set up and fire fast enough?"

"I'd rather not ask them to perform a miracle on a minute's notice."

"Our people won't need it, and the locals couldn't do it no matter how much time you gave them."

That was an injustice and an insult to the section of 120-mm tubes riding with the Federal company from the 2nd Brigade that made up the other column of the task force. At least Parkes hadn't seen any of the local liaisons around; he knew better than to look around while Podgrebin was lecturing.

"All right, Captain," Forbes-Brandon said.

"Any more questions?" Podgrebin said. "Dismissed."

"Some brandy in your coffee?" came Forbes-Brandon's voice behind Parkes.

"No thanks."

"It's private stock, not local."

The bouquet had already told Parkes as much. On impulse, he grabbed the bottle and took a healthy swig. The Amazon's blue eyes widened.

"Nervous in the service, Sergeant Major?"

"If I was—"

"You'd be damned if you'd tell me? Sorry. God knows I don't like having my mind read, either. But you look like you have something on yours."

"Well, Lieutenant—if I were in your position, I'd be sure there was a complete observer team with both columns. Artillery, air, and resupply. I don't know if that's so now."

"With a little help from you, it can be. Maybe not before we move out, but at our next stop."

"You'll have it, Lieutenant." Parkes started conjuring up a mental list of the qualified N.C.O.'s. "We want to hit anything we find as hard as we can."

"Hard enough to let us break contact?"

"We shouldn't—"

The blue eyes, the striking face, and the clear voice all hardened. "Don't play soothe-her-down games, Sergeant Major. That's an order."

"Yes, ma'am."

"And *don't* salute. I don't need sarcasm, either." A sudden smile. "That's a suggestion, not an order."

"Okay. I wasn't trying to scramble you. I don't think we're likely to run into more than the bad guys' reconnaissance in force. That could still mean superior rifle strength. We'll need firepower as an equalizer."

"Very much my own thinking. Now, who do we sneak into the Federal column?"

The patrol that had left Task Force Magnusson's HQ at midnight returned nine hours and twenty-nine kilometers later.

"It looks more like scouting for L.Z.'s than anything else," said the corporal who'd led the patrol. "Scouting a lot and picketing a few."

"Were they improving any—sorry, Lieutenant," Dozer di Leone said.

Magnusson ignored both the question and the apology. *Not perfect, but better than he was a day ago. The man started off as a clerk, but he might just end up as an officer.*

"Not that I could see, sir," the corporal said.

"Very well. Then they may be building up for a major airmobile operation into this area. *If* they have the assets for it."

"We don't know that they don't," Dozer said, answering the implied question. "We got on the scoreboard with the raid on Eggerstadt, but what the score is . . ."

"Probably four goals to one, their favor," Magnusson said with a wry grin. "Well, the game's no more than well started. I want to get word of this out."

"Break radio silence?" Dozer asked.

"I was thinking of another patrol, our four best pairs of legs. We don't want to move by day, and we might have to, if we break radio silence." His grin broadened. "Don't look so surprised, First. My mother's an accountant. I don't know much about fighting, but I do know something about keeping the people on top informed—or not, as circumstances suggest.''

Dozer smiled. ''Yes, sir.'' She'd still have sold her retirement bonus to have Vela or the Fruit Merchant here, but just maybe they could manage with what they had.

''Thank you, Corporal,'' Magnusson said to the patrol leader. ''Don't be surprised if you get a citation for this. Now get off your feet, all of you, and relax.''

''Okay, Lieutenant. Is Captain Klin—?''

''He died two hours ago.''

''Damn.'' The corporal spat into the gravel. ''Thanks. Okay, people. Break time.''

Dozer and Magnusson watched the patrol disappear under the trees. ''Can I make a suggestion, Lieutenant?''

''Could I stop you by saying no, First?''

''We've got some extra time and some extra hands, with those twelve workshop locals who came in last night. I think we ought to modify the hovers, one for low signature and one for high speed.

''If it was just the fit people, I'd recommend ditching the hovers and hiking out. But we've got too many people who can't walk. I don't know if it'll be safest to sneak them out or run them out. We ought to be ready for both.''

''You take charge of that, First.'' Magnusson sat down, pulled off his boots, and began massaging his feet. ''I'd like to bring all three hovers out, if we can. Sort of like the gunners bringing out their tubes.''

''Got any good-luck tokens?''

''No. Can a Lutheran burn candles to the saints?''

''Saint Jude listens to anybody who's in hip-deep.''

''I'd say we're in up to our bottom ribs. Count me in for ten dollars of candles to Saint Jude, scare up a tube of Pedex if you can, and get to work.''

''On the way, Lieutenant.''

The patrol from Task Force Magnusson made contact with the point of Task Force Blair just before 1500. Their message gave Captain Podgrebin new energy. After hearing the captain's orders, Parkes would rather it had made him drop dead in his tracks.

''Left column, laager up here'' —he slapped a map display— ''with both launcher sections. Forbes-Brandon, shift all your observers to the right column. Parkes, you have an hour to round up some extra civilian transport."

"Permission to get some help from the Feds?"

"That'll take too long."

"Sir, with their local knowledge—"

"If you can't tell a truck from a scooter, Parkes—"

"Sir!" He didn't dare look at the Amazon. Fatigue had sharpened Podgrebin's paranoia without dimming his sight.

With only an hour to conjure a couple of trucks out of a countryside of small farms, Parkes didn't have much time to spare for the Amazon. He still gladly swigged down another ten cc's of her beatific brandy, then contemplated doing it again.

"Nice case of Singleton's Syndrome, isn't he?" Forbes-Brandon said. "Here, give me a turn. That's the last bottle I packed along."

A captain in an otherwise obscure Peace Force campaign fifty years ago, Samuel Singleton had tried to rescue some P.F. prisoners with a reinforced company, run into an enemy battalion, and lost his whole command.

"The Command Course has a week they call 'Horrible Examples.' He's right up there with Custer and Crassus."

"Podgrebin must be thinking that the first P.F. officer to bring out some of our strayed sheep is going to get a medal. He's probably right, if he succeeds. We're going to be pretty close to extreme range for the launchers if they stay here."

"Air should be sending somebody over to investigate those L.Z.'s pretty soon. I can ask them for a few tactical loads."

"What if you don't get them?"

"I'm going to make some arrangements with the Feds' artillery chief. Nothing you need to know about."

Meaning you don't want me involved if Handy Andy decides to string you up.

"Okay. But—don't get your tail in a crack over this."

"Sometimes that's where a tail belongs. Better than being wiggled at the likes of Dietsch, anyway. Don't choke on that brandy, First. Either drink it or give it back. And—you keep your head down, when it doesn't belong up."

"I'll do my best."

Another enemy round burst in the trees. Branches, bark, and leaves showered Dozer and Magnusson. Dozer brushed off her helmet.

"I wish Handy Andy hadn't announced he was coming to the rescue. It didn't improve our morale and it did improve the bad guys' intelligence."

Another round. Magnusson looked like a man who badly wanted to flinch, but knew that too many people were looking at him. "No doubt," he said. "We would both have been surprised."

"Lieutenant!" the radio operator said. "Security Two reports enemy infantry in the West Ravine."

Without looking at Dozer, Magnusson asked, "Strength?"

"Looks like part of two companies, one from the Avengers and one from the mercs—the Chosen."

"Engage with grenades, then shift," Magnusson said. "If Two has snipers, have them engage officers and rocket teams. Maintain observation of the ravine if they can. We can't be more than an hour or two from being able to call in fire."

Dozer grinned as the orders were relayed. Magnusson should have known whether Security Post Two had a sniper. That was his only mistake—pretty good going, considering how long it was since anyone around here had slept well or eaten a hot meal—

Grenade launchers thumped for about two minutes and ten rounds. The radio reported that the enemy was going to cover.

"Now, if I was in that ravine, I'd try to work a platoon or so around to the north and infiltrate through the woods," Magnusson said. He had adopted the "if I was" formula to ask Dozer for advice without openly seeming to. *It probably doesn't help much with the veterans, but they're keeping their mouths shut, thank God, and so far none of my advice has got anybody killed . . .*

Before they could decide on the best response to that threat, the whine and rumble of fast-moving vehicles filled the grove. Dozer whirled, chambering a round, then whooped with delight as two P.F. all-terrain wheelers raced up.

They'd barely stopped when their doors popped and a dozen P.F.'ers stormed out through the settling dust. Dozer saw the Amazon with a complete O.P. team and a security squad with an L.M.G., the Fruit Merchant with Dietsch, a couple of aidmen, and some warm bodies humping ammo.

"Good afternoon, people," the Amazon said. Her face was caked with dust, but her teeth seemed to glow. She looked as cheerful as Joan of Arc on a good day. "Any high ground around here for an O.P. site? We can have an air strike in a few minutes if I can show them some targets.''

''We're short of high ground, but we can talk targets,'' Magnusson said. The two officers went off to brief each other and position the O.P. team. Dozer realized that Parkes was looking at her as if he wasn't quite sure she was real.

''Hey, come on, Fruit Merchant, it's really me. Feel?'' She guided his hand to her shoulder. ''Pinch me, it's all right.'' Then she threw her arms around him in a bear hug. ''Nice to be around to say hello.''

''Nice to hear that hello,'' Parkes said, returning the hug. ''Banshee missed fire?''

''For me, so far. Not for others. We lost Klin, Schmidt, Dugan—'' She ran down the list of the dead and missing Parkes had known. She stopped when his long face started growing longer.

''Let's save the rest until we've got something to drink. Magnusson told me to get the wounded on the way out, then do my best for the other two hovers. If you'll take the wounded, I can scare up crew for the hovers and—''

''Dozer, since when do you take orders from a commissioned clerk about salvaging hovers?''

''Since he turned into a fighter. Take my word on Magnusson, Fruit Merchant. I don't know where he found it, but he's got a pretty good grip on—''

The radio's Red Alert alarm screeched. Dozer flipped her helmet set to the all-hands frequency and heard a frantic Security Two reporting infantry launchers deploying on both front and right flanks. The report ended in the hiss of incoming rockets, explosions, and silence.

''The ambulance driver has standing orders. He'll come out here,'' Dozer said.

''Fine. Dietsch, you'll guide the ambulance as far as the task force C.P. Any I.F.F.?''

''No, but plenty of visual ID—''

Two hundred meters away, the edge of the ravine where it left the woods sprouted human figures. A moment later bullets churned dust from the ground and chewed bark chips from the trees.

''People who like to play berserker can spoil your whole battle,'' Dozer said. ''Fruit Merchant, don't go away. Ferrand, Chalky—move it!''

The ambulance driver was starting her turbines as Dozer sprinted for the two empty hovers. The last of the walking wounded scrambled through the open tailgate as the hover slewed around and began to accelerate. Through the dust it raised, Dozer saw Parkes practically throw the chunky Dietsch into the open cabin door. Then the ambulance was roaring away to the south, a roostertail of dust behind it, as the Amazon and Magnusson came sprinting back from their conference.

Ferrand and Chalky dove into the second hover as Dozer scrambled into the first. She started the turbines, then the windshield starred and cracked into a dozen pieces. Dozer plucked two out of her skin, ignored the trickling blood, and fed power to the fans.

The hover turned 180 degrees in place. Ferrand gunned his machine and raced along the edge of the irrigation ditch, teetering but not quite going in. Dozer opened the throttles, a blue-gray shape swept by low overhead, and two bomblets burst just under the skirts of her hover.

The combination of extra power, blast, and suddenly unbalanced lift threw the hover totally out of control. It wobbled toward the irrigation ditch; Dozer called on all God's saints and all her coordination. The hover reached the ditch, lurched, and toppled in.

The impact tore Dozer's seat loose from the floor. She was slammed forward against the control panel, feeling ribs snap inside her flak vest. She tasted blood in her mouth, tried for a firm grip to pull herself free, and realized she was jammed between the cabin bulkhead and the control panel.

What stinking luck. Mama Dozer wasn't going to walk away from this one; they'd have to pry her out and carry her—

Then fuel leaking from ruptured cells struck shorted circuits and hot turbine blades. Flames swallowed Dozer from feet to waist. She heard screaming, thought briefly of the banshee, then realized it was her own in the moment before pain wiped out all thought.

Parkes was on the move from the moment he knew Dozer had lost control of the hover. This gained him all of six seconds before he had to dive for cover again. Grenades and bullets were flying in both directions; both combat reflexes and common sense told him a dead friend couldn't help Dozer.

The O.P. L.M.G. yammered and the incoming fire slackened

briefly. Parkes sprinted the last fifty meters to the ditch, reaching the edge as Dozer started screaming.

He dove into the ditch, rolling to come up on his feet. The screaming wavered. Parkes looked into the cabin, long enough to know what to do, not long enough (please, Wise One) to fray his sanity.

His rifle lay at his feet. *A recruit's carelessness.* He picked it up and fired three shots. The screaming stopped.

More grenades, bullets, and Brotherhood war cries, rapidly growing louder. Parkes crouched beside the burning hover, where he could look west without seeing the cabin. He'd see the Brotherless before they saw him, and he had plenty of ammo—

From the north, the thud of bombs and the tearing-cloth noise of aircraft guns. From overhead the howl of launcher rounds, plunging down into the west, then explosions and screams (or were the screams wishful thinking?). The L.M.G. again, louder and closer.

The Amazon appeared, leaping into the ditch without breaking stride, slamming the barrel of the L.M.G. in her arms down on the far side. A loader plunged after her, landing on his face, getting up with his nose streaming blood but his arms full of ammo drums.

More launcher rounds, landing closer. This time the screams were real. No Brotherless war cries anymore, either.

A couple of would-be Brotherless heroes in sight, though. Parkes picked off one with a head shot and put three rounds into the other's chest as he dove for cover. Then a second M.G. opened up, firing high.

Probably from the wheeler.

Dozer's dead.

We're hitting them with air, artillery, and M.G.'s.

Dozer's dead.

They can't take that.

Dozer's dead.

If they go on playing berserker, they're going to be pretty badly wasted.

Dozer's dead.

Parkes didn't know which voice in his mind was replying to which. After a little while they blended into a chorus.

Then the Amazon was slinging the L.M.G. over one shoulder and holding out a hand to him.

"Sergeant Major—Parkes—hey, Fruit Merchant! Get your finger out. The party's over."

"Dozer's dead."

He'd thought it might not be real if he didn't say it out loud. Had he just killed Dozer all over again?

"She's got a whole Brotherless company as an honor guard, First." She slung the L.M.G. to leave both hands free. "You have your nose packed yet?" she asked her loader.

"It'll do as it is, I guess."

"Good. Then give me a hand with the First. I think he banged his head a little."

"No." Parkes shook off all four helping hands and scrambled out of the ditch.

10

THE LAST OF the enemy aircraft (a mixture of P.F. Shrikes and armed Federation vertis) vanished to the south. The smoke from their strikes began to thin.

"All right, people," Hiko said. "Back to work."

Hiko's Teams and the tank crews emerged from ditches, holes, and under the tanks, brushed themselves off, and picked up tools, lube cans, and ammunition pallets. Both units had been quick to learn what the other needed, when it came time to resupply and repair the tanks or resupply the Teams and evacuate their wounded.

Hiko would miss Green Squadron when it was pulled back to its parent Salamanders. He'd heard that one squadron had gone west to pursue the Security Police and the P.F. toward Nordshaven, while the rest were engaged against withdrawing Federal troops to the east. He would be happy to find this rumor held truth, unlike the stories of the sinking of the west coast landing ship and the Proctors taking hostages. With the Salamanders dispersed, his Teams would have their armored comrades-in-arms at their backs for a while.

A captured civilian car rattled up. Four women climbed out. Hiko recognized Ruth's walk and was on his feet before she hailed him.

"Team Leader, in the Lord's name, I greet you."

"As I do you, Commander. What business of the Lord's brings you here?"

"My company and I are to reinforce this position. Then the rest of the First Daughters is to pass through us, along with the Avengers and the Chariots, for an advance southward."

It was too public to speculate on exactly where in the south the brigade's objective lay. Probably the Kocher Pass.

"May the Lord's favor and your own valor give victory." *Al-*

though if the Lord's favor also keeps you and your company in reserve until that P.F. column is cleared from our path—

"Did the air strike do much harm?"

"Not to us. The Avengers and the Chosen were engaged with the P.F. They were the main target. I've heard that their casualties were heavy."

"Avengers and the Chosen together?"

"A company of each."

"Doubtless time was short, and surely they are equal in valor." Their eyes met, saying what could not be put into words: *time is never so short that it is wise to send in two companies from different battalions against a determined enemy.*

Ruth turned to one of the other women. "Platoon Leader Ryan, order our people to double-time. The Avengers and Chosen will doubtless need help evacuating their wounded."

Ryan frowned, then saluted. "Yes, ma'am." Hiko knew that Ryan probably resented starting off the campaign as a glorified nurse. Some of the Brothers would still like to reduce the Daughters to such work. But then, no faith was without its fools.

"There is no loss of honor in tending those wounded in fighting the Lord's battles," Hiko said. "Still less in recovering the bodies of those the Lord has taken to Himself." *Or their pieces, because that's all air strikes and artillery often leave.* "Your valor will be well tested." *Not to mention your stomachs.*

"Yes, sir."

Ryan withdrew. Ruth stepped close to Hiko. "Team Leader, have you heard the rumors about the Second Daughters?"

"Just that—rumors. The enemy is silent, and they would certainly claim a much smaller victory. They need to encourage their people in the face of the Lord's blessing on our cause."

"It is not unknown to hold one's peace, in order to encourage one's enemies to overconfidence."

I hope no one overhears, who would call that defeatism. I would call it a shrewd guess. With only minimal satellite or air reconnaissance, the Second Daughters' ship would be easily found, then easily sunk. Many of Ruth's friends may well be dead.

"Both are possible. Only the Lord knows which is the truth, if either. Let us do our duty to Him and those we lead and go on."

Ruth seemed content with that. Did she believe, or was she wise enough to know that he had become reluctant to lie to her?

• • •

"What in the name of God is *that*?" Vela asked.

Dallin stared at the jet verti settling on the pad fifty meters away. "An old-model Shrike. Looks like it's been fitted with extra seats for training. I don't know if those underwing pods are electronics or guns."

"That's your transportation," Warrant Officer Cecchi informed them. Their escort since Lieutenant Liebermann brought them to Jaeger HQ, he was a mobilized reservist, a high school computer teacher in civilian life. "We're putting most of the tactical air into holding Nordshaven. The fields are more secure, and the targets are fat enough."

"That thing looks like a pretty fat target itself," Vela said.

The verti's canopy popped open. "Hurry up, people," the pilot shouted.

Cecchi handed Vela and Dallin their Jaeger-issue bags, stepped back, and saluted. "Good hunting. We were honored to have you with us. Although I imagine you could have done without the honor, to be with your own people."

"Got it in one," Dallin said. She ran toward the verti. Probably nothing had fallen apart without her and Vela, but this was too damned big a war for field-grade spectators!

From the cockpit consoles, Dallin judged that the verti was an old attacker converted not only for training but for airborne E.C.M. and communications. The pilot confirmed her guess.

"I flew on the strike against the *Margarethe Bulow*," he said.

"The what?"

"Oh, you hadn't heard?"

"Pretend we've been out-system since before the shooting started—" Vela began. Dallin cut him off. The pilot looked ready to talk all the way home if given a quarter of a chance.

"Would that be the ship that launched the decoys and missiles against Ponte d'Oro?"

"Not just that. She had a big load of women soldiers on board. Put some of them off in fishing boats, maybe some more in minisubs. A lot were still on board when we had a positive ID and invited surrender."

"Did they?" Vela asked.

The pilot slammed the canopy and began powering up the engines before answering. "Daughters surrender? They probably figured that drowning was better than rape by us and execution after they got home."

The engines built to a shriek that made all conversation impossible. Dallin and Vela had to stare at each other until the verti transitioned into horizontal flight two hundred meters up. Then the shriek died back to a distant howl.

"They believed that?"

"The ones the Navy picked up did, or so I've heard. Excuse me, I didn't get much sleep last night, and we're going to be low all the way."

Dallin realized she hadn't strapped herself in. She remedied that, then helped Vela, whose shoulder was still aching and stiff.

"Please God, it's not going to be that kind of war," he said.

Dallin wanted to reassure herself and him with a cheerful answer. She looked north instead. From the Pfeiffer Tunnel, dust rose like the smoke from a forest fire. The engineers must already be at work.

She told herself to think about all that was being done to repair the damage, her chances of getting in some combat flying, how to reorganize Transportation Company—anything but Vela's question.

"We have to advance and maintain contact," Podgrebin said. "Nothing else to do. We broke those two companies. We can break their friends."

His words were slurred and his voice had a roughness in it, like a turbine with a bent blade. Forbes-Brandon shook her head.

"Captain, I'd recommend against an advance."

"Officially?"

So he was going to be regulation about this? Not surprising.

"Yes. We'd do better to break contact, evacuate the wounded, then find a secure position with good observation. If we force them to concentrate, they'll be better targets for our air and artillery."

"And if they don't concentrate?"

"Then we can be reinforced and go hunting them in detail."

"I'm glad all your thinking isn't defensive, Lieutenant. My answer is no. We can get just as much air support if we advance and keep up the pressure on the ground."

"That's not correct. We won't have another air strike for at least four, maybe six hours."

"I knew the Feds were useless. Has our Air Group lost its spine, too? Never mind, you might not know and you probably wouldn't tell if you did. You—'' He broke off, wiping his mouth with a shaking hand.

''Never mind,'' he said again. ''I'll order up a platoon of the Feds, to guard the wounded. They should be able to do that. We'll advance when they arrive.''

Podgrebin lurched off to the far side of the boulder that marked the task force C.P. Forbes-Brandon looked at Parkes, sitting cross-legged with his hands on his knees and his eyes staring into space, or maybe into some other dimension in search of Dozer di Leone.

Come on, Parkes. I'm in over my head. I think *I can swim, but I'd like to know you'll throw me a life preserver if I need it. Technically I can supersede Handy Andy, but standing on technicalities with the enemy five kilometers away—*

She looked at Dietsch, sitting with his back to the boulder and her L.M.G. across his lap. He pulled the cleaning kit out of the butt slot and unfolded the rod. He didn't meet her eyes, either, but she could have sworn he nodded slightly.

Podgrebin's shout was almost a scream. The captain lurched around the boulder, kicking up gravel, face as red as if he'd been scalded. His hands clawed at the air.

''Damn it! What motherrammer ignored my orders about keeping the tubes in the rear! Those pissing Feds sent them up and a platoon for security. They can't spare anything for the wounded!''

''Captain, I don't know who—''

''Oh, yes, you do. You know exactly who.'' Podgrebin's gaze focused on Parkes. His eyes held glee, anger, and exhaustion, but very little sanity. ''Lieutenant, I am placing Sergeant Major Parkes under arrest for insubordination. If he cooperates, I may not raise the charge to mutiny.''

''If—'' began Forbes-Brandon. Then rage choked her, as it swept away everything but the urge to put a bullet through Podgrebin's empty head.

It wasn't just the paranoia, the stupidity, the criminal folly of arresting Parkes. It was the obvious bribe to her. *Back me up in my feud with the Sergeant Major,* Podgrebin was saying, *and I won't accuse you.*

Forbes-Brandon thought that she had never been so insulted in her life. She could hardly have felt dirtier if she'd been raped. Her thoughts about Podgrebin turned to shooting him in the groin before shooting him in the head. Or maybe staking him out and having her old Morris dance troupe trample all over him—

"Lieutenant, that's an order."

"Captain, it's not a lawful order. Neither is your order to advance in the absence of air and artillery support. Under the circumstances, I must conclude that you're temporarily unfit for command. I would prefer that you turn over command of this task force to me—"

Podgrebin gobbled in his throat, but his hands stayed in view. Forbes-Brandon went on, the part of her mind that wasn't frantically searching for soothing words hoping that neither he nor Parkes would do anything drastic.

"My date of rank as first lieutenant makes me senior, and I'm command-certified. That means—"

"You mutinous bitch! You—you—Dietsch, disarm them! Both of them!"

Dietsch hesitated just long enough for the lump in Forbes-Brandon's throat to turn from cold lead to hot steel. Then he turned to her.

"Ma'am?"

Podgrebin hissed like a snake and his hand darted for his pistol. He'd just gripped the butt when Dietsch flipped the L.M.G. end for end as deftly as a drum major with a baton, then drove the butt end hard into Podgrebin's stomach. He doubled up, then toppled and lay gasping and retching, one hand almost touching Forbes-Brandon's boots. The pistol landed muzzle-down in the gravel.

Forbes-Brandon bent down, picked up the pistol, and rolled Podgrebin over so he wouldn't inhale any gravel. She was pleasantly surprised to find her hands steady.

"Thanks, Dietsch. I'd kiss you, except that I have the feeling it might be misunderstood." She looked at Parkes, and felt like singing when he met her eyes.

"Yes, ma'am," Dietsch said. He knelt by Podgrebin and started tying the man's hands behind his back with his belt.

It's not a life preserver I need. It's more like a parachute.

"All right. Dietsch, get a medic for the captain. Say he suffered a seizure."

"A Julius Seizure—" Dietsch began. Parkes and Forbes-Brandon together glared him into silence. "Yes, ma'am."

"Parkes, take over at HQ. Bring Lieutenant Sharpe up here on the double. I'll do the explaining. Then we'll put a second platoon of the Feds with the launchers. They and the wounded can go out together. All units will rendezvous on the south bank of the Kimli, half a kilometer west of Hill 206, by 1730. Then we'll see about finding that defensive position and updating HQ on the situation.

"Parkes, as soon as you're not needed here, I want you to take over Magnusson's people—"

"No."

He was suddenly on his feet, standing close to her. He was also slumping a bit and she was standing very straight, so their eyes were exactly on a level, blue meeting gray.

"No?"

"Magnusson—Dozer"—two syllables and a whole universe of pain in the second one. "Dozer"—this time it came out easier—"she said Magnusson was pretty much on top of things."

"If he was good enough for Dozer, then he's good enough. He still may need some help. Dietsch, you are a very local, very temporary, very acting sergeant, reassigned to Task Force Magnusson."

Dietsch thought a lot of things quite loudly, but only said, "Yes, ma'am."

Parkes was almost smiling. *Keep it up, and I'll have that parachute.* "Lieutenant Sharpe will run Third. The Feds won't need any changes. Magnusson can stay where he is. Anything else?" *And if you don't answer, Sergeant Major, I may get down on my knees and beg you.*

"If we can manage a hot meal for everybody when we rendezvous . . ."

"That somewhat depends on where we dig in. If it's 206, no problem. If we have to make a night march to reach our position, time might be short."

That's almost the right answer but not quite, as far as I can judge from his expression.

"Parkes, we'll go over the maps together, and pick three or four good positions. Then we can move to the closest one that's in range of the Fed artillery. We can have some hot food sent in with the medevac and resupply missions."

He's really smiling. I must have said the right thing. Maybe I even hid my suspicion that the medevac and resupply may take a while.

"All right, people. It's been a bad day, but I think it's about to get even worse for the Brotherbuggers."

• • •

"Come in! Raoul, two more places for lunch!"

Duchamp himself threw open the door to his office and ushered Vela and Dallin inside. "Sit down and have a drink. What they call *eau-de-vie* here, I call *pis-de-chameau*. However, I am saving the brandy for when we have something more to celebrate."

Dallin nearly gagged on the drink but felt warmth spread up into her head and down into her stomach. Duchamp emptied his own glass in a single swallow, shoved a pile of papers off his desk, and leaned back with his hands behind his head.

"Welcome home. I fear my welcome will be to hear your adventures, brief you on the situation, and send you back to your battalion—you were saying, Colonel?"

"Only 'Thank God,' sir."

"If you insult Raoul again, he may put laxatives in your omelet . . . But no, I appreciate your sentiments. Indeed, I honor you for them." Duchamp poured three more glasses. This time he sipped and Dallin didn't gag.

Telling the general of their adventures took Vela and Dallin through the soup and half their omelets, plus a glass of wine apiece. Duchamp frowned at Vela's recounting the rumors about the *Margarethe Bulow*.

"All of the prisoners seemed to believe the tales of rape," he said. "At least, when they were together. Interrogated alone, some of them seemed more skeptical. Few seemed to believe they would be shot for surrendering. The Brotherhood produces fanatics, but we know well enough that it does not produce fools."

Over the rest of the omelets and a desert of local pears with ration chocolate sauce, Duchamp briefed them.

"I am giving you the strategic picture because the colonel at least may soon be making decisions of strategic consequence. The Federal chief of staff and I agree that the Brotherhood's objective is to seize as much Federal territory as possible, to use its population as hostages.

"Their primary objective was the north shore, which they have largely achieved except for Nordshaven. They will not have the city; the Federals are making its defense *their* primary objective.

"First Company of your battalion is also withdrawing into the city. Two companies of Seven are being deployed north as soon as the area around Dietrich's Bay is secure. The defense of Nordshaven also has priority for air support and airlift.

"The secondary Brotherhood objective seems to be the area east of the Kevo River. They appear to be advancing toward it along two axes, one over the Kocher Pass and the other here—" with a tap of the display at the east end of the Serpents.

"The heavier thrust and the more dangerous one seems to be the western one. We estimate a full brigade with armor, artillery, and air support. Their eastern one will emerge into sparsely held territory, a long way from anything except a great many stubborn Finnish farmers.

"So our secondary objective is defeating the thrust over the Kocher Pass. At the moment Task Force Blair is in contact with the enemy thirty-two kilometers north of the pass. Unfortunately, Colonel Blair was killed in action this morning, and the T.F. came under the command of Captain Podgrebin—"

Vela winced as Dallin hadn't seen him do since his shoulder was set. It didn't escape Duchamp, either.

"One day you must explain to me why you winced at Captain Podgrebin's name, Colonel Vela. It now appears that Captain Podgrebin has had a seizure, and that the task force is temporarily under the command of Lieutenant Commander Forbes-Brandon."

It was Dallin's turn to wince, but Duchamp either didn't notice or decided he'd used up his quota of pointed remarks. "Colonel, you will proceed to task force HQ and take command. You will have roughly two Federal battalions operating in your area, one in your rear with artillery support and another retreating from the north. Their brigade commander is an old Jaeger officer, Colonel Majo. He seems to know his business."

One elongated arm swept across the map, eastward from the Kocher Pass to the edge. "Colonel MacLean will be in command of Peace Force operations here. That includes Battalion Five, which starts landing tomorrow.

"Major Dallin, you are temporarily without a command. You will proceed to Colonel MacLean's HQ and coordinate transport for both Task Force Blair and Battalion Five, until their own Transportation Company is fully operational.

"You will also supervise the fitting of ten Tollhouse kits to light vertis. Once operational, the Tollhouse squadron will provide reconnaissance, light tactical air support, and harassment against enemy airmobile operations."

Dallin decided not to ask about flying missions with the Tollhouses. It was always a lot harder to be court-martialed for disobeying orders you hadn't received. The thought of Kat's sticking her head into a noose chilled Dallin for a moment.

A second thought deepened the chill. "What about enemy air? Tollhouse vertis really aren't meant to tackle fighters or even attackers."

Duchamp shrugged. "Both sides' air assets are spread like a single pat of butter on a meter-long loaf. Both our cover and their fighters will be few and far between. We did major damage with our strike on Eggerstadt, but we have not been able to repeat that."

"Can't orbital fire—?" Vela began.

"Two-thirds of what we have is devoted to substituting for the Skyguard system and protecting our satellites. As to unleashing the rest—you know the Rules of Engagement. If Colonel Vela can force the Brotherhood to deploy major units in an area free of civilians . . ."

"I understand, sir."

Duchamp stood up, emptied his glass, and wadded up his napkin. "I am meeting the Federal chief of engineers in half an hour, to discuss restoring land communications with Nordshaven. After that I will arrange your return to Fourteen. My quarters are at your disposal, if you want an hour or so of sleep or a bath. If General Lindholm has not returned from Nordshaven before you leave, Major Kiley will give you a supplementary briefing."

"Thank you, sir," Vela said. Dallin started to ask if the briefing would include casualty lists, then swallowed the words. She didn't need to know how many of her friends were gone. In fact, she needed *not* to know for the next day or so, until she was too busy or too tired to hurt.

Duchamp gripped their hands and kissed both of them. "You are returning to a battalion that has conducted itself in the highest tradition of the Peace Force. It was an Englishman, Lord Nelson, who said it, but it was said well nonetheless: 'They fought like one man, and that man a hero.'

"Au revoir."

Forbes-Brandon turned off the map display with more force than the switch required. She felt a personal grievance against the map for not showing her that last slope on Hill 1242.

Hill 1242 was only three kilometers' comparatively easy walking south of 206, or so the map said. It had water, good command of all likely approaches, plenty of concealment, and a wet bar. Captain Relander of the Feds, Magnusson, Sharpe, and the Federal artillery commander (by radio) all agreed.

No one knew and the map didn't say that the last kilometer to the best position was over a variable slope strewn with glassy volcanic debris and loose scree. It was like walking over knife blades and ball bearings, an ordeal for tired soldiers in the fading light.

Forbes-Brandon pushed herself to arrive at the head of the column, ignoring increasingly indignant muscles. She sensed Parkes's disapproval, but quite irrationally she felt that if he hadn't protested her choice, he shouldn't complain about anything else she did.

Everybody's morale was nearly as ragged as the slope by the time they'd settled into position. Mending it came from the outside, with the arrival of a pair of vertis. A sedated Captain Podgrebin and five other casualties of the march went out; hot food and ammunition came in. So did good news: the Federal artillery was in position; the ambulance had reached friendly lines with everybody as alive as they'd been.

The hollow feeling of having botched her first field command slowly faded. Forbes-Brandon forced herself to eat some hot food and stay off her feet while she did it. Obviously her first impulse was still to be a perfectionist, but at least her second thoughts were coming faster!

She punched the last few ranges into the computer and turned it off. She was folding up the blackout hood when she heard footsteps behind her.

"Ma'am?"

"Dietsch?"

"Yeah. I brought up the party for Magnusson's share of the goodies."

"Want a drink? I think there's something in—"

"What I'd really like is the rest of that bottle, for the First."

"Where is he?" She couldn't quite ask "How is he?"

"Down with us. Placed the M.G.'s, inspected the holes, then started asking people about Dozer. How she looked, what she said, what she did."

"I hope everybody's being polite if they can't be truthful."

"Magnusson's going to knock them down and I'm going to

jump on them if they slip. Really, it's no big problem. Old Mama Dozer went out swinging. Magnusson's going to write her up for all kinds of medals. Nobody's got a bad word to say about her."

"Then what's—no, I suppose I know what's bothering Parkes. Dozer's death was the one-too-many that can hit even an experienced soldier? At least that's what the book says." Even in her own ears, that sounded like a particularly lame excuse for even lamer phrasing.

She hadn't expected that Dietsch would laugh. "Lieutenant, just 'cause the books say something is so doesn't mean it isn't. Dozer and the Fruit Merchant, they go back a long way. Bifrost and even before, maybe ten, twelve years from what I've heard."

Twelve years ago I was dreaming of winning the Sword of Honor again, until we heard about David.

"Were you on Bifrost?"

"Platoon sergeant in Three. Nothing very glorious, but—"

"Platoon sergeant?"

"Well, they were hard up, and—"

"Just a minute. You were a private when we went to Bayard. How many times—?"

"Have officers and me not gotten along? This'll be my third shot at stripes, if they stick after we come off this hill. But I didn't want to dump on you with my memoirs. What I wanted was the brandy, and to ask if maybe you could keep an eye on the First."

"I'm his C.O., not his mother."

A long silence, ending in another laugh. "Maybe what he needs is a little of both, right now. Thing is, Lieutenant"—and now Dietsch was practically pleading—"I can't do the job. Not like he needs, without bugging out from where you sent me, unless he stays down with Magnusson.

"He won't do that, either. He won't cut down Magnusson, not when the lieutenant's really shaping up. Besides, he knows you need him free to move."

"He hasn't said a bloody word to me."

"He would, if you gave him a chance. Even if he doesn't say anything, it'll be better if you're around. The way he's feeling, he might get careless and—"

"Get himself killed?"

"Or somebody else. That'd be just about as bad. He might feel that he wasn't a good soldier anymore. Then—I'm probably talking out of turn—"

"Dietsch, you don't have anything to lose by talking. If you stop now, on the other hand . . ." She couldn't think of a threat dire enough.

"Okay. It's just that you and he are a lot alike, from what I've heard. Being the best possible soldier is the whole damned world for both of you. Take that away, and what do you have?"

What, indeed? Forbes-Brandon knew intellectually that N.C.O.'s discussed officers and each other with a frankness that made women discussing their lovers look reticent. She hadn't expected to have those discussions sneak up on her like a low-flying missile and hit her with a personal *and* professional dilemma.

If she kept too close an eye on Parkes, wouldn't she be neglecting the rest of her command? If she did that, wouldn't Parkes notice it, know why, and feel an even heavier burden of responsibility that might further impair his judgment?

Possibly. Just as likely, Dietsch was right, and she was Parkes's best hope. Not to mention that keeping Parkes functioning was part of her duty to this oddly assorted command, which only a miracle could keep from having to fight one of the decisive battles of the war.

There's such a thing as defining duty in a way that leaves out people. Maybe you don't win any more battles, by throwing that one out the window. But you sleep a bloody sight easier at night!

11

THE FORWARD ARTILLERY observer punched the final range into his computer. Ten seconds later, the radio squirted half an hour's accumulated data back to the waiting guns in thirty seconds.

"It is in the Lord's hands now," the F.A.O. said.

Hiko hoped the Lord wasn't meditating or out for a drink. The twelve tubes of the Hammer of God battalion weren't much against a position like Hill 1242, held by a determined opponent with twice as much artillery in support. If they were to do more than provide targets for counterbattery fire, the Hammers were going to have to come down *fast*.

For at least the tenth time since midafternoon, Hiko wondered why his Teams hadn't been ordered to infiltrate past Hill 1242, then locate and harass enemy artillery. They would have been in position by now if the orders had been given after lunch.

Of course security for the F.A.O.'s was important. The Peace Force at least was known for aggressive sniping and local counterattacks. If they eliminated too many of the F.A.O.'s, the supporting fire against the hill would be much less effective.

Just as certainly, the Brotherhood lacked orbital reconnaissance and was short of both air and electronic assets. Not using their best available infiltrators against the enemy artillery could make the enemy a present of unhampered artillery fire, called in from a commanding position by experts.

What was causing this sudden new uncertainty in the Brotherhood's tactics? Green Squadron had received three contradictory sets of orders in four hours, before finally moving north to protect the Brotherhood's left against Federal counterattacks. Neither of tonight's two assault battalions had eaten a hot meal. Vehicle spares were already running short—and not just for the impressed civilian machines.

Was the War Council simply in beyond its depth? Or were the Teams serving an authoritarian regime with all of such regimes' traditional fear of initiative by their armed forces? Were Hiko and his men being held back because the Brotherhood didn't trust them to operate where Proctors feared to tread?

The night split in flame and thunder as the Hammer of God opened fire. Illuminating rounds, H.E., and clusters poured down on Hill 1242. Its fanged crest jutted up against the night, silhouetted by the shellbursts on the reverse slope.

The F.A.O.'s had worked hard, but Hiko didn't expect too much of the bombardment. Not against the Peace Force and a regular Federal unit. Some casualties and a great deal of confusion would be the limit, but probably enough when two Brotherhood battalions were ready to attack—

The flame and thunder seemed to double. The light silhouetting the crest grew brighter; some launchers up there had survived to shoot back. Most of the new uproar was rockets and shells arching high overhead, from far in the rear of Hill 1242.

Hiko looked north, to watch the return fire plunge down toward the Hammer of God's positions. The hills hid the explosions, and the bombardment hill drowned them out. Had the Peace Force done what his Team should have been doing, sent ground observers to within visual range of the Hammers? They seemed to be getting onto their targets with a speed that hinted of continuous observation.

Airbursts rolled over Hiko's position. He hastily buried his chin in the rocky ground, as bomblets enveloped him in fragments, bits of rock, and acrid fumes.

Fragments disemboweled the F.A.O.'s computer and mangled his right arm. More fragments glanced off Hiko's helmet. Someone screamed, "Lord, help me!" loud enough to be heard over the bursts.

Then sudden, if only relative, silence. Hiko watched and listened, realizing that the airbursts were coming four at a time, and creeping back and forth across the foot of 1242. The launchers on the hill—they sounded like 120-mm's.

Never mind the enemy's artillery. They might have been too far in the rear to be reached on the ground. Infiltrating Teams could at least have harassed the hill launchers' crews, perhaps exploded some of their ammunition.

The artillery duel went on. The enemy's counterbattery fire

was beginning to hurt; fewer Brotherhood rounds burst on the hill. The launchers started firing three-round salvos, then pairs.

Jamshir Singh grinned. "They are losing tubes."

"May it be so." They might also simply be moving the weapons.

Far to the right, the slope of 1242 lit up with tracers and the trails of infantry rockets. Grenade bursts followed. During the next lull in the artillery duel, Hiko heard small-arms fire building steadily.

"The Avengers are going forward!" Jamshir shouted.

"May the Lord grant them victory," Hiko said. They'd need the help of the Lord or *somebody* who could answer prayers and snatch victory from folly. The Avengers were going forward alone, with no sign of the Daughters on their left even being in position.

The Avengers were largely recruited in the far northern Protectorate, the most conservative area. Had they attacked unsupported to prove they needed no help from women so lost to propriety as to be warriors? Or had they simply been unable to endure the enemy bombardment?

A final 120 round burst three hundred meters away. Hiko froze, then dressed the F.A.O.'s arm, sent Jamshir to collect casualty reports and check ammunition, and drank some water.

The C.O. of the Avengers didn't survive to explain his battalion's premature attack. At least he had no reason to be ashamed of its performance once it moved. All that saved the defenders was the lack of any supporting attack or even fire from the Daughters. Forbes-Brandon managed to shift not only fire but even a half-platoon "fire brigade" under Parkes from one danger point to another until the Avengers stalled. Then fire from the three repositioned 120's wrecked the Avenger's reserve company, and the danger from them ended.

By then Federal counterbattery fire had beaten the Hammers down to the level of a nuisance. Most of the artillery shifted to the Daughters, catching them massed for their jump-off on ground short of both cover and concealment. They suffered thirty percent casualties before the order to move even came.

The survivors did everything possible, but they'd lost too many leaders. Squads and even platoons ended up as gaggles of near-strangers, under junior sergeants. Then Peace Force fire lashed at them.

The Daughters' courage couldn't hide the fact that the attack was doomed. Not from their enemies, not from themselves. That courage kept them going, though, until a half kilometer of slope was littered with their bodies, and the cries of the wounded and dying nearly drowned out the last of the firefights around the Peace Force positions.

"That ravine, here," Forbes-Brandon said.

Parkes stared at the map display. His eyes didn't want to focus and his ears were ready to take a vacation in some quieter spot.

"Yeah. It comes right up under the Knuckle." The monolith they'd christened the Knuckle marked where Third Company's position met Magnusson's company. "Nice concealment, too close for the heavy artillery. What about the launchers?"

"They're displacing again. Count them out for oh, ten minutes at least."

"Make that fifteen, on this kind of ground."

"Point taken."

"So you want the fire brigade down there?"

"Unless you think we're going to have more trouble here?" She drew a finger along the front of the Feds and Third Company.

"We might. Nothing as bad as a platoon coming up that ravine and getting into our rear, though."

"Rather what I thought. You'll have two L.M.G.'s and a Mark VII."

"Extra ammo for Magnusson's people?"

"If there's any to spare."

"I'll see."

"We can move out as soon as we have the ammo and Scavullo gets his leg bandaged."

"What hit him?"

"Bullet. A couple cees into his thigh, that's all. He can move if he doesn't have to hurry."

A T.O.T. salvo from all the supporting artillery made conversation and even thought impossible for a moment. In the dying glare and roar, Parkes thought he saw the Amazon smiling. Then she gripped him by both shoulders.

"Take care of yourself, Parkes. If we lose any more officers, you may make the difference for holding this bloody hill!"

The Amazon warned all friendly positions that the fire brigade would be moving. Parkes felt it was safe to take a shortcut, from the rear of Third Company into Magnusson's rear. The sixteen soldiers of the fire brigade had covered about two-thirds of the six-hundred-meter diagonal when the platoon of Daughters came out of the ravine.

For the fire brigade, this cut both ways. They were outnumbered. They weren't outgunned, and they could use their firepower with less risk of hitting friends.

Parkes gave one order, sent one message, and fired two shots. The order was "Open fire." The message was a report of the enemy attack and the fire brigade's position. The first shot was a warning. So was the second.

Half the enemy were down, along with three of the fire brigade. Almost at Parkes's feet, an enemy corporal was trying to put a fresh magazine in her rifle, in spite of having a hand and a knee smashed. Somebody drew down on her; Parkes knocked the soldier's rifle aside, fired a shot past his ear, and picked up the Daughter's rifle.

As Parkes straightened up, an L.M.G. opened fire from near the C.P. So did Magnusson's people, tracers flying both forward and backward from their position. The remaining Daughters in the open didn't last long. The ones who took cover survived until Dietsch led a squad out from Magnusson's position with grenades.

Parkes slid down into Magnusson's C.P.

"Hello, First. Casualties?"

"Two dead, three wounded. Dietsch's people are bringing them in, also a couple of prisoners. We've got some ammo for you."

"How much?"

"Three thousand rifle and fifty grenades."

"Better than a belly wound."

Parkes wondered how much of Magnusson's casualness was an act. Of course, he was keeping his own hands in his jacket pockets because he couldn't quite trust them not to shake . . .

The night grew noisy again, as the 120's began searching for Daughters still lurking in the ravine. Ten minutes later they fell silent.

"Hope they didn't shoot themselves dry," Magnusson said. "These are fairly determined people over there. Evicting them isn't going to be easy."

"No. If I were you—"

"Parkes, would you shove the etiquette and save time?"

"Okay. I'd suggest putting a couple of sniper teams out to your front. A marksman with night sights and a security element in each team. The Daughters are pulling back already. A few more casualties might keep them on the move."

"Makes sense. Any names for the teams?"

"Sanders, Dunkerley, Hagstrom—" Parkes listed four more names.

"All right. I'll take your advice. Just don't put yourself down for leading a team."

Damn her.

"Her? Are you a Goddess-worshipper, Parkes? Sorry, it's none of my business."

"That wasn't the Her I was thinking of."

"Me neither. Do—Sergeant Major di Leone said Captain Klin would be a bad ghost to have haunting me. I think she would be much worse."

That wasn't the Her, either, but he'd be damned if he was going to discuss it with Magnusson!

From all three units holding Hill 1242, snipers and patrols slipped out into the darkness. The physically and psychologically battered Avengers and Daughters found bullets picking off exposed people where they'd thought they were nearly safe.

Some of the Brotherhood's soldiers broke completely. A few of these were shot down by their own officers. Other officers refused to apply such Draconian discipline and were noted down by the agents of the Proctors as unreliable.

More of the Avengers and Daughters resorted to wild firing, hoping to suppress the snipers and patrols, careless of whom they hit. One Federal patrol lost half its strength.

A good many Brotherhood casualties also should have gone in the books as "friendly fire." Many officers and a few medics were too afraid, either of the Proctors or for their units' reputations, to be entirely honest.

With both assault battalions shaking like gelatin molds, the first Peace Force air strike came in on the Hammer of God.

Hiko knew the air strike was hitting the Hammer of God. Distance and terrain kept him from knowing how hard. Not that the Hammers were that much of an asset anymore, against superior enemy counterbattery fire. Good soldiers would still be dying, and the morale of the brigade facing Hill 1242 further battered.

He looked over the rim of his hole and noticed several of his men half out of cover. "Are you servants of the Master or sacrifices to the Destroyer? Get down, you fools!"

Most obeyed at once. All but one obeyed quickly enough. The rifle shot that killed him might have been inaudible even without the air raid. The meaty *chunk* of the bullet tearing his head apart sounded like a thunderclap. His helmet flew off, landed on a slope, and rolled clattering away into the darkness.

"Jamshir," Hiko said.

"Team Leader?"

"Man the C.P. I think it would be well to organize a patrol to deal with that sniper."

"As you wish."

The sniper inflicted two more non-fatal casualties by the time Hiko had his patrol organized. He had also begun to doubt that there was only one sniper. If not, then the Peace Force might have local fire superiority. That could be opposed most effectively with his Teams' rockets, at the cost of making the Teams highly visible to those cursed P.F. M.G.'s!

There was also the risk of inflicting casualties on the Daughters. He'd had no reliable intelligence of their positions since they broke off their attack—which also meant no reliable intelligence about whether Ruth's company had gone in, been hammered before it could move, or sat out the whole slaughter in reserve . . .

Hiko returned to the C.P. as the air strike ended and tried to put a message through to Daughters HQ. The tactical network seemed to be a thorough mess, between panic, casualties to people and equipment, sheer ignorance, and probably enemy jamming.

What he finally heard was an order to withdraw to a set of coordinates that turned out to be eight kilometers to the rear. In conjunction with the reserve company of the Daughters (Ruth's company, and he was glad the darkness hid his face when he learned that), he was to patrol aggressively to the east, engaging small Federal units and reporting larger ones.

"It would seem that the enemy's 6th Brigade is about to take a hand in the fight," Jamshir said. "I had hoped that they were either dead, dispersed, or fled over the Serpents. But hoping is a great waste of effort in war, is it not?"

"I can hardly think of any greater."

Hiko knew that he was not following his own advice, as he hoped for a chance to sit down alone with Ruth. She could tell him about the Daughters, and he could give her advice. Before long, she might be the senior surviving officer of the Second Daughters.

The fighting flared up again about 0430. The point company of the Second Lions reached the Avengers' position and made a reconnaissance in force against the Federals. Without reliable guides from the shaken Avengers, the company advanced too far and had to fight its way clear of both the Federals and a Tollhouse air strike.

Being elite troops, they came back in good order, bringing their casualties with them, along with some of the Avengers'. The Lions' C.O. decided that the enemy was more to be feared than the Proctors. He would wait until enough of the Lions were on hand for a formal set-piece assault, relying on his own political connections and the high reputation of the Lions to turn aside any Proctors' doubts.

This last fight cost the defenders of 1242 one Tollhouse verti and nearly the last of their ammunition. An hour later the refueled and rearmed Tollhouses escorted a nine-verti resupply and medevac mission. The seventh verti brought reinforcements, in the form of one (Acting) Lieutenant Colonel Jesús Desiderio Vela.

Forbes-Brandon was rubbing cream on cracked lips when a polite cough made her look up.

"Colonel Vela?"

"The last time I looked in the mirror, yes."

"The sentry should have stopped you."

"He did, but quietly. He thought you were asleep."

"I probably ought to be, but I'm not." She put the cream away and stood up. "Welcome to Hill 1242. How are things going in the world?"

"The west and Nordshaven are secure except for mopping up. The Feds are coming in on the left of the people facing you, and also holding the Salla Pass in the east. Battalion Five is landing in that area, but I don't know what's planned for them."

"What about reinforcements here? We're in shape to hold off the people who attacked earlier. They're pretty badly knocked about. But the Brotherless seem to have brought up at least one battalion of the Lions. Is there anybody else you can throw to them besides us?''

''The 2nd is sending up one company as soon as we can be sure daylight movements are safe. MacLean should be able to release our own Second Company and Major Katsouros before dark. I'll be in overall command on the hill, and you'll stay with Third Company and Magnusson's people.''

''Thank you.''

She was surprised how relieved and grateful she felt. Not being the Old Lady for the whole hill was a blessing, but it would have hurt to lose Third Company as well.

''Thank Duchamp and MacLean. The general wants to ask you a few questions, but says he can wait on the tactical situation. He gave MacLean discretion, and MacLean told me to relieve you only if you were unfit for duty or had mishandled your command.

''You obviously haven't mishandled your command, but as for the other—when did you last sleep?''

''I'm not sure. I'll get my head down as soon as I've shown you around the position.''

''What about letting Parkes do it? If he's still on his feet.''

''He's asleep. He was leading the mobile reserve all night.''

''All right. When he wakes up, though, I'll have some bad news for him.''

''What?'' Had she kept the panic out of her voice? From Vela's expression, she probably hadn't.

''Don't look so horrified,'' Vela said, with a faint grin. ''Our sergeant major is now a first lieutenant—field commission.''

''This time I suppose it's an order?''

''Unless he wants to argue with Duchamp.''

''I'll try to talk him out of that, if he wants to.''

''Good. Don't you do anything stupid, either. This battalion's been chopped up worse than any P.F. unit since Bifrost. You and Parkes are going to be worth your weight in cesium for getting us through the rest of this campaign.''

''We endeavor to give satisfaction, sir.''

Vela shook his head. ''I think we need a drink.'' He pulled out a thermos flask. ''Coffee laced with *Rotwasser*. I don't know if that refers to its color or its politics, but it does bite.''

The local herbal vodka did indescribable things to the coffee's flavor, but Vela was correct about the bite. With a cup of the brew inside her, Forbes-Brandon felt almost human again. Better give Vela his tour before the feeling wore off—

"Now, what about looking over the position?"

"Katherine, I thought I said you were going to have somebody else give me the tour. I won't ask you to sleep until Parkes wakes up and I get back, but—"

"Is that an order?"

"Yes."

Forbes-Brandon suppressed insubordinate mutterings but couldn't do the same with her thoughts. Who else could she trust, besides herself? It had to be somebody who not only knew the position but knew that Vela should be steered away from Parkes.

The sergeant major—no, the lieutenant—was a long way from asleep. He was sitting down with Sergeant Brezek, recording the formula for Brezek's legendary home brew and operating instructions for his still. Both were battalion institutions, and while the still was safely back at base, the only other people who knew the formula and how to run the still were M.I.A. in the north.

Brezek had to trust somebody with a written record, and he'd chosen Parkes. If Vela stumbled over Parkes under these—call them *irregular*—circumstances, his new field commission might be one of the shortest in P.F. history.

Forbes-Brandon held out her cup for a refill. Another throat-searing slug, and she had an idea. "Palm Leader to Palm Three," she said into the radio. "Status report—Yo-Yo."

"Ten-ten."

"Roger. Yo-Yo ten-ten. Have Yo-Yo report to Palm Grove on my 23."

"Roger that. Yo-Yo to report to Palm Grove on your 23."

She switched off the radio. "Dietsch can give you a better tour than anybody else. He'll be up with the ammo party in about ten minutes."

"Yo-Yo. Not a bad code name. How's he doing?"

"Like he wants to keep his stripes this time."

"He wanted to keep them the other times, too. He just wanted even more to tell an officer the right thing at the wrong time."

Vela sat down and stretched his legs, then held out his thermos again. Forbes-Brandon shook her head. Any more and she'd be asleep before Dietsch arrived.

After a minute she realized she hadn't asked about orbital fire support. The Company Commander really *had* swallowed up the Naval Liaison Officer.

"How are things in orbit?"

"We have a little firepower to spare from zapping meteors. Now all we need is targets far enough from any civilians, friendly or otherwise. That's one reason we've got patrols out north of the Serpents. They're looking for targets and evacuating or warning civilians to give us a clear shot."

"Any word on how the Brotherhood broke the Skyguard security?"

"Tegen secured his files a little too thoroughly. Singer's been trying to crack into them for two days."

"Wait a minute. Where's Tegen?" The little intelligence computer expert had gone with her on the mission to the República de las Montanas on Greenhouse. They were less than good friends, but a lot more than strangers—

"Dead. Murdered. The night the Brotherjammers attacked."

"How?"

"A microfilament *rumal.*"

"A *rumal*? That's the Thuggee strangling cord, isn't it? And Thuggee means—"

"May mean the Game Master. Did I say I had only good news?"

"No, you didn't."

Forbes-Brandon looked up at the stars, then held out her cup again.

12

CARDINAL PARONA LAID the sets of graphs and charts side by side, with the summary sheets on top.

"I'm glad you provided the summaries," he said. "They're almost in layman's language. The rest—" He shrugged.

"Actually the summary was my brother's work," Chancellor Biancheri said. Professor Bahr glared, and Professor Biancheri hastily added:

"We were short of time, with all the departmental business and not knowing how long you'd be visiting."

"Thank you," Parona said, impartially to all three. He suspected that without the senior professor's intervention he'd have been asked to draw conclusions from a mass of vulcanological data somewhat less intelligible than Ancient Aramaic.

"From the summary, I should say that the Teuffelberg is preparing to erupt. Comparing the data from its last eruption with what you've gathered lately, it looks like a violent eruption."

"There can hardly be a one-to-one correlation between pre-eruption indications and the actual—" Bahr began.

"I didn't say there was," the cardinal put in. "I would ask you, though—if you were wagering on the violence of this coming eruption, where would you put your money?"

Bahr nibbled on his lip and looked everywhere but at his companions. "Several times the violence of the last eruption, at least. There are also indications of an eruption that won't follow the usual pattern. Not that we really have enough data for the Teuffelberg that we can speak of a 'usual pattern,' of course."

He sighed. "I have said since I was a student that building Nordshaven here went against three centuries of environmental wisdom. I'm not the only one to say it, either."

"It would have gone against even older wisdom not to build a city on the best harbor on the north shore," Professor Biancheri said. "If our economy had been completely independent of water transportation, it would have been another matter."

"Let us also remember that no one anticipated that the city could be cut off from easy evacuation, both by land and by sea," the chancellor added. "An evacuation in the depths of winter would have been slowed by the limited number of privately owned vehicles in the city. It might have been dangerous to the very young, the very old, and the sick. It would not have faced a hostile army."

"This one may not, either," Parona said. "The Brotherhood's offensive seems to have been slowed, if not stopped."

"If you were placing bets, Your Eminence, would you put your money on the north shore being clear before the Teuffelberg erupts?" Bahr grinned.

Parona shrugged. "I have to concede your point. So what do you want me to do? If it is something that you could and should have already done yourself—"

"Read this, Your Eminence. It's what I asked from those fascist clowns on the General Staff. With this, we'll have plenty of warning of the eruption. With the evidence in hand, we can lay it before the Protectorate's War Council. Even the Proctors won't argue against a truce to let us evacuate Nordshaven."

The memorandum called for continuous air and orbital surveillance of the Teuffelberg. As soon as security permitted, manned monitoring stations should be set up at six to nine places. These stations should be continuously linked to each other and to a central computer. In addition, the possibility of using orbital lasers or ground-implanted fusion devices to affect the volcano's activity should be explored. Not being familiar with the capabilities of Federal or Peace Force weapons, Professor Bahr would request information on them before advising on their use.

"Sensible enough, as far as it goes," Parona said, returning the memorandum. "My only question is—did you call them 'fascist clowns' to their faces? If so, when?"

Bahr's glare gave Parona most of his answer. "I asked when," he repeated.

"After they threw 'military exigencies' at me," Bahr said sullenly. "Damn it, people may be killed over this—"

"People are already being killed, including soldiers and civilians for whom the General Staff is responsible," Parona said. "Did that occur to you when you lost your temper?"

"I suppose it should have," Bahr said. He still sounded sullen, but Parona detected the beginnings of contrition.

"It *certainly* should have," he said. "You have sinned by vanity and by wrath. Since you are not a Catholic, I cannot ask for your confession or demand penance. I do suggest that you apologize to the General Staff, however. If nothing else, it may keep political investigators out of the Geology Department!"

"Those bastards are running off with their tails between their legs!" Bahr said, suddenly cheerful.

"Perhaps. That doesn't mean they can't or won't retaliate when they stop running. I have as much experience with politicians as you have with volcanoes. Both tend to be unpredictable."

Parona looked at his watch. "It's an hour before evening mass. If someone will drive me to the cathedral, I think we can compose a memorandum about the Teuffelberg to General Duchamp. From what he told me last night, he'll have enough troops on-planet to spare some, as soon as the battle for Hill 1242 is finished."

"Duchamp won't go against the General Staff," the chancellor pointed out. "Or at least he's not supposed to, except in a total emergency."

"This may be one. Also, I doubt if the General Staff will issue him a direct order not to watch the Teuffelberg with his own people."

"I will pray they have that much wisdom," the chancellor said.

"Pray that there's something to eat in your brother's kitchen," Parona said. "I had no breakfast, and my lunch was that alleged food called 'Peace Force rations.' "

Professor Biancheri smiled. "It will be fish, bean soup, and bread, I'm afraid."

"Any coffee?"

"Well—"

"Call it a work of mercy. I'll only ask for one cup."

"I think we have that much."

As Parona sat down at the living room terminal to compose the memorandum, Bahr set a glass of brandy beside him. Parona reached for it, then stopped with his hand in midair.

The house was shaking, violently enough to make the amber brandy dance in the glass.

A vapor trail scrawled itself across a patch of blue sky. *Probably Peace Force,* Hiko thought. *Not likely to be headed this way, however.* The Federals were still building up their strength on the Brotherhood's left flank, not preparing the kind of attack that would benefit from close air support.

A Team sentry shouted, almost in chorus with two Daughters. A line of Proctors was emerging from the stand of dwarf wheeltree halfway down the hill. Two lines, actually, with a ragged line of civilians between them.

"Refugees," Ruth said. "Thank the Lord that they have found safety."

Hiko nodded. A second look suggested hostages rather than refugees. Some of the civilians were barefoot or partly clad, few carried much gear, and all looked sullen, scared, hungry, or all three. A few showed fresh bruises, and one a freshly bandaged cheek.

As the new arrivals began to climb the hill toward Hiko, a woman stumbled. Hiko raised his binoculars and saw that she was carrying a five-year-old girl on her back. Two Proctors broke from their line and hauled her roughly to her feet.

Voices rose. A man was shouting that if the Proctors had provided basic proper medical treatment, the girl would be walking and his wife wouldn't have stumbled. Two Proctors stepped forward, to pull him back. He swung on one of them; a third stepped back and raised his pistol.

"No!"

A girl of about twelve threw herself at the pistol-wielder. He swung his pistol against her cheek; the sound of its hitting and her falling reached Hiko.

"Kari!"

The man jerked an arm free and lunged for the pistol. He made the mistake of leaving his back exposed to one of the other Proctors. Three shots and the man fell beside his daughter, a broad red patch on the back of his work shirt.

The woman screamed and swayed, but didn't faint. Instead she knelt, wiping her older daughter's bloody face with the hem of her dress. The younger daughter started to cry, a thin wail. Hiko turned away, unwilling to watch any more and hoping he would hear nothing.

"Poor fire discipline," he said. "They were lucky not to hit any of their own men."

"The Lord—the Lord—the Lord was with—" Ruth began in a strained voice. She stood with one hand clenched at her side and the other clapped over her mouth. He took a step toward her, and the clenched hand rose to fend him off. Discipline, fear of the Proctors, and a lifetime of chastity joined to make her refuse any comfort of man to woman.

Hiko turned away again, to spare Ruth any witness to her fight for self-command. To his relief, the rest of the family was back in line and moving with it. The girl Kari was carrying her younger sister, although her cheek was still bleeding.

Hiko still wanted to examine what Ruth might call his soul or his conscience, but which he preferred to call his concept of duty. If the Proctors were taking hostages and treating them this way, the Game Master's Teams faced new dangers.

The Convention of Clovis was ambiguous about its definition of complicity in illegal acts of war, as such documents usually were. It definitely didn't require preventing such acts by force, did require not volunteering for them, and left in a vast gray limbo the rest of the choices that might confront a soldier. Little help there, not that Hiko had expected much.

Nor was it likely that his men would have to worry about legal penalties. The Master's orders against being taken prisoner were explicit and enforced by hypnotic conditioning. Most of the Team people wouldn't have needed the conditioning; they'd learned war in places where a soldier was either free or dead.

It was the effect on his men's professional standards and morale that concerned Hiko. Even the devout worshippers of Kali did not kill like weasels in a henhouse; an undedicated victim gained one no favor. Could he keep his men and the Proctors apart from now on?

Perhaps, with luck and a little help from the mercenaries, who *would* be concerned about legal penalties. He would have to keep such help concealed from both the Proctors and the Master's Representative, of course—

The thought of the Representative brought him to a halt. What if the Representative ordered him to avoid the mercenaries or even aid the Proctors? He could even hear the full, confident, complacent voice saying, "It will aid the Master's plans, and that is your purpose."

When loyalty to his men clashed with loyalty to the Master, which loyalty was higher?

Above the sunset glow in the east, Wotan climbed into a star-flecked sky. Automatically Dallin looked for the moving stars, the ships and satellites, and counted them. Then she disengaged the automatic pilot, and watched her winger land behind the four cargo vertis they'd escorted. As her winger taxied in, Dallin began the delousing circuit of Andrus Field, looking for any unusual activity. Two-thirds of the way around, she spotted a high dark-colored truck pulled off to the side of the road from town.

"Pillow One to Andrus Tower, there's a truck parked near the 683214 crossroads."

"A civilian all-wheeler. Cargo body and dark paint?"

"Far as I can tell. I'll use the IR scan—"

"Don't worry. That's the mobile library. They were coming out to the base an hour ago and blew two tires. The driver decided to patch before going on, then discovered he was out of patches."

"Pillow One to Tower, thanks."

"You're welcome. You're also cleared to land after this circuit."

Five minutes later, Dallin put her verti on the strip, less than fifty meters from the assigned field revetment. A light civilian all-wheeler fitted with towing gear hauled the verti the rest of the way. Dallin climbed out as the ground crew hauled the armorcloth shield across the front of the revetment. She noticed that the revetment already had a tenant, an identical verti with Battalion Five badges on the doors.

The sergeant who'd ridden with Dallin climbed out, staggering under the weight of her pack of microwave spares. She was an earnest young Afroam woman who treated officers as if they might suddenly start radiating lethal frequencies.

The tow truck took them both to the field's HQ, in the living room of a house that must have been there long before the airfield. A tired lieutenant handed Dallin a small recorder.

"Any enemy activity?"

"None I'd swear to."

"Then record your flight here. If I have any questions, I'll ask them in the morning."

"I may not be here in the morning."

"You're at the limit for flying hours, Major. You may not have any choice. The report just came through, so I have to—"

"You and which brigade have to do what?"

The sergeant was trying to blend with the walls. The lieutenant frowned. "I'm not trying to make trouble, Major."

"Neither am I. If you can find another pilot to take my bird home, I'll hold an orgy and invite you. If you can't, I fly her back."

"I'll look, Major."

"You do that. You also find this sergeant's transportation to the Recon Company and something to eat for me."

'Recon's a hundred meters the other side of the tower. Gilliam, take the sergeant there. Bar and grill's downstairs."

"Thanks."

Dallin lit a cigarette and went downstairs. The "bar and grill" was more bar than grill; the house must have had at least one recent incarnation as the local watering hole. The two supply privates still had a supply of nonalcoholic potables laid in for pilots, and a miscellany of rations and local procurement for Dallin's rumbling middle.

As Dallin sipped her fruit juice, she noticed an Australian bush hat on the bar. "Is there a Captain Reinhardt anywhere around?" she asked.

The cook straightened up and waved toward the back of the room. "You mean Major Reinhardt? She's back there."

Dallin put her drink down and was turning when the bathroom door opened.

"Marcy!"

The blond officer in a blue flying suit stopped, then grinned.

"Sonny!"

The two flying-school roommates embraced. "That your bird, out in Four?"

"Six hours out of the crate. This base is the western end of our A.O. I decided to test *Appaloosa* and check the field on the same flight."

"I was just about to have something to eat. Want to join me? It's only the usual local wurst—"

"How did you spell that? Never mind, I've been living on soy bars and peanut butter sandwiches since we hit orbit. If it doesn't eat me first, I'll eat it."

Over sausages, coffee, and more fruit juice the two pilots compared notes. Reinhardt was Transportation Officer for Battalion Five, and her leaves were new but permanent, not chalk-ons like Dallin's.

"Not that you won't be growing leaves soon enough, I suspect. Proving the Tollhouse concept has to be worth *something*."

"Likely enough. Maybe not Steve Hughes's neck, though." She lifted her glass. "Absent friends."

"Absent friends," Reinhardt said. They clinked glasses, and she pulled out a map and unfolded it on the table.

"We've got two rifle companies and a composite support company deployed twenty kilometers south of the Salla Pass," she said. "The Feds are holding the pass itself with two battalions, one from the north shore that's kind of chewed up but regular, and one fresh militia."

"Don't sell the militia short. There's a story about one who spotted an enemy patrol on his farm, took out half, and captured the rest. Then he made them repair a gate they'd broken before he turned them in!"

Reinhardt laughed. "I believe it. We've had six livestock claims already. Anyway, we're using our spare airlift to resupply the Feds. We're not supposed to get involved in the ground defense of the pass unless the Feds can't hold without us. Once we're fully airmobile, we're going to jump the hills and try to take the Brotherhood at the pass in the rear."

Dallin looked at the map. "That'll put you pretty close to their overland supply line."

"I thought they were bringing in most of their stuff by sea."

"They have been. But word is, we start orbital interdiction of all sea traffic in the gulf tomorrow. Then we move attackers right into Nordshaven and start hitting their dumps. Duchamp may just have big plans for you people."

"I won't complain. Why should a newlie outfit like Fourteen hog all the credit?

"No reason at all." Dallin looked at the bottom of her empty glass. "This campaign may set a new record for P.F. casualties as a percentage of the number engaged. We'll be happy to accept contributions to the statistics from other battalions. You can't *believe* how happy we'll be."

13

THE DECISION IN the battle for Hill 1242 came on the third day, when the reinforced defenders repulsed a full-scale attack by the Lions. In proportion to the numbers engaged and the firepower used, it wasn't a particularly bloody battle. Good body armor, well dug-in defenders, and attackers who knew how to use cover kept the death toll down.

It still left the defenders stretched thin, with many positions held by walking wounded. It left the Lions too battered to launch another attack, but not short of teeth for defending themselves. It left everybody suffering from the most common shortage of high-tech warfare—ammunition.

That shortage finally decided the outcome of the battle. The Brotherhood couldn't attack, and with the Federals moving against their flank they were in danger of being cut off. The Peace Force and Federals could hold indefinitely, but didn't have the ammunition to blast the Lions out of strong positions. They could only encourage the Brotherhood's decision to retreat.

They tried more. Three airmobile operations tried to block the Brotherhood's retreat. Each time, the Brotherhood launched a desperate counterattack, once by the Lions, once by the Daughters, and once by an improvised battalion of guerrillas. All three times they suffered heavy casualties, the guerrillas especially. Each time, they drove the allied blocking force off its position and cleared the line of retreat.

At last the Brotherhood broke contact and retreated forty kilometers in one night. Van Doorn and De Lisi, the local Federal commander, decided they didn't have the troops or supplies to follow that far. They settled into a perimeter a few kilometers beyond where Fourteen's Third Company had first engaged the enemy.

Third Company and Magnusson's people went into brigade

reserve, ten kilometers to the south. Of the 238 field and support people Forbes-Brandon and Parkes had led onto Hill 1242, they had 135 left. Some of these were in worse shape than some of those medevacked.

"I'm going to ask Dietsch to pick another house for our billet," Parkes said.

Forbes-Brandon dropped her bag in the middle of the bare foam-tile floor and looked around the living room. "Why? This is big enough for us and the C.P., too. Save time and walking around, and right now I want a sedan chair with bearers to go more than six meters!"

"Yeah, but—remember that family that gave us breakfast when we came through, the first day." He still couldn't manage "the day Dozer was killed" easily, and knew that the Amazon noticed it.

To hell with her hovering. He wished they weren't the two senior officers still on their feet in this pickup P.F. company. They had to work together and it made sense for them to be billeted together, but he wasn't sure how much either of them wanted the other's company.

"What about them?" the Amazon asked. "If they come back, we can move. Or they might be willing to double up with somebody else for a few days. I don't think we'll be here even as reserves once Eleven lands."

"I was thinking they might not be coming back."

"Hostages?"

"Maybe."

Nobody had wanted to believe the reports of the Brotherhood taking hostages when they first came in. The Peace Forcers were professionals; atrocity propaganda wasn't part of their military universe. The Federals called the P.F.'ers naive; they turned out to be right. The Brotherhood had collected somewhere between 1,500 and 2,200 local civilians as hostages and were withdrawing with them.

There was little the allies could do about it, either. They could file a complaint with the Interstellar Juridical Commission and restrict their air attacks on unidentified personnel targets. They could strengthen their scout teams behind enemy lines, hoping to rescue weakly escorted parties of hostages. They could wink at occasional failures to take Brotherhood prisoners. They could pray.

That was all, short of winning the war. This promised to take longer than anyone cared to leave civilians at the mercy of the Brotherhood. The combat units could be more or less trusted, particularly the elite units like the Lions or the Daughters. The Proctors were another matter.

Forbes-Brandon picked up her bag. "I'll send a message to Dietsch as soon as there's somebody to take it. Meanwhile, what about baths?"

Parkes tapped the nearest light switch. The overhead panel glowed. "We've got juice. Do we have water?"

"I'll go see."

"If we don't, we can wait until the village sauna's back on line. Dietsch found a case of vodka and persuaded Guslenko to get to work on it."

"I thought that was the worst way to get work out of Guslenko."

"He's pretty much off the stuff now. But he might like a bottle or so to unwind. Also, he'll take a couple more—trade goods, you know."

"I do, but I won't let anyone know that I do. Fair enough?"

"Lieutenant—hey, what do I call you now that we're both members of the leisure class?"

"How about 'Katherine' or 'Kate'? 'Kathy' gets—something unpleasant. I'll figure out what when I've had a chance to sit down."

"Okay, Katherine. Which bedroom do you want?"

"Eeny, meeny, miney, mo—the right-hand one's the way to go."

"Fine. Shout when you find out about the water."

Forbes-Brandon discovered that the water, like the electricity, was still on. The water heater, however, was deader than the Prophet Shimo. She shouted to Parkes and got a muttered reply that suggested he might be falling asleep.

She decided to let him sleep. He certainly needed it. So did she, but *after* a bath. Thank God this was a coolish planet and both Hill 1242 and the weather had been dry. She didn't feel as she had coming in from the field on Greenhouse, as if she needed to take off her skin, beat it on rocks, and scrub her bones with a stiff brush before she'd feel clean.

She stripped and sponge-bathed from a kettle of water heated on the stove, then pulled her one-piecer back on and sat down on the bed to brush her hair. She'd never realized before how ecstatic it could be to feel a worn carpet under her bare feet. Probably anything else that proved you were alive would have done as well, but she'd always liked to go barefoot whenever she could—

A sense of being watched made her look up. Parkes stood in the bedroom doorway, fully dressed except for his battledress jacket.

"The water heater's down but the stove's—" she began, then took a second look at Parkes. She'd seen people dying of internal bleeding who looked like that.

No, Parkes was worse. The dying knew where they were going. Parkes looked as if he was already in Hell without having gone through the formalities of dying.

"John. What is it?" He swallowed but said nothing. The urge to bark an order came and went in the same heartbeat. "What is it? A body in the other bedroom? You can flop here—"

"No."

"I won't molest—"

"No." His voice was rusty and grating. "No body. That—it was the girls' room. Kari and a—baby sister. Four or five Standard, I guess. There was a chest of her—toys, dolls, things like that. Somebody—somebody had ripped open all the dolls."

"What with?" *Fight off the silence, even if you sound like an idiot. Silence has the power to harm you both.*

"Knife, bayonet. I don't know. I—I can't go to bed there. Not—no." His throat and mouth worked but no sound came out. Forbes-Brandon didn't want to look at him, but she couldn't take her eyes off him.

As she stared, she remembered where she'd seen a similar look. The last photograph taken of her brother Donald, ten days before he OD'ed. The look of a man who knows that the world has no mercy left, if it ever had any at all.

And did his eyes look like that when he popped those last half dozen tabs of Extasine that left him dead in a cheap hotel on Clovis? Did anyone recognize the look? Nobody helped him, that's for sure.

Could I have done more, before he left home? I was busy being super-cadet, but could I have made a difference without giving up my own life?

Parkes did a better job for his sister Louise than I did for

Donald. She's alive. He's tied himself up in knots for her sake, but he's alive, too, to untie them. With some help, maybe.

With a lot of help. He's not my brother, either. I can help him any way he needs.

I can help him any way I want *to.*

It was surprising how easily that last thought turned into a positive decision. It might have taken three heartbeats instead of one, but by the fourth heartbeat it was fixed.

All right, but don't be gross about it, Katherine.

She walked over to Parkes and put her arms around him. "John, you're dead on your feet. I don't want to be left running this outfit all by myself. Sit down, please."

She touched the side of his neck. It surprised her how easy it was to touch him. It didn't surprise her that once she'd done it, it was hard to stop there.

"My God, what do you use for neck tendons? Woven microfilament? Sit down, I said. I want to rub your neck before it snaps and I have to screw your head back on."

Parkes's voice was still rusty. "A Japanese bathboy taught you?"

So he remembers that foot rub on Bayard. We do have a history, come to think of it. A longer and better history than a lot of Article Forty-six get-togethers—or some marriages, in fact . . .

"No. A Filipino *escrima* instructor. Very handsome, but quite impersonal."

"Like you."

She stuck her tongue out at him, but he'd withdrawn again and didn't even blink. A firm push, and he sat down on the edge of the bed. A gentle push, and he bent his head. She knelt behind him on the bed and went to work.

A tendon at a time, his neck relaxed. Forbes-Brandon moved her hands down under his shirt, to his shoulder blades. They stuck out so far she was almost afraid of bruising her hands on them.

A centimeter at a time, she opened his shirt and worked down his chest. His breathing seemed to be quickening; she knew hers was.

Please, God, don't let him be so much in awe of me that I have to tear off his clothes and push him into bed. Or the other way around—

Parkes turned half around and kissed her. The kiss turned open-mouthed almost at once. She felt his hands on her shoulders, then undoing the upper seam of her one-piecer.

The lower seam followed naturally, if not as fast as Forbes-Brandon would have liked. Then matters went about as quickly as possible, until Parkes's clothes littered the floor, the one-piecer was rucked around her waist, and a simple upthrust of her hips settled them both in place.

Parkes ran his fingers through the Amazon's thick blond hair, finding this as pleasurable as he'd imagined. He didn't think that either of them had slept. His watch said it was only half an hour since he'd walked into the children's bedroom. If they'd slept, it would be tomorrow morning at least.

Forbes-Brandon moved against him and let out a contented sigh. The sigh eased one of Parkes's fears. He couldn't recall such a muddled lovemaking since the time he learned that bourbon and sex don't mix well. But if Kat had reasonably pleasant memories of it—

Wide blue eyes opened and looked into his. "R.H.I.P., and thank God," she murmured.

Parkes's body stiffened and his tongue went into action before his brain caught up with either. "Another damned bribe to make me take the commission!"

Then his body had to run ahead of his brain, because the Amazon was uncoiling like a striking snake. He deflected one chop with his left forearm and caught a clawed hand centimeters from his eyes. They sat frozen like that for a moment several hours long, before the clawed hand went limp.

The Amazon remained sitting. Then she began to shake as if she was chilled through, even though the room was comfortably warm. The shaking did things to her breasts that Parkes would have enjoyed under other circumstances.

He ignored them, because his wits were finally catching up with the rest of him. What they were telling him was not pleasant hearing, but he had to listen.

She keeps everybody on their feet for a week, you included, and risks her career to save you from Podgrebin. All that time she's been wanting to go off and pound down a couple of stone walls with that lovely head, but she's got the same sense of duty you have.

Then when she asks your help, you give it with one hand (or body) and take it back right afterward with your goddamned big mouth, calling her a whore!

Parkes, maybe it would have been better if Podgrebin had *shipped you back under arrest!*

At that point Parkes knew that his wits weren't speaking anymore. He was hearing the old, ugly voice of guilt. For a moment he let the waves of guilt wash over him.

Then the moment passed. For the first time Parkes could remember, other thoughts followed naturally and easily.

All right. You mucked it. Start off by apologizing and see what happens. It can't do any harm and being the Man of Sorrows can't do any good. Not for Kat, and you'd have owed her something even without this. She was one hell of a good officer and let you be something less than a perfect N.C.O.

"Katherine." She didn't move. "Kat." She stared. "Katy Kat." She closed her eyes, and silent tears streamed down her cheeks. Parkes held her, tasted the salt of the tears, and muttered into her ear.

"Katy Kat. I'm sorry. That was stupid and vicious and nonsense. I'm too tired to know what I'm saying, but that's no excuse. You're as good a woman as you are an officer—"

Something that mixed a giggle, a sob, and a hiccup. "Only one session, and already he knows my limits? Talk about male vanity!"

"I didn't mean—" began Parkes, torn between panicky apology and leaping hope.

"I know you didn't. Thanks for the compliment, though."

Her voice wasn't quite steady, but he could hear a note of amusement. He guessed that this kind of misunderstanding could be funny—afterward, and as long as you still had the other party around—

Someone knocked on the bedroom door. Parkes resisted the urge to tell the visitor to bugger a cliffcarpet, swung his legs out of bed, and groped for his pants. He pulled them on, added a shirt, and walked to the door.

"Who is it?"

"Dietsch, First—I mean, Lieutenant."

"Okay." Parkes opened the door. The first thing he saw was Dietsch's jaw dropping halfway to his navel. Parkes looked over his shoulder and groaned. Lack of sleep was an explanation but not an excuse for failing to study the layout of the room. The mirror over the dresser gave anyone standing at the door an excellent view of the bed and anyone in it.

What might have been a telepathic link formed. With grace and dignity the Amazon slid down under the blankets until nothing but her head and one bare shoulder was on display. Parkes gave Dietsch a death's-head grin.

"Sorry, Lieutenant."

"Don't be sorry, Dietsch. Just be quiet." Parkes put a hand under Dietsch's jaw and gently closed his mouth.

"Sir, that's a court-martial offense, now that you've joined the leisure classes—" Dietsch began. A hoot of laughter from the bed interrupted him.

"Dietsch," Parkes said quietly. "Two words of advice. One is to keep your tongue between your teeth. Otherwise you get a suspended sentence. I will suspend you by your tongue from the first place I find that's high enough to keep your feet off the ground.

"Two—is this a social call? If it is, either it or you will be terminated in ten seconds."

"No, Lieutenant. Well, we do have a little present for you and the—Lieutenant Forbes-Brandon. Iron Mike gave up a bottle and we found some apples and cheese." He handed Parkes a basket that looked like the sort of thing medium-priced hotels put in their honeymoon suites.

"Thank you all too much. Anything else?"

"Well, Magnusson's back from hospital. He says he'll take the duty until midnight, to let you people catch up on your sleep." The hesitation before "sleep" was barely noticeable. "Dubnick's got the C.P. gear all ready to unload, if you want it here. He thinks the office of the village meeting hall would be better."

"What about housing the refugees when they return?" Forbes-Brandon said.

"They can mostly go straight home," Dietsch said. "There's maybe two, three houses knocked about so they can't be lived in. Otherwise, not even much looting."

Parkes looked away. If they didn't put the C.P. in the living room, he and Kat would have at least some of the privacy they could now put to such good use. Did the outfit think he and Kat had earned it? No way to ask that straight out, either. Call it a tactical decision that couldn't wait . . .

"The village hall sounds fine by me," Parkes said. "Katherine?"

"No problem for me," came the voice from the bed. Fortunately for his next of kin, Dietsch's grin stopped short of turning into a leer.

"Anything else?"

"Oh, almost forgot. Battalion Five came in with a double-strength N.L. team. They're sending six people over our way tonight, for a briefing. The Old Man wants to know when you'll be up to meeting them."

Forbes-Brandon pulled her other arm out and looked at her watch. "Twenty-one hundred at the C.P., and come by to wake me at 2000."

"Yes, ma'am. Sleep tight."

"Dietsch, do you want to walk or bounce?"

Dietsch grinned again, saluted, and walked.

"Sorry about the mirror," Forbes-Brandon said as Parkes turned from the closed door.

"What's done is done," he said. "They can only court-martial us once, anyway."

"I suppose we haven't heard the last about Podgrebin," she said. "Anybody heard what happened to him after he was med-evacked? If he's started foaming at the mouth I don't imagine we have much to worry about."

"I suppose I could find out. Although I think they'd be relieving you of more than the N.L. job if they were really pissed."

"Don't try to soothe me."

"Sorry, ma'am." Then they both laughed.

He was now close enough to the bed to let her touch his stomach. "Two things you're going to have to get used to, with me. One is, I snore. The other is, when I try to make witty remarks afterward I usually muck it."

"I'll remember that, the next time." He started taking off his shirt. "But the next time is going to be *after* I have a bath. Unless you want to know what it's like to sleep with a dead goat."

"I'll pass on the experience."

Forbes-Brandon tossed the one-piecer onto the floor the moment Parkes left the bedroom. The effort seemed to drain the last of her strength, like pulling the plug on a bathtub. She curled into a ball, knees halfway to her breasts, and barely managed to wrap her arms around Parkes when he came back, smelling of soap and no more than two days' grime.

Right now they could give each other warmth and maybe freedom from nightmares, and that was enough.

14

"THIS IS NEW," Hiko said, pointing downhill at the village.

"Indeed," Ruth replied. Armed Proctors now manned checkpoints at both ends of the main street. More Proctors stood at either end of the bridge across the stream that divided the village from its fields.

"Not all in these villages submit to the Lord's servants," Ruth added. "It is as well that we are protected from their unholy vengeance."

Unless a lip-reader had a high-magnification scanner on them, it was unlikely that anyone would know what Ruth was saying. Hiko still appreciated her caution. No one who did not know her would have suspected her sincerity.

The slope turned their progress into a near-scramble. Past a fenced grove of tunbush, they came into view of the Proctors at the near end of the village.

"Halt, in the name of the Lord. Who are you?"

"Hiko the Valiant Defender and Ruth Sworn-to-do-Battle-for-the-Lord."

"The commander in the Second Daughters?" Hiko told himself that he would have heard sinister implications in a Proctor's blowing his nose.

"The same."

"Then pass, in the Lord's name."

They walked into the main street. The village had seen little fighting, except for one enemy air raid by microwave drones, aimed at an Air Defense C.P. The meeting hall/sauna showed the banner and door insignia of a Proctor Band HQ. Two others showed the insignia of messes, and one the banner of the Chosen.

Hiko badly wanted a meal of something besides rations, but doubted there was anything else left in the village. Besides, the more public his meeting with Ruth, the better. They would only be discussing who among their people deserved honors for the recent fighting against the Federals. With the Proctors growing more militant and suspicious as the campaign stalled, there was the need to appear virtuous, not just be so.

They sat down on a bus-stop bench across the street from the mercenaries' rendezvous. As Hiko pulled out his notes, an all-wheeler with Chosen insignia drove up to the Proctors at the far end of the street.

"Now, I have witnesses for the valor of each of these men," he began. "But if your Daughters can also bear witness to as many of them as possible—"

"Servants of the Lord!" one of the Proctors shouted. Hiko and Ruth jumped up, knowing the rallying cry but wondering what the Proctor had in mind.

The all-wheeler's motor whined and it shot into reverse, away from the Proctors. Not looking where he was going, the driver sent it into the ditch. He and his passenger hurled themselves out, seemed to fly up the side of the ditch, and sprinted across the field.

One of the Proctors went on shouting. The other knelt, leveled his rifle, and squeezed off three shots. Hiko had never been impressed with Proctor marksmanship and was even less so now; the two fugitives vaulted the nearest fence and vanished unhurt.

Meanwhile, Brotherhood soldiers were swarming into the streets and running toward the Proctors. Proctors were pouring out of their HQ and running toward the mercenaries' rendezvous. The street was too narrow to hold everybody, so a first-class traffic jam developed in front of Hiko and Ruth.

"Sister Commander, the Lord has given you favor in the Proctors' eyes. Ask them what is going on."

She nodded reluctantly. Hiko knew the reason for the reluctance. Ruth's two uncles in the Proctors had helped her career but given her a too-intimate knowledge of the Protectorate's not-so-secret police.

Hiko stuffed his notes in his battledress pocket, unbuttoned his shoulder holster, and headed for the Chosen rendezvous. Enough of the mercs knew him that it was likely he'd find somebody willing to talk—*if* the Proctors were out of the way.

By the time Hiko crossed the street, he'd abandoned hope of that. The whole HQ complement was surrounding the rendezvous, thirty-odd burly men in grayish-brown battledress. Every other Proctor in the village was coming in as well, except the checkpoints and sentry posts.

The door slid open, and Captain Ngomba led out twelve mercenaries. Their rifles were slung, but Hiko saw unbuttoned holsters and hands casually close to those holsters.

"We heard firing," Ngomba said. It was not a question.

"One of our sentries showed poor judgment," the Band Commander said.

"Did he show poor marksmanship as well?"

"Yes."

"Then we have no claim against your men, as long as they have no claim against ours. Is this so?"

The Band Commander nodded slowly—and reluctantly, Hiko thought. "Their vehicle is disabled. We shall provide another."

"Thank you, but we'd rather march."

"The enemy's air force—"

"May show up unexpectedly. We'd rather be a small target."

"The orders we received were to provide you with a vehicle."

"Will it be enough to provide us with a marching escort?"

In other words—are you concerned for our convenience or for keeping us under control?

The Band Commander hesitated. Hands moved millimeters closer to pistols, and rifle slings crept centimeters down shoulders.

"I know the Proctors are fine soldiers, ready to face hardship to aid the Brotherhood's allies," Ngomba said. His smile did not reach his eyes.

The Band Commander nodded, even more reluctantly than before. The hands and slings moved back. The commander turned and started shouting out names. When he'd named six men, he handed Ngomba a sealed envelope. They exchanged salutes and the commander strode off toward his HQ.

Half of Ngomba's men disappeared through the door. In a minute they were back, each wearing his own pack and equipment and carrying another's. In two more minutes the mercs were lined up in two squads of six, each with a Proctor at the point and rear. Ngomba fell in between the two remaining Proctors.

"Let's move out, people."

Proctors and soldiers made a path as the odd procession marched off toward the hills. The last detail Hiko noted was that Ngomba hadn't opened the envelope.

As the street cleared, Ruth hurried up.

"A major in the Chosen has been arrested," she said. Breathlessness and nerves made her voice pleasantly husky. "Did the Proctors know the charge?"

"No. That is, I assumed they had the Lord's justice on their side and would not question it."

Again, no one who didn't know Ruth quite well would suspect she was reproaching Hiko for expecting her to ask a stupid question.

"Indeed, the Lord will grant us knowledge in His own good time." Hiko would have prayed this was soon enough for his and Ruth's people, if it had been in him to pray.

"Will—what will the mercenaries do? They know not fear of the Lord."

"They know fear of the Lord's good soldiers, who outnumber them ten to one." Probably more than that, after the Chosen casualties in the retreat from Hill 1242. But the mercs were concentrated, and they'd be more so if the Proctors or even the War Council were going to pull in all their outposts.

"Madmen do not know fear."

"The Chosen aren't mad." Angry, almost certainly. The Brotherhood wouldn't be taking all these precautions if the anonymous major had been arrested for something clearly forbidden by military law or the mercenaries' contract. No good mercenary unit expected to get away with murder, and the Chosen were certainly good.

Such units also had their own ways of dealing with employees who broke contracts or made other kinds of trouble. Such ways were often subtle, seldom made good songs, but were usually effective. The Master's extensive files on mercenaries showed no more than half a dozen such cases in the last ten years.

"We need have no fear for our backs, Sister Commander. Not from the Chosen."

At least as long as the Brotherhood and above all the Proctors recognized the signs of subtle opposition and responded intelligently. If they chose to regard any opposition as mutiny and applied the harshest of their laws . . .

The distant artillery fire grumbled into silence as Cardinal Parona entered Dr. Laughton's office. Idly he wondered what somebody had found that was worth shooting at. Both sides had to be miserly with their ammunition these days.

The Peace Force and Federals had shot off most of their—"basic allowance"—was that the phrase? That, and most of the Federal stockpile and the prepositioned Peace Force dumps as well. They were receiving more with the two new Peace Force battalions, but the two battalions also added to the number of guns that had to be fed.

Not to mention that the Thorshammer Shower had struck one orbital ammunition dump. Nothing exploded, but tons of artillery shells and rockets were drifting uselessly in orbit instead of going into P.F. tubes.

One could console oneself that the Brotherhood was even worse off. They'd used most of their basic allowance. Now they had to slip their supplies by road around the end of the Great North Gulf, harried by air attacks and ambushes.

If the war went on, the Protectorate's factories would come under attack, from orbit, air, or ground raids. The Federal factories would go on turning out new supplies, and the Peace Force would go on bringing in whole shiploads.

If the war went on, it would again become a butchery. This made the Brotherhood's almost inevitable defeat somewhat less than consoling to Cardinal Parona. Evil causes had to be fought, but could they ever be fought without killing good people?

That, Parona concluded, was a question General Duchamp was probably better equipped to answer than he was, red hat or not. For a moment he contemplated "military theology" as a new branch of learning. Then he pressed the buzzer plate.

"Come in!" Dr. Laughton sounded harried.

The door slid open and Parona entered. The doctor—it was hard to think of her as an officer—was seated behind her desk. She wore a P.F. sweater, civilian slacks, and low boots with mismatched socks. Her auburn hair was roughly gathered into knots above either ear.

She rose. "Forgive me, Your Eminence. I asked you to come to me only because—"

"Your duties would not let you come to me? Well, I am here. Take the forgiveness as granted, and remember that I have duties, too. One of them is visiting the sick and hurt in this hospital."

"Thank you." From her tone, Parona half expected her to kneel and kiss his ring. He moved toward a chair, she pushed it toward him, and they collided. She laughed uneasily.

Parona decided to sit down before her unease infected him. "Would you have any coffee?"

"I'm a tea drinker myself—"

"That will do as well."

An enlisted orderly brought the tea. Laughton waited until the door closed behind him, then locked it. Sitting down, she fiddled with something under the overhang of her desktop.

"There. Unless the Security Police have come up with something new since a war started . . ."

Parona forced a smile. "I remind you that cardinals no longer have their ancient skills at intrigue."

"I never thought you were an intriguer, Your Eminence. You wouldn't have threatened excommunication for Security Police atrocities otherwise."

"Perhaps not. But it proves little that one can see the wisdom of encouraging good soldiers or police at the expense of bad ones." He set his cup down. "Have you discovered evidence for those rumors of Security Police torture of guerrilla prisoners?"

"I don't doubt that it's happened, Your Eminence. That's not what I have here, though. It's a recording of interrogations of guerrilla prisoners speaking freely. It's what they said that I want you to hear."

She rose and began to pace up and down. "Since we came into the Nordshaven perimeter, I've been following the media." Her pacing broke off as she nearly stumbled into a chair.

"You might have done better to catch up on your sleep."

"Who's the doctor, Your Eminence? Forgive me. It hasn't been that bad, at least since the refugees stopped coming in. Your bishop has been a tower of strength, too."

"He will be happy to hear that. But—the media?"

"They've been pumping out hate propaganda against the guerrillas. Emphasizing their atrocities—"

"Which are real enough."

"I know. But they could all have been committed by a few hundred out of the thousands, or by Proctors disguised as guerrillas. I think they were. I think most of the guerrillas aren't even religious fanatics. They wanted the Security Police off their backs, they wanted freedom to worship according to the Brotherhood's principles, and they wanted the thrill of being soldiers. Half the prisoners on that recording are under eighteen. Frightened, cold, hurt children who've learned that playing soldier with real guns isn't nearly as much fun as they thought."

"That could be said of new soldiers in almost every army, in every age."

"It's not being said about the guerrillas. The propaganda is whipping up everybody to the point of giving them no quarter."

"Not the Peace Force, I trust?"

"No, although after we lost some wounded in at the Meierwald—I don't know."

Parona looked at the shiny brown sliver nestling in the doctor's hand. He truly wanted to believe, but . . .

"This scrambler's only good for about half an hour, before I have to plug it into something. Then there'd be a power drain somebody might notice. The recording's a good two hours."

"Was this recording made covertly, or is it a copy of Security Police material?"

"Covertly. Nobody's threatened the Security Police for being secretive."

"That would be an exercise in futility. Exactly what do you want me to do with this recording?"

"Pass it on to the Federal government. I have another copy, and I'll give it to my own people. I swear it. But the Peace Force has to work with the Security Police, particularly around Nordshaven."

"I'm glad you have *that* much trust in your superiors," Parona said. It seemed to him that with Professor Bahr and now Major Laughton, he was dealing with more than his share of those who rushed in where angels fear to tread. "My influence with your General Duchamp is considerable, but not, I suspect, without limits.

"One other matter, and then you can summon someone to escort me out. Is there possibly a Security Police witness to these interrogations? Not somebody with an independent recording, that would be too much to ask for. But somebody who could offer evidence that you hadn't faked the whole piece."

"He'd have to be ready to sacrifice his career."

"Did you think of that before you made the recording?"

"Yes, but probably not as much as I should have."

Parona would not pray to be delivered from the zealous. They were a two-edged sword. He would pray that wisdom came to join to their zeal.

Laughton hesitated. "Marius Abrams, the Transportation Officer of the 4th Field Battalion, came out with us. He was the senior police officer in our column, really. He deferred to the line lieutenants, but they did let him sit in on some of the interrogations.

"I don't know if he's ready to give up his career. He did hint that he was a friend of our Field First, Sergeant Major Parkes—he's a lieutenant now, for his work on Hill 1242. Maybe that will help."

"It can hardly hurt. Thank you, Dr. Laughton. Will you be able to visit me at the chancery tomorrow evening around 1700?"

She grinned. "If I'm not under arrest, I should be." The grin faded. "If I come—Your Eminence, will you hear my confession? It's—God only knows how long it's been. Too long, anyway."

Parona had long known that the inability to be greatly surprised was part of being any kind of priest. "Of course, Doctor. Meanwhile, God keep you."

Laughton looked torn between kneeling and saluting. She compromised on a handshake as the orderly arrived to let Parona out.

15

THE WINDOW OVER Parkes's desk gave him the same view of the Teuffelberg as it had the previous six mornings. A wisp of steam crept from halfway up the southeast side of the main cone. Otherwise nothing had changed. Parkes turned on his portable computer, unfolded the keyboard, and began writing a letter to Betsy Tyndall.

4/22/07 (NF Cal)

Dear Betsy,

By the time this reaches you, no doubt the New Frontier media will have given an account of the opening stages of the Zauberberg campaign. They probably won't give too many details, and right now the only ones I could give myself are those of my own part in it.

Kat—

He hesitated, then substituted "Lieutenant Forbes-Brandon":

Lieutenant Forbes-Brandon and I did do a good job defending Hill 1242, although we had a lot of help. Don't let anyone convince you that the Triple Federation's people aren't good soldiers. They aren't as professional or as experienced as the Peace Force, most of them, which means they took longer to shift from peacetime to wartime attitudes. Once they'd made the shift, they were first-class allies.

Battalion Fourteen has been pulled out of the Serpents and is now P.F. security and logistics in Nordshaven. Battalion Seven is in the field east of the city, along with two Federal brigades.

Never mind that the two "brigades" were each about two understrength battalions, and that everybody was still short of ammunition. It wouldn't be critical when the time came for the big push on the north shore. Facing Nordshaven, the Brotherhood probably had no more than two battalions of regulars and a few thousand guerrillas. It would be a hard fight, but with time, ammunition, and airmobility on the side of the Good Guys, it would be a successful one.

Those of us who were on Hill 1242 have been lucky. After a big fight like that, it's a real killer to be shoved straight back into action. As it is, we've had a few days of not watching our heads and backs when we're awake, and sleeping in real beds when we're not. A few more days like this may be all—

A familiar footstep sounded outside the door. Parkes couldn't have picked it out of a crowd yet, but certainly out of a medium-sized party.

"Hi, Kat."

The footsteps stopped behind his chair. He smelled gardenias. He turned and saw she was wearing full-dress uniform.

"Why the full rig?"

Instead of replying, she looked over his shoulder at the screen. "Are you trying to maintain security or bore Betsy out of joining up?"

"Security, mostly. It's too late for anybody to keep her out of uniform. She's passed the physical for the Support Battalion of the New Selkirk Rifles. Hell, she'd have passed the physical for P.F. Recon if they'd let her take it!"

"Sounds as if you've given up arguing with her."

"I'm thinking about it. You can argue with a uniform-happy teenager. You can't argue with a young woman with a vocation. Or at least I'm not going to."

He stood up, saved the text, and hugged Forbes-Brandon. "You look good. But as I said, why?"

"We've been invited to an audience. Duchamp is in town."

" 'We,' Comrade Lieutenant?"

"We, as in you and me. The heroes of Hill 1242."

"Oh well, as long as they don't bust me back below corporal, I'll serve out my thirty."

Suddenly, she was hugging him back. She had to stoop too

much to rest her head on his shoulder; instead she pressed her cheek against his. "Damn, John. I'm scared."

"Welcome to the club." He gently pulled free and began untying his bathrobe. "Now, do I still *have* a full-dress outfit somewhere around here—?"

Duchamp's traveling HQ was in the penthouse of the Rienzihof, one of Nordshaven's two luxury hotels. The Peace Force had taken it over, and the Federal troops the other, the Schwarzwalder. (Rumor said that Duchamp and the Federal commander in chief had arranged this between them, to push the Security Police into second-rate housing.)

Brigadier General Lindholm, Duchamp's chief of staff, met them and personally led them to Duchamp's office. This proved nothing; staff work might be light this morning. She also neither spoke nor smiled, which proved even less. Without being dour or disagreeable, the Valkyrie smiled less than any other senior officer Parkes had ever known.

They stopped in front of a polished ragwood door set with quartz panels.

"Come in!"

Given a choice, Parkes would rather have been back on Hill 1242 facing the Lions. Ignoring seniority, he and Forbes-Brandon marched through the door abreast.

Duchamp was seated at a field desk, wearing battledress and a neutral expression. The desk held only a platoon of papers, instead of the usual company. One was a copy of the Action Report on the Hill 1242 fight. A hotel robot stood beside the desk.

Duchamp rose and returned their salute. "If you haven't had breakfast, I can arrange something. If you have, the robot has coffee, tea, hot chocolate, and fruit juice."

Parkes took coffee and told his stomach firmly to like it and shut up. Forbes-Brandon took hot chocolate.

Duchamp poured himself a cup of coffee, fished an envelope out of the papers, and handed it to the Amazon.

"Congratulations, Lieutenant Commander."

To Parkes, Forbes-Brandon looked simultaneously surprised, about to cry, and absolutely gorgeous. He kept his eyes resolutely to the front.

"I knew I was being considered for deep selection," she said finally. "But—well, I'll thank you for a start, sir."

Parkes knew what she meant. As senior P.F. officer on Zauberberg, Duchamp had the authority to hold up the promotion, retirement, or transfer of anyone under his command—if that person was under charges that might lead to a court-martial. Letting the Amazon put up her half stripe meant that here and now she was not.

Of course there were several kinds of investigation that might lead to such charges. He and Kat weren't out of the swamp yet, although maybe not in quite as deep as he'd feared.

Duchamp sat down and sipped coffee, until the silence would have had Parkes ready to fidget, if pointed lessons from a couple of D.I.'s more than twenty years ago hadn't come to his rescue. His eyes were still to the front when Duchamp put down his coffee cup and lifted the Action Report.

"The facts are all here, and they reflect much credit on both of you. Also on those officers under you, who took the situation you had created—the somewhat anomalous situation—so well."

He slapped the report down with a pistol-shot crack that made them both jump. "What I do not find here is the real *why* of your relieving Podgrebin. Lieutenant Commander, did the possibility of a charge of mutiny even occur to you?"

"Yes, sir. It did."

"Then I ask again—*why*?"

Forbes-Brandon took a deep breath. "Sir, Podgrebin was trying to settle—some grievance—against Parkes, right there in the presence of the enemy. He was going to deprive his people of an experienced troop leader, probably the most experienced around. He was also trying to bribe me into ignoring this, by leaving me out of any trouble he made for Parkes. That was splitting his Command Group, also in the presence of the enemy.

"When I realized what he was doing, I knew he was such an utter damned bloody fool that he could do *anything*! I didn't want to be court-martialed for mutiny. I didn't want to get anybody else killed, either."

"Indeed. And—your personal relationship with Parkes?"

Parkes jumped and knew that if Duchamp was guessing, he'd just confirmed the general's guess. The Amazon shook her head.

"There was no personal relationship. At least, nothing except that of two old comrades who were facing a sticky situation. That probably did influence me. But I hope I would have been just as reluctant to let a bastard like Podgrebin throw anyone else to the wolves!"

"From your record, I rather suspect you would have been." Duchamp refilled his coffee cup. "Lieutenant Parkes. Do you have anything to add?"

"No—well, yes. The—Forbes-Brandon was making a hell of a big bet that I was in shape to benefit from her help. I was pretty much one of the walking wounded, after Dozer—Sergeant Major di Leone's death."

"I won that bet, didn't I?" the Amazon said.

"Yes, but—sir, it's not down there in the report, but—I—I used my rifle on Dozer when she was trapped and burning—" The lump in his throat grew until it stopped his voice.

An arm went around his shoulder and a voice whispered in his ear, "Might as well be hung for a sheep as a lamb."

"I'm not going to hang anyone yet," Duchamp said, clearly trying not to laugh. Before he could go on, the intercom made a sound like a giant spitting on a hot stove. He slapped it and produced an ear-piercing squeal, then Lindholm's voice.

"Yellow Alert for meteorites, sir."

"Thank you, Kirsten."

Duchamp handed Forbes-Brandon another cup of hot chocolate. "I appreciate your frankness. Now I must be frank in return. Captain Podgrebin is currently in Medical Category Four. He can neither be charged nor bring charges until he is certified down to Category Three. By the time that happens, this campaign will be over. If we win, it is unlikely that Peace Force Command will be zealous in making trouble.

"It is still more unlikely, because I have unanimous testimony in favor of both of you from every other senior officer of both Battalion Fourteen and *Ark Royal*. Not to mention several Federal officers, to whom Captain Podgrebin seems to have failed to endear himself."

The lump in Parkes's throat seemed to grow a little more, almost enough to cut off his breathing. The whisper in his ear came again: "Who says it's only the English who can make a fine understatement?"

"I can conclude one of two things," Duchamp continued. "Either some dozen or more experienced Peace Force officers should all be tried for perjury and mutiny, or Captain Podgrebin had been working up to his—ah, lapse of judgment—for some time. I prefer to believe the former.

"However, the fact remains that your relief of Captain Podgrebin was somewhat irregular. Therefore, it would not be reasonable for you to expect any awards for your work on Hill 1242, although under other circumstances you would certainly have earned them."

Parkes and Forbes-Brandon exchanged looks, then shrugged in unison. "Good," Duchamp said. "I also have to warn you that there may be trouble about the list of awards you submitted with the report. Everyone on that list is technically a party to your irregularity, except for Sergeant Major di Leone. Acting Sergeant Dietsch should consider himself lucky not to be charged with assaulting a superior officer in the presence of the enemy."

"Will he be?" Parkes blurted.

"Since he was obeying the orders of Lieutenant Forbes-Brandon, whose right to give those orders has so far not been called into question—I should say he can expect to go free. He had best be very careful if he wants to keep those stripes, however."

That was some consolation, but not enough. The lump in Parkes's throat dissolved in pure indignation with overtones of rage. Now he knew how the Amazon had felt. Except that Duchamp not only had more rank than Podgrebin, he had more sense.

Take it slow, Parkes, take it slow. It's beginning to look like you'll keep your commission—and you want to, now. Don't sacrifice it in a frontal assault on an entrenched general.

"Sir, I'll have to protest that decision, if it is a decision. Everyone else on that list ought to get something, particularly Magnusson and Sharpe.

"I seem to recall one of your articles, where you said that no military force in history has ever been as dependent on the initiative of junior leaders as the Peace Force. They can affect the future of whole planets. I think we've just proved that, if it needed proving.

"Maybe that's why Kat and I aren't being court-martialed, because we exercised a legitimate initiative. Magnusson did the same thing, and pulled more than a hundred people out of the fire. He couldn't have done it without Dozer, but I don't think she could have done it without him.

"The same thing's true of pretty much everybody else on the list. Take—"

"Assume I'm literate, Lieutenant Parkes, and get to the point."

"Sir, it's been Peace Force custom to reward initiative by junior leaders. Break this custom, and what else are you breaking? That's why I have to protest.''

''How far are you prepared to protest?'' Duchamp's voice was dangerously quiet. Parkes didn't care. The Amazon had said it for both of them.

''I'll insist on a court-martial over Podgrebin's relief from command, so that I can make my case.''

''Lieutenant, you didn't initiate the relief from command.''

''So court-martial me,'' the Amazon said cheerfully. ''Or court-martial us both under Article Forty-six. We don't want to push you on that, sir, but with all due respect—''

''I should not care to be someone to whom you think all respect is not due,'' Duchamp said. ''You have both made your points. It is not unlikely that—''

The intercom screamed. So did Lindholm. ''Red Alert! Red Alert!''

''The meteorite?''

''Yes. Impact—impact in this quadrant. Four minutes or less.''

''Thank you, Kirsten.'' Duchamp stood up as the window shutters slammed into place.

''A quadrant is a fairly large place, but still—if you have any farewells or religious duties, for which you require privacy . . .''

''Thank you, sir,'' Forbes-Brandon said. ''But I think we're in good company right now.''

Duchamp smiled. It struck Parkes that the Amazon almost certainly hadn't won any promotions by sleeping with superiors. Charming them was another matter. Was it that charm she was using on him, and did something lie behind it that might affect their long-term—

Parkes told his doubts to go take a running jump at themselves. *If you spend what may be your last minutes of life doing anything besides hugging Kat, you deserve to have the next rock drop straight on your empty head!*

Parkes took his own advice. The Amazon returned the compliment. Two oversized noses did somewhat get in the way of kissing, but they managed.

Somewhere in the middle of the embrace, the building quivered. A window cracked with a vicious *pnnnggg*, plascolor chips popped off the walls, dust rose, and papers fell from the desk.

The intercom was also a casualty, so Lindholm delivered her report personally. ''They diverted the main object, but it sloughed off a fragment. Then the fragment split up, so low they couldn't hit it in time. We had two strikes, one on the northwest face of the Teuffelberg and the other out to sea, about a hundred kilometers west of Dietrich's Bay."

"Peste," Duchamp said. Ocean strikes were more vicious than land ones, thanks to the tsunamis and possible weather effects. Everything permanent on the coasts of Zauberberg was at least ten meters above high water, to allow for that.

"Strike yields?" the general asked.

"Five to seven MT equivalent on the land strike, from the seismic data," Lindholm said. "No data on the ocean strike, but they've ordered everyone to head for high ground."

Thanks to the rugged topography of Zauberberg, that wouldn't be far in most places. One place where it would be hard to find high ground was near the mouth of Dietrich's Bay, where Federal and P.F. engineers were finishing the repairs to the Ponte d'Oro . . .

Praying had seldom seemed so futile, but there had seldom been so little else for Parkes to do.

"Thank you, Kirsten," Duchamp said. "My friends, your new assignments may be a trifle more exciting than I had anticipated. Lieutenant Commander, you are to take a Naval Liaison team and repeat your survey of the Teuffelberg for orbital and aerial resupply. Also for both laser and explosive fires, in case we need to divert lava flows. I cannot imagine that a five-MT kick in the *cul* will make the Teuffelberg more peaceful.

"Lieutenant Parkes, you are now an acting captain. You are also in charge of security for the volcano monitoring teams, including evacuating them if necessary. You will be reinforced if we need to start evacuating the whole Teuffelberg peninsula."

"A vos orders, mon général," Forbes-Brandon said.

Duchamp threw her a pained look. "Your efficiency ratings, your command presence, and I presume your sex life have all improved. Your Francone, however, remains execrable."

The shutters rattled and squealed open. At first Parkes thought the Teuffelberg's main cone had entirely disappeared. Then he saw that it was still there, shrouded from peak to base in a vast somber cloud of dust.

16

THIS CLOSE TO the water, Dallin had to fight to keep the verti's engines running on air and fuel instead of spray. She adjusted the fuel feed to run the engines hotter. She didn't need too much endurance but she absolutely had to stay in the air. If she went down into Dietrich's Bay now, her chances of rescue would be somewhere between small and nonexistent.

Steep gray pyramids roared back and forth across the hundred-kilometer width of the bay, colliding, trampling one another, dissolving and recombining. Most wore beards of foam. Dallin strained her eyes, trying to see *anything* but water down there, hoping to see survivors or at least wreckage.

The wave from the ocean strike came roaring into Dietrich's Bay twenty meters high, swamping the causeway and dropping two spans of the bridge into the channel. No railroad out of Nordshaven, not for months. Not much hope, either, for the fifty-odd engineers and A.D. people caught by the wave. The western bay had already been covered by Federal air patrols who reported bodies and wreckage but nobody alive.

The shoreline wasn't Dallin's problem, either, although she'd heard an estimate of the death toll that made her cringe. High ground was close enough; the problem was people who'd started too late.

''Wreck, bearing 65, about four thousand meters,'' the copilot sang out. A banking climb gave Dallin a better view.

''Overturned oyster boat,'' she said after a moment. She descended to within meters of the wave crests, then circled. Three circles showed no signs of humanity except the white bottom. Shellfish flourished in unpolluted Dietrich's Bay, both native and altered Terran and Helvetian strains. *Had* flourished.

A quick fuel check, and on to the next search area. Dallin

climbed to the transit height of two hundred meters and started feeding in the new course—

"What the devil's that!"

The copilot frowned. "It looks like—it looks like the old ferryboat from Porto Roccanegra."

"Yeah, but that thing hasn't been in service for years! Not since they built the bridge."

"Didn't they have her out for a few days, until the pontoon bridge was in place?"

"Couldn't prove it by me, but—I'll be damned! There's a *crew* on board."

One wing of the ferryboat's midships bridge was folded down to the passenger deck. On the other, two men were standing, waving frantically.

"Are those distress signals, or what?"

As the verti circled, another man climbed out of a deckhouse hatch and scrambled aft. When he reached the stowed rafts, he began making hand signals. On the second circle, Dallin recognized the Universal Code for "Await radio communication."

"Shift to the Sea Survival band," she said.

The S.S. band was a busy place, signals punching straight through one another. The ferry's survival radio was the closest source, once it started transmitting.

"We started *Donna Lucrezia* offshore the minute we heard the Yellow Alert," the man said. "We met the wave far enough out to ride over it. We lost one man overboard, but we still have a crew."

"Do you need assistance?"

"Can you fly out a portable pump and some fuel?"

"It would be safer for you—"

"We will not leave her!" The spitting on the circuit might not have been static. "The worst is over. Besides, you soldier people may need us. The pontoon bridge is all smashed to pieces."

That didn't surprise Dallin. The man's next words did.

"The pontoons are all sunk or scattered. The highway bridge fell, too."

"What!"

"I was aft lookout. I saw it fall. Not when the wave came, but after. Was there an earthquake?"

Dallin had been airborne since ten minutes after the strike. She didn't know but wasn't going to admit it, either. She should have asked.

"Any other earthquake damage?"

"God only knows."

Somebody closer to hand probably did, but they might be busy if local faults really were letting go. God might still be needed, though, if the new picture in Dallin's mind was correct.

The pontoon bridge gone and the pontoons destroyed. The highway bridge down. The next bridge upstream over the Roccanegra bombed out in the first days of the war; never repaired because of limited engineer assets. The bridge after that, serving a little backcountry two-laner and in guerrilla territory to boot.

The meteorite strike had just cut Nordshaven off from all secure land communication with friendly territory.

"Where to?" Warrant Officer Gallagher said.

"Camp 1160," Forbes-Brandon replied. Parkes nodded. They climbed into the verti and were airborne before they'd finished strapping in.

"E.T.A.?" Parkes asked.

"Ten minutes, unless you want me to crest-hop?"

"The bad guys' air has better things to do, what's left of it," Forbes-Brandon said.

"Then I'll take it straight and level."

The verti climbed to a thousand meters and increased to standard cruise. Forbes-Brandon sighed. With a twenty-minute flight, she'd have been tempted to remove her boots. No, too much risk of not getting them back on again. She'd been on her feet and on the run except for a few short verti hops since the meteorite strike.

From the way Parkes sank into his seat, he felt much the same way. He'd probably been even busier, pulling together two scratch platoons out of Fourteen's support people and getting them out to the slopes of the Teuffelberg.

Damn it, security teams for the vulcanologists were supposed to have been assigned ten days ago! Was Duchamp trying to soothe the Security Police, or being cautious about offending the Federal brass by implying they weren't doing their job? After the Security Police attempt to investigate Marian Laughton, Forbes-Brandon was sure the Security Police didn't need soothing. Shooting, maybe, but better to try soothing a strangler in *must*.

"Think we need to talk to Professor Bahr?" Parkes said at last.

"I'd rather talk to Biancheri, but yes. We ought to check my D.Z.'s and your outposts with him. No point in putting either over a magma vent."

"We could do that by radio."

"The university doesn't have secure equipment, the last I heard. Besides, they must have had a busy day. A little encouragement won't hurt."

She wondered if he'd asked that last question to test her reasoning. She *was* feeling a little blurred, and it was surprising how much she valued his approval—and respected his judgment. No, the respect had always been there, just submerged.

Five minutes later the verti slanted down toward a long narrow valley, winding uphill toward one of the Teuffelberg's secondary cones.

"Doesn't look like anybody's home—no, they're moving uphill," Gallagher said. He set the verti down fifty meters east of the camp, as several field-clothed figures hurried out of it. A light all-wheeler was creeping up the slope to the south with more people aboard it, while a third group erected a tent on the ridge at the top of the slope.

The leader of the approaching figures turned out to be Professor Bahr himself. Forbes-Brandon climbed out, reached to shake his hand, then stopped, hand outstretched. The ground was quivering under her feet.

"It's been doing that since the war started," Bahr said dismissively. "Somewhat more since this morning, but not critically."

Forbes-Brandon looked at Bahr. In his natural environment, there was nothing of the loud-mouthed political zealot about him. He seemed entirely in command of both himself and the situation.

Bahr would make a poor soldier, but then, Forbes-Brandon realized she would make a wretched vulcanologist. When she had solid ground under her boots, she wanted it to stay solid.

"Mind if I ask why you're moving?" Parkes said.

Bahr pointed toward the secondary cone. "It's not about to erupt, but it's showing signs of steam venting. We could have a mudslide coming right down the valley."

"Can we help?"

"Indeed you can. If your verti would carry the rest of our heavy equipment—it can be slung outside—"

"No problem."

"Then, if you have room for a passenger back to Nordshaven, could you—ah—transport His Eminence?"

"Now, Professor—" began a polished, urbane voice Forbes-Brandon remembered from the prefect's reception. A second look told Forbes-Brandon that the man who looked like a spry retired professor in graduate student's field gear really was the primate of Zauberberg.

"Your Eminence, I don't wish to be insulting," Bahr said. "But how fast can you climb the hill to that ridge? The university verti is evacuating the teams from the far side of the mountain, otherwise I would let you wait for it. As things are . . ."

"We flew over the far side, surveying for D.Z.'s and security outposts," Forbes-Brandon said. "If we'd known your people needed help—"

"Thank you, but how could you have known? We need better communications among the university and military elements of the volcano watch. Always excepting the Security Police, of course."

To change the subject, Forbes-Brandon asked, "Any of your people hurt?"

"Some burns and sprains, but nothing crippling. There is just no stable site on level ground left on that side of the mountain. We do not even know if the meteorite drove through the crust into the magma."

"I'm no vulcanologist, but as far as we could see it hadn't," Forbes-Brandon said. "What hit was only a fraction of the rock, and it split in two when it hit atmosphere. Both chunks must have lost a fair amount of mass and velocity before they hit." She decided not to mention the Nordshaven situation. "We'll make all our data available to you, of course," a promise she prayed could be kept.

Bahr nodded and returned to his original quarry. "Your Eminence, would you at least accept a verti lift to the top of the ridge? We can pack the equipment while you're on your way."

"Very well. I am not one to rely on prayer to counteract the force of gravity, and we *are* downhill from that cone. If—"

The ground quivered like a furiously beaten drumhead. Then it heaved sharply upward, sank down, and repeated the pattern. Cracks appeared in the hillside; nothing came out of them, but they zigzagged crazily across both sides of the valley.

"Lift out!" Forbes-Brandon shouted.

"Wait for the cardinal!" Parkes and Bahr yelled almost together. Parkes and a university woman virtually snatched the cardinal off his feet and hustled him toward the verti. Gallagher flung open the door with one hand and started the engines with the other.

The cardinal and his bearers had just reached the verti when the ground opened under Forbes-Brandon's feet. She dropped a meter between one breath and the next, landing with a thud and falling back against the side of the crack.

Parkes gave her one frantic look, then turned back to loading the cardinal. The ground heaved again, the crack narrowed enough to squeeze the breath out of her, and slabs of rock fell in on either side. Then Bahr gripped both her hands, dug in his boots, and heaved. She flew out of the crack like a cork out of a bottle as the ground closed behind her fast enough to nip the toes of her boots.

She landed on top of Bahr, too weak with relief to get up at once. It wasn't only the relief at being alive, either. It was relief to see Parkes showing the professional's reflexes, rather than the lover's.

She'd been in danger, but his duty lay elsewhere and somebody else had been close enough to save her. That was double good luck.

'Thank you, Professor Bahr."

The verti's taking off drowned out his reply.

Parkes's turning his back on Katherine wasn't entirely a stern decision in favor of duty. It was also a total refusal to watch her crushed when the crack snapped shut.

When he turned back, she and Bahr were sprawled on the ground, both with all limbs attached and intact. It wasn't entirely the next shock or the prop blast from the verti that drove Parkes to his knees.

He lurched to his feet, Katherine's lips moved thanking Bahr, then the verti took off and Parkes fell again. He really wanted to lie there, hugging the ground until it stopped shaking and tasting the pleasure of having made the right decision.

If he'd reacted as lover instead of fellow-professional, what he and Kat had might have ended almost before it began. Article Forty-six was sometimes enforced less than rigorously. There was no avoiding the conflict that was built into any relationship with a comrade-in-arms. With Kat a man had only one choice. (And come to think of it, it probably went both ways, because being an officer was really beginning to look like an opportunity rather than a punishment.)

Parkes rose to his knees. The Amazon reached down to help him up the rest of the way. Bahr looked up, following the flight of the verti toward the ridge.

Then from the uphill end of the camp, someone screamed:

"Mudslide!"

Parkes lurched to his feet and looked up the valley. The whole face of the cone seemed to be moving. At the head of the valley something writhed toward them, like a vast brown dragon exhaling steam, growing larger as he watched.

"Uphill!" Bahr and several others shouted quite unnecessarily.

Parkes was already moving. The university student who'd helped him load the cardinal stumbled; he dragged her up and along.

The two sides of the valley were about the same distance away. The south side was steeper, but the north side was covered with patches of loose stones and those damned volcanic glass ball-bearings. Parkes headed south.

He wanted to look up the valley, but the swelling roar of the mudslide told him enough, and he didn't dare stumble. Kat was well out ahead, already mounting the slope. She'd be safe even if she did stumble.

Sulphur-reeking steam reached Parkes as he reached the slope. He flung a hand over his mouth and nose and plunged upward, leaping cracks he barely saw, somehow not landing arse over apex. His lungs threatened to burst their way out of his chest, and blowtorch heat seared the back of his neck.

Then Kat's hands were gripping his again. He let the grip remain just helpful for a moment, then tore his hands free and threw his arms around her.

In due course, the outside world returned, in the form of Bahr's decorous cough.

"That was a small mudslide, as such go. I suggest we climb a trifle higher before a large one comes along."

With sulphurous steam pricking their nostrils and lungs, they climbed to the ridge. Gallagher had already landed, and Parona was sitting staring toward the mountain.

"Your Eminence," Bahr said. "There is really nothing I can

say that doesn't sound like 'I told you so.' Please—for all our sakes, return to Nordshaven and pray for us."

Parona managed another wry grin. "I came out here to see how your work was going. I have seen it. I can return with a reasonably clear conscience, since to do so will let you get on with it. By the way—and forgive me if I intrude—I thought you were an Anti-Clerical."

Bahr frowned. "I do not think religion needs hierarchies. As for believing in God—do not soldiers say, 'There are no atheists in foxholes,' whatever they are?"

"Something like that," Forbes-Brandon said.

"Well, there are few atheists facing volcanoes. Although we perhaps find it easier to believe in the wrath of God than in His mercy . . . Thank you for your help, by the way. We would have been in a tight place without it."

Forbes-Brandon looked down at her legs for the tenth time since Bahr pulled her out of the crack. She wanted to be sure they were still there. "I'd rather nobody mentioned tight places for a while, if you don't—what the devil is that?"

She pointed to a verti circling over the valley. "Did I inhale too much sulphur, or is that a security verti?" She fumbled for binoculars until she remembered that hers were now under several meters of boiling mud. Parkes raised his own, then nodded.

"The securities, all right." He shifted frequencies on his radio. "Hello, Security Police verti. This is Camp 1160 Sub-one, Captain Parkes speaking. Come in, Security Police verti."

"Hello, Fruit Merchant," came a static-ridden but robust voice. "Captain Abrams here. Can we land safely? This isn't a joyride, you know."

Parkes looked at Gallagher, who gave a thumbs-up. "Affirmative."

The Security Police verti plunged down with a recklessness that reminded Forbes-Brandon of Dallin's piloting. It landed beyond the P.F. verti, and a large Security Police captain climbed out, followed by a medium-sized woman lieutenant in a Nordshaven police uniform.

"People, meet the Wondering Jew," Parkes said. "This son and brother of rabbis was always beginning sentences with 'I wonder.' He still flunked philosophy."

"Well, Fruit Merchant, you didn't do any better in logic, in spite of Denise's tutoring. So I guess both of us were doomed to wind up officers. Congratulations, I think."

"Since this wasn't a joyride . . ." Forbes-Brandon said, more politely than she felt. Old Comrades' Day could wait.

"Sorry," Abrams said, sounding anything but. He pulled out an envelope and handed it to Forbes-Brandon. "All the details are here, but I'll give you the predigested version." He looked at Bahr. "Professor, if you don't mind—"

"Does it affect his work?" Parona asked.

"Yes."

"Then he has—what is it called, 'a need to know,' I think?"

"Your Eminence, you can't excommunicate me. You do have a point, though. Very briefly, the Brotherhood is staging a medium-sized offensive, from just south of the city down through the Serpent's Tail. Mostly guerrillas, but there's been one assault with a company of Angels. Many reports of movement, some sniping with rockets, a lot with small arms.

"Fourteen's going back to the field, including the security detachments. I know you just got here, but don't blame me. I'm just the messenger boy. Get on my radio, and tell the vertis we're sending where to pick up your people."

Forbes-Brandon and Parkes had meanwhile torn open the envelope and authenticated the contents. They nodded, then looked at each other.

"Order," Forbes-Brandon said.

"Counterorder," Parkes replied.

"Disorder!" they shouted in unison.

Abrams sighed. "As I said, I'm just the messenger boy. Well, not quite. I'm in charge of getting your people out and the new people in."

"Who *are* these new people?" Bahr shouted. "*Bei Gott,* if they are the Security—"

"They aren't, except for some pilots. Some shrewd calculator noticed that Security was short-handed but had plenty of transport. It wasn't being used, either, now that we weren't in the field.

"On the other hand, the Field Company of the Nordshaven Municipal Police had plenty of idle hands but no transport. So they're coming out to protect you volcano-watchers in our vertis. Meet Lieutenant Ursula Krieger, of the Field Company."

While Lieutenant Krieger introduced herself to Bahr, Forbes-Brandon led Abrams downhill out of hearing of the rest.

"Are you the one who helped derail the investigation of

Laughton, by confirming her tapes? If it's none of my business—''

''It is, but don't go overboard thanking me. The old professionals are trying to take back security from the youngsters. If they succeed, I may get a promotion out of it.''

''And if they don't?''

''Are you always a pessimist, ma'am?''

''I'm a veteran.''

''Good point. I still think I can take care of myself. You just take care of the Fruit Merchant.''

''Is that any of your—?'' she began, then realized she'd be the pot calling the kettle black if she complained of Abrams's nosiness. She turned uphill, to watch Parkes climb into the verti with a map board in one hand.

17

Eight kilometers away, somebody was fighting on the slopes of the Schneeheim. Somebody using rockets or launchers, to be visible here at Fourteen's HQ. To Parkes that meant P.F., Federal Jaegers, or Brotherhood regulars. The guerrillas had shot their heavy stuff dry in the first few days of their offensive. They'd done some damage with it, but they'd still need a resupply before they could do more. Allied air strikes and deep-penetration raids were trying to make that resupply a long slow process.

Parkes contemplated tapping into the tactical net and finding out who was doing what to whom. As he did, a verti floated into the HQ strip, cutting engines and lights the moment it touched down. Guerrilla snipers with telescopic sights and explosive rounds still popped up randomly. Maybe that verti was bringing word of the truce negotiations? Parkes laughed. In the ten days since the Serpent's Tail offensive began, "when the truce team returns" had become the local equivalent of "when they find the Azteca Expedition."

Parkes yanked shut the light- and heat-opaque shades and sat down at his desk. Rereading Betsy Tyndall's letter took him five minutes. In another five he was deep into his reply.

> —not such a good idea, applying for an age waiver without telling your parents. Normally it's granted without parental consent only if the parents have been legally declared incompetent or unfit. I was one of the few exceptions—

That was one of the things for which his stepmother had never forgiven him or his sister Louise. It was something for which she might never have forgiven his father, if she'd known how many people felt they owed Oscar Parkes the favor of letting his eldest boy escape into the Peace Force.

—but I had a lot of help. Much of it was from people who knew my home situation. You won't get that kind of help, because your family has and deserves a good reputation. Those same people who helped me will think you're signing up (or trying to) in a fit of rebellion.

It also won't help your relations with your family. I know that at your age it's not always easy to think of the long-term consequences of being on bad terms with your parents. It's also desperately important, if you're planning on a career as a professional soldier. It's a lonely, dangerous, stress-loaded profession. All the human contact you can have is none too much.

I had already lost so much of mine when I signed up that I thought it wouldn't make any difference. I was wrong—

—although I don't think I realized how wrong until suddenly, there was Kat—

—and you would learn that you were wrong a lot sooner. Withdraw that waiver application, apologize to your parents, serve out your year in the Selkirks, and you'll have a better career in the long run.

If you haven't already stopped reading this letter, you certainly would if I gave you a detailed account of what I haven't been doing lately. Since Fourteen moved back into the field, I've been doing everything except the one thing I'd really like to do, which is lead a rifle company in action.

I've been in charge of HQ security. I've been liaison to the Jaegers on our right. I've been unofficial deputy adjutant to Major Katsouros. I've been George for everything that doesn't require staff training and a few things that do.

What I haven't been, is shooting or being shot at.

This isn't really anybody's fault. We've got more qualified company commanders than we have companies to command—

—to be specific, five commanders for two companies, but let's not get specific in case somebody who shouldn't reads this—

—and not much prospect of vacancies soon. The worst of the fighting against the guerrillas was done by the Jaegers and Battalion Seven, before Fourteen arrived. The enemy did his worst and got badly hammered, although there's a fight going on as I write this.

I could transfer to Seven, but I'd rather spend the rest of this campaign with the people I know. This will probably be my last campaign with Fourteen, anyway, at least for several years.

There's an Advanced Command Course being set up on Helvetia for people like me. We're first-class company commanders as we stand, but these days it's not really safe to give anybody a company unless he can also take over the battalion if necessary. If I'd ever had any doubts about the wisdom of this policy, Hill 1242 would have killed them as dead as Marshal Zhukov. We'd have been in very deep toxics if Forbes-Brandon hadn't known a hell of a lot more than there was any reason to expect her—

The familiar footsteps sounded behind Parkes again. No gardenia this time, just healthy woman needing a bath and the faint nose-prickling smell of impregnated battledress. It suited her as well as the perfume, just as battledress, full dress, a sweat suit, or bare skin all suited her at the right time.

"Hi, Kat—" Then he was on his feet as she raised a hand to her throat. A vein was throbbing in the long neck.

"What is it?"

"The truce negotiations have been broken off. Those—the Brotherhood is refusing to allow the evacuation of Nordshaven, unless they get free withdrawal of all their troops and an amnesty for the guerrillas."

"What about their hostages?"

"They'll take the hostages home to the Protectorate. They will be released when and if we and the Feds have complied with the other provisions of the armistice."

"Those damned . . ." He couldn't talk. He wanted a Brotherhood member—any age or sex would do—to strangle slowly with his bare hands.

"Oh, they won't be damned. They are strong in the defense of the Lord. They . . ." She closed her eyes and started crying silently. Parkes put his arms around her until she stopped.

"We'd better tie up any loose ends and pack for the field," he said when his own voice returned. "I have a feeling we're due for a Command Group meeting before we get to bed."

• • •

For once, Parkes was wrong. The Command Group didn't meet until after breakfast the next morning.

Forbes-Brandon suspected part of it was sheer mental paralysis. It took an hour for the word to spread through the battalion, another hour for everyone to regain their ability to talk and think coherently.

By then orders had come down calling MacLean, Vela, and Dallin to a Force Command Group meeting in Nordshaven. Everybody else was on Yellow Alert—the guerrillas on the Schneeheim *had* been resupplied with heavy-weapons ammunition and were expected to attack elsewhere in Fourteen's A.O. before dawn.

The alert ended around midnight—Forbes-Brandon didn't remember exactly. By then she would have been ready to crawl into bed with Parkes on a planetwide TV hookup, just for the sake of being held. Both of them were physically incapable of violating Article Forty-six.

Instead they scrounged coffee and a midnight snack, then she sat down with a report on the Schneeheim attack. It provided the first good news she'd had in quite a while. If the guerillas insisted on forcing a major engagement around the Schneeheim, their supplies would have to come across the kind of open ground where orbital fires could do a lot of damage.

"Therefore, the guerrillas will probably attack everywhere else, once they think they've got our attention focused on the Schneeheim."

"Eh?"

"Sorry, John. I was thinking out loud." She repeated herself.

Parkes nodded. "Yeah. The Brotherless have been a lot of things, but not dumb. Not yet."

They both heard the verti descending at the same moment. Parkes went out to meet the returning officers while Forbes-Brandon started tidying up her desk.

The minutes dragged on, until she began to suspect this wasn't MacLean's verti. At ten minutes, she stood up. She had her hand on the doorplate when it slid open.

Parkes stood there, a small boy asleep on his shoulder and a slightly larger girl holding on to his free hand. Behind him trailed three more children, two boys and a girl, ranging from nine up to thirteen Standard.

Forbes-Brandon decided that silence involved the least mental and physical effort. Parkes managed a weary grin, handed her the boy, and herded the others into the room.

"No, the guerrillas didn't hit an orphanage. These are the children of some of the Jaeger officers. They're being evacuated from Nordshaven, on a space-available basis. MacLean's verti had room and lift, so he brought them out. We're supposed to bed them down—somewhere—until arrangements can be made."

"What kind of arrangements?"

"I don't know. I will tomorrow, though. I've got a new helmet—Evacuation Officer."

"Fine. Take it off and go to bed."

"Kat, you've been working a lot harder than I have these past few days."

"Not that much harder. We can at least split the job until you get things organized."

"Too bad Dozer isn't here. She'd be singing Sicilian lullabies to them in half an hour."

It would have made her feel good, Parkes's easy reference to Dozer, if she hadn't seen his eyes. That room with the mutilated dolls still haunted him. He wanted to make up for the girls he hadn't been able to save by knocking himself out for these children.

"John, don't make me pull rank. I'm too tired to pull it or anything else." *Also too tired to censor my words, but who the devil cares at this point?*

"All right. You baby-sit while I scrounge some rations."

"And some help. Some *nice* help. These kids are scared."

"There aren't any nannies on the T.O. of an Expeditionary Battalion."

"I mean, people with children of their own. I'll volunteer Chief Schrader. He's part of a group marriage, nine kids or something like that."

"All right. The one you're holding is Camilla. This is Rudolph. The others—"

"Michael."

"Leon."

"Dirdre."

"How do you do? Welcome to Expeditionary Battalion Fourteen. I'm Lieutenant Commander Forbes-Brandon—"

"The Amazon of Hill 1242?" Dirdre said, wide-eyed. "We all saw you on the television!"

"Well, I did command there. If you'll all sit down and be

quiet, I'll tell you about it. Captain Parkes is going out to find you some food and beds and other people to take care of you. Dirdre, would you take care of Camilla?''

''Yes, ma'am.''

Over Camilla's dark head, Forbes-Brandon's eyes met Parkes's. He sketched a salute, smiled, and went out.

Losing sleep doing something for the children was almost as good as sleep itself. Or at least Parkes felt as if he'd had eight instead of four hours, when the Command Group met the next morning.

MacLean repeated the Brotherhood's conditions for a truce and added that the Triple Federation had tentatively rejected them.

''Tentatively in this case means subject to being overridden by the Union Council. Duchamp has recommended against such action. The Teuffelberg is only a probable threat. Having to do the whole job over again in a few years if we give in is a certainty. Not to mention what all the other people who want to behave like the Brotherhood would think.''

He turned to the map. ''We're supposed to get a major resupply of all consumables plus a draft of two or three hundred individual reinforcements in another ten days. In another ten to fourteen after that, the 8th Brigade under General Kuroki will be in-system. We have to do the best we can with what we have, at least until the resupply.

''After that, Duchamp will balance the danger from the Teuffelberg against the danger of expending Federal and P.F. strength before Kuroki arrives. It would be jumping out of the frying pan into the fire to let the Brotherhood take Nordshaven.''

Parkes felt that MacLean could have chosen a better metaphor, but didn't disagree with the principle.

''The main burden of any offensive will be borne by the Eastern Division, including Battalions Five and Eleven. Our Western Division has the primary responsibility for the defense and evacuation of Nordshaven, as well as clearing the guerrillas out of the Serpent's Tail.

''For the evacuation, I'll turn you over to Major Dallin. Incidentally, Major, I'm happy to inform you that you can put up real permanent leaves now.''

''Good God, sir. What did you hide?''

"Nothing. I just told the Promotion Board that you could walk on water anytime you didn't have a verti—"

Dallin choked, pressed the heels of her hands into her red eyes for a moment, then nodded and stepped up to the map.

"All right, people. The evacuation of Nordshaven is now officially under way. The priority groups, in order, are the sick and disabled, children, the able-bodied elderly, and other dependents of members of the Peace Force and Federal Armed Forces. They're still arguing about who comes after that, but that's not our problem. By the time we're through with the priority groups, they'll have it straightened out."

"They'd damned well better," was nearly a chorus.

"We're using airlift and Highway 75, until one or the other bridge over the Roccanegra is restored. Forget the Ponte d'Oro. Airlift will be both military and civilian vertis, and fixed-wings as long as they can operate. As you know, the main Nordshaven airport is on the Teuffelberg side of the city. That's the largest patch of level ground above the tsunami level, so putting the airport there must have seemed like a good idea at the time.

"We'll be operating convoys over Highway 75, using primarily heavy-duty civilian hovercraft. Each unit from Nordshaven south to the Roccanegra has appointed an Evacuation Officer, to organize the passage of the convoys through his A.O. Captain Parkes is our Evacuation Officer, and right now he's probably the most important man in the battalion. If he says he needs a fur-lined toilet seat for the head in a medevac hovercraft, *try* to get it for him.

"Senior Evacuation Officer is Colonel Fribourg, of the 2nd Engineers. His deputy is Major Abrams, of the Security Police. They'll be arriving later today, to give a more detailed briefing."

"What about evacuation by sea?" Acting Captain Sharpe asked.

"There's no place to house any large number of sealifted evacuees north of Nuovo Milano. That would make transit time prohibitive.

"However, the next supply convoy that comes into Nordshaven will be sent back with a full load of evacuees." Dallin looked at MacLean, who nodded. "If the convoy is attacked at sea, General Duchamp will retaliate with nuclear weapons."

"What about guerrilla attacks on refugees traveling overland?" Lieutenant Magnusson asked. "Any retaliation for that?"

"Conventional only. That's from Peace Force Command."

"*Why?*" The word held a load of heartfelt rage.

"Guerrillas are more ambiguous than air forces. They may not be fully under control of the Brotherhood's government."

"Control, my ass!" Magnusson snarled. "I think we ought to unambiguously bomb the Protectorate into radioactive glass!"

MacLean fixed Magnusson with a look that slowly turned the red of anger into the red of embarrassment.

"Sorry, sir. I was out of turn—"

"You were. I doubt if you're the only one in this room who thinks that way. You might even be right. But our orders are different. Our first duty is to obey those orders. Otherwise we undercut a century's trust in the Peace Force and give fifty worlds over to the likes of the Brotherhood.

"Major Dallin, any more?"

"No, sir."

"Fine. The mess is now open, for late breakfasts, early lunches, or drinks."

Mostly drinks, Parkes suspected—except that he wasn't going to lay anything stronger than water on his stomach for a while. He caught the Amazon's eye as the meeting broke up, and they went out side by side.

Halfway down the hall, the Amazon stopped and leaned against the wall, a hand over her face. She brushed Parkes off with the other.

"No, no. I'm—pretty much all right. Maybe I should have got more sleep. But—this is turning into such a filthy business. It's making *me* feel filthy. Do you know, I think I could *enjoy* calling down a Mark V on the Protectorate?"

A Mark V was *Ark Royal*'s big gun, with six 200-kiloton M.I.R.V.'s. There wasn't a city on any inhabited planet a single Mark V couldn't reduce to rubble, ashes, and dead, some of them not too dead to scream.

This time she didn't brush him off. Parkes remembered an Old Terran playwright Denise had discussed, someone who'd written a play about the Trojan War in Francone. The face of war, someone said in the play, was like a monkey's backside, red and scaly.

Parkes had looked at that face often enough. As a Naval Liaison Officer, Kat had always faced the possibility of having to kiss it.

18

MAYBE THE HARVESTER'S PEACE in South Pamar had been austerely furnished even before the war. Or had it been looted during the war? Certainly it now offered little more than walls, floor, ceiling, and basic furniture.

This did not bother Hiko. A childhood spent outside what had been Osaka, *ninjitsu* training, service with the Master, and temperament—all let him accept austerity as a natural condition,

In the Harvester's Peace, austerity also had practical advantages. The Proctors would readily let alone an uncomfortable room offering neither alcohol, drugs, cigarettes, nor any other prohibited vice. So it had quietly become a refuge for the Lions and anyone they chose to allow in, including Daughters, Chosen, and Hiko's Teams. This hospitality agreement was highly informal, but the Proctors seemed to know that it would be enforced.

Even here, Hiko would not sit with his back to the front door or without someone watching the back door. He'd just exchanged hand signals with Jamshir Singh at a rear table when Ruth walked in.

She moved as if she was tired, which indeed they all were. Preparing to meet the enemy offensive meant long days and sleepless nights. Tonight Ruth showed something more, less common but oddly familiar.

Hiko stared until she flushed. He realized that he was seeing on her face the same expression he'd seen on his own this morning, as he shaved after his interview with the Master's Representative.

Interview? Briefing? Names hardly mattered. "An Imperial Rescript" would be accurate if tactless. Certainly the Representative had spoken as if he was either emperor or at least free to invoke the emperor's name at will.

"The decision to oppose evacuation of Nordshaven will be supported with all our resources," the Representative announced.

"All?"

That request for clarification was a mistake. "Yes. We must even support the Proctors' work against any who oppose the decision."

"I shall do so, although we have had few dealings with the Proctors."

"By all means feel free to approach them through me. They will listen with more attention than if you approached them directly."

They would also doubtless listen attentively if the Representative reported Hiko for not approaching him. Then the least that could happen would be intensified Proctor surveillance of the Teams. Hiko expected that his men could take care of themselves, but not without time and effort wasted at a critical time. Possibly, also, not without Proctor casualties who would be missed.

Even worse, the Proctors might start withholding ammunition from the Teams. Since the Proctors gained virtual custody of the reserve ammunition, the Lions had received their share only because anything else would lose the war in a matter of days.

"Anything I learn, you and the Proctors shall know," Hiko had promised.

Looking at Ruth's face again, remembering his own, Hiko suspected he was about to break that promise.

"Greetings in the name of the Lord, Sister Ruth." He pushed a chair toward her. She almost collapsed into it. Hiko signaled the waiter for two glasses of apple juice and some cheese.

"In the name of the Lord, I thank you." She drank thirstily, but didn't touch the cheese.

"The body must be kept fit, for the Lord's service."

"Oh, I am not hungry. Not for the body's food, at least. I hunger for knowledge, of what I should do for Platoon Leader Ryan."

"Ryan? What has happened to her?"

"The Proctors have arrested her."

"Indeed, that is great zeal in the Lord's service, as one has come to expect in the Proctors." What else they had both come to expect in the Proctors was better left unsaid.

Ruth's look made Hiko wish he had said either more or less. "They are blinded by that zeal, I know. They have arrested her for an unholy love of another woman. Ryan, as chaste as a Sworn Handmaid!''

''Indeed, she seemed most unlikely to do anything so Godless.''

Or foolish, which was the worst Hiko would have thought of her. If there were gods, it did not seem to him that they had reached any agreement on homosexuality. But spitting in the eye of the Proctors that way would have been the act of a madwoman, which Ryan was not.

''I will tell you what I think happened. One of Ryan's squad leaders was led astray by her zeal, into becoming an Eye of the Lord.''

Stripped of religious euphemisms, a police informer. The Proctors were less than the most professional police force Hiko had seen in action. They were also spread very thin. Inevitably, they relied heavily on informers, and everything else followed naturally from that reliance.

''Did this squad leader then neglect her duty?''

''Yes. She also defied Ryan's orders, so that Ryan had to punish her to keep authority over her platoon. How could she serve the Lord's cause otherwise?

''Yet there are those among the Proctors who seem to think that punishing an Eye is rebellion against them. As Ryan left the hospital where she had been visiting another squad leader, she was arrested. She is charged with taking that squad leader as her lover. It is said that the other has confessed.''

Quite possibly the other had, out of fear for herself, the delusion that this would help Ryan, or possibly simply drugs mixed in with her medicine. True believers confronted with secret policemen were always at a disadvantage, even in good health.

''What do you wish me to do for Ryan?''

''For Ryan, nothing except pray. But—you have knowledge of where those who wish to avoid the Proctors can do so?'' The words came out as painfully as might be expected in any patriot proposing to commit treason.

''I have some knowledge. What I do not know myself, I can learn.''

''The Lord be praised! It seemed to me at first that such people might find their refuge among our supply units. But they contain so many who doubt the Lord, I thought they might corrupt true souls.''

She probably believed that. She also must know, as well as

he did, that the Children of Martha and the Good Shepherds were under even tighter Proctor surveillance than the combat units. Anyone with an "Unreliable" stamp on their political or religious record was barred from a combat unit, except the penal companies. The supply outfits were more lenient.

"Indeed, you are wise. Had the Proctors more of your wisdom along with their zeal, they might see the truth more clearly. Ah well, the Lord will show them the way in His own good time. I will seek what we need to know, and tell you as soon as I can."

"Blessings upon you. I—there is nothing I would not do, if this saves others from Ryan's fate." From her blush, Hiko judged she was even prepared to barter sex for her people's escape route.

He would not ask that, even as a joke. But if she was prepared to trade something for the escape route, what should he ask?

He considered the Proctors' control of the ammunition reserves. If rumors had it right, the enemy was going to concentrate their offensive in the Kocher Pass area. Attacks on the Brotherhood's supply lines would be left to their Air Force, assuming it had any planes to spare from protecting and evacuating Nordshaven.

Ammunition would flow freely—into the hands of the Proctors, if nothing was done. With proper information, something might *be* done, probably without the consent of the Representative (not a pleasant thought) but with the blessing of many soldiers who had a better claim on Hiko's loyalty.

"I wish to learn everything you know about where the reserve ammunition is kept and how it is guarded. I may be able to suggest to the Proctors better places and ways."

"What I know, so will you."

"Then let us pray to the Lord, to open the Proctors' eyes to their zeal and to give us strength to forgive them."

Ruth's mouth set like titanium. "The Lord will have a large task, to make me forgive the Proctors. Ryan has been sentenced to death."

Forbes-Brandon drained her third—or was it fourth?—scotch and stared hard at the circular stage in the middle of the White Swan's dining room. The singer, the synthesizer player, and the guitarist went on mutilating "Eye of My Heart." It was the eighth song they'd mutilated this evening.

The blue eyes wavered, then focused, then turned hard. Parkes kept his face expressionless. Interesting things tended to happen around Kat after the third drink. Sometimes they reminded him of the old Chinese curse "May you live in interesting times."

Not dangerous, though. Besides, if things did get out of hand, Parkes was junior man at the table. Vela, Abrams, Reinhardt, or Dallin could all step in more effectively. It was nice to know that being an officer didn't always put you at the head of the line for troubleshooting details.

Forbes-Brandon shifted her gaze to Reinhardt, who was staring just as intently at the guitarist. As the song ended, the two officers exchanged looks. Parkes desperately willed the applause to silence.

"For God's sake, people, don't encourage them," Dallin muttered. Vela added something in Hispanic that sounded alarmingly like a curse upon the performers' ancestors, teachers, and instruments.

Parkes sipped his second drink.

After eight grinding days of evacuation duty, Parkes found himself in Nordshaven with a free evening—or at least without anything clamoring to be done yesterday at the latest. So did Dallin, Vela, Reinhardt, Abrams, and the Amazon. A party of six emerged with hardly a word spoken, and headed straight for the White Swan.

Its new clientele of Security Police had evaporated after the first day of the war. As the old-line professionals reasserted themselves, those Security people who had any time to drink at all did it in private.

The university might have filled this vacuum, if both students and faculty hadn't mostly been furloughed or mobilized within three days of the war starting. The only remaining university activities were the volcano watch and the medical school's hospital, and Parkes had just spent two days helping to evacuate the latter. (He'd been helped by a fur rancher who donated his whole stock to provide extra bedding, although he'd stopped short of lining any lavatory seats with brushtail or bluecrest pelts.)

So the Peace Force and the Feds had the Swan nearly to themselves, with the grateful owner ready to do almost anything to please customers he'd despaired of finding until both the war and the volcano quieted down.

Anything, it seemed, short of either improving or terminating his "live entertainment."

• • •

The applause followed the entertainment into silence. Parkes was so relieved that he'd ordered another bourbon on the rocks before he realized that the Amazon and Reinhardt were both gone. Looking around, he saw the guitarist sitting at a table with three P.F.'ers, one of them Dietsch with his new sergeant's stripes on his jacket. Parkes thought the guitarist looked disgruntled.

A moment later the owner trotted out onto the stage, signaling the enviroconsole operator to bring up the lights.

"Ladies and gentlemen, I have the pleasure to announce an unexpected addition to tonight's entertainment. Major Marcia Reinhardt and Lieutenant Commander Katherine Forbes-Brandon!"

Amid cheers and whistling, he vacated the stage with a haste that suggested a desire to flee.

The two officers hopped up, Reinhardt carrying the guitar. The Amazon emptied another glass, set it down, and toed it off the stage. Then she knelt, unfastened one boot, sent it after the glass, and started on the other boot.

"Take it off!" someone shouted. Parkes suppressed atavistic impulses to use the heckler for medical research—what limbs would fit into what orifices and how firmly were his teeth attached to his jaws?

The second boot went the way of the first. A waiter appeared with two more glasses and a full bottle, set it down between the two women, and retreated as fast as the owner.

The Amazon refilled her glass, planted her feet wide apart, cued three rapid chords from Reinhardt, and began to sing.

"Kiss me good night, Sergeant Major.
Tuck me in my little wooden bed.
We all love you, Sergeant Major,
When we hear you bawling,
'Show a leg!'

"Don't forget to wake me in the morning,
And bring me 'round a nice hot cup of tea.
Kiss me good night, Sergeant Major.
Sergeant Major, be a mother to me."

Parkes didn't know if his impulse to crawl under the table was atavistic. He knew it would be desertion under friendly fire.

No one ever noted how long the much-livelier-than-before entertainment went on. The two women synchronized and paced themselves as if they'd been performing together for years. One solo vocal, one accompanied vocal, one solo guitar. Reinhardt's playing was the same quality as the Amazon's singing—nearly professional. Her repertoire also seemed to include most of the Amazon's old war songs.

Somewhere in the middle of "MacDonnel on the Heights," Dallin whispered to Parkes:

"Marcy could do even better if she had her own twelve-string. You can't see her fingers when she's on that one."

Parkes nodded, afraid to break the magic by speaking. *It's going to be very hard not to be in awe of Katherine. It's also going to be very necessary. She doesn't want to be worshipped. She has all the pride in the world, but not the kind that demands worship.*

Somewhere in the middle of "When This Bloody War Is Over"—after trying not to choke at "I will kiss the sergeant major"—Parkes noticed that the guitarist and Dietsch's party were gone. He also noticed that his glass was empty again. He raised it as a signal to the waiter at the same moment Vela raised his. The two glasses collided in midair and dropped to the floor.

Dallin shook her head. "A midair collision can ruin your whole—"

The floor shook, sending the fallen glasses rolling crazily. It shook again; the lights flickered, a waiter dropped a tray, and bits of decorative tile pattered down around the table.

Somebody screamed. Several other somebodies leaped up, knocking over chairs and a table. A rush for the door boiled up out of nowhere. Under shellfire most of these people would have known what to do. Faced with the prospect of being buried alive (if they were lucky), too many of them had slid to the edge of panic.

Reinhardt struck a chord on the guitar, so hard that Parkes heard strings snapping. Then she settled down to a soft melodic strum as the Amazon began to sing again.

"Underneath the lamplight, by the barracks gate,
Darling, I'll remember how you used to wait—"

By the time she reached the last verse of "Lili Marlene," the incipient panic had faded. Vela, Dallin, and two of Dietsch's party went into the kitchen to herd out the staff. Parkes and Abrams divided the other military personnel into search parties, to make sure no one had been hurt or left behind.

"Or slept through it," Abrams said. "After all the little jolts and jiggles, this one may not feel different to some people. I don't agree."

"Neither do I," Parkes said. He knew little about volcanoes, but all his instincts for danger were on Red Alert.

When the last civilians and inessential military personnel had streamed out the door, Parkes gave the Amazon and Reinhardt the "cut" sign. The guitar rippled into silence; the Amazon flowed down onto the stage and began groping for her boots.

"Here, Kat," Parkes said, holding them up.

She was steady enough tugging them on, but leaned against him when he pulled her up.

"Need a sober-up?"

She frowned. "Can I afford to be flat on my back for half an hour while it works? I think the Teuffelberg's voted against that idea."

"I didn't know volcanoes had the suffrage on—"

The floor heaved again and all the lights went out. Parkes snapped on his belt light as Vela shouted from the doorway:

"Come on! The panic's all outdoors now!"

Arm in arm, they followed Vela out into the night.

Outdoors Parkes found little or no panic. Everybody seemed to be in an undignified but not frantic hurry toward an open square, the edge of the built-up area, or anywhere else not overhung by tall buildings. Nothing had collapsed that Parkes saw, but a lot of buildings had shed windows, ornaments, planters, and entire balconies.

About half the buildings had also lost their power. In the off-again, on-again pools of light, Kat's hair looked gray. Parkes reached to pat it, and found the grayness coming off on his fingers. He looked down, and saw that they were leaving footprints on the street.

"Volcanic ash," he said.

The emergency P.F. rallying point was the medical school parking lot, about six hundred meters across the face of University Hill. Parkes fought down the urge to break into a run every millimeter of that way. He didn't want to start a panic but he wanted to get to work.

At least there seemed to be few casualties. He saw only two people being carried, and three more limping. *Have to organize a citywide search, though, to make sure nobody was trapped and overlooked.*

The parking lot was half full when Parkes and the Amazon arrived. Parkes wondered irritably why the early arrivals hadn't already moved out, when he had his first clear view of the Teufelberg.

Streaks of fire laced the flanks of the main cone. A glow around the summit of the nearest secondary cone told of magma welling up inside it as well. The main cone also jetted steam from three vents. The glow of the magma streams lit up the base of a cloud of ashes, towering from the main crater and already starting to blot out the stars.

Overhead a meteorite died in a silver-yellow blaze. Parkes barely noticed, and forced his eyes away from the volcano before it destroyed his night vision.

Beside him, Vela muttered something in Hrothmi.

"What's that, sir?" the Amazon asked.

" 'The mountain is walking,' " Vela replied. "The Hrothmi call a volcano a 'walking mountain.' " He looked at the Teufelberg again. "Coming our way, too."

Vela and Abrams moved off, routing people out of their daze and press-ganging them into work parties. Parkes put his arm through the Amazon's, patted her hand, and followed his seniors.

He'd just passed out of her hearing when he saw Dietsch and the rest of his party unloading hampers full of canned and freeze-dried food.

"Thought we might need to feed some casualties, so we raided the Swan's kitchen," the sergeant explained. "No sense in its being buried. We left a proper receipt, don't worry about that, sir."

Parkes led Dietsch away from the others. "Sergeant, why were you out by the kitchen?"

"Well, sir—"

"Keep it short and try to keep it truthful, if you don't mind."

"Okay. It was that guitarist who shouted, 'Take it off!' Me 'n' McKee thought we shouldn't allow that, and the others agreed.

So we settled things with the guitarist, real nice. At least, we would have, if the volcano hadn't interrupted—''

Parkes recognized techniques he himself had used on officers in similar situations. *One day I may get used to it, just as I may get used to being called ''sir.''*

''The man's not hurt, is he?'' *Stick to essentials.*

''No, sir. We had to grab him kind of hard when he learned McKee wasn't going to drop her pants for him, but he was in shape to run fast. I guess he believed all the things we'd been talking about doing to him—''

''Dietsch.''

''Sir.''

''This conversation never took place. Understand?''

''Yes, sir.''

19

"FIRING SQUAD—IN the Lord's name, attention!"

The twelve soldiers came to attention.

"In the Lord's name—present arms!" The Proctor certainly had an impressive voice.

Twelve rifles rose. Four were carried by Daughters, four by Saints, four by Avengers.

Hiko shifted, trying to gain a better view of the condemned prisoners without staring into the sun or attracting notice. The Saint corporal sentenced for insubordination had soiled his trousers. Ryan was sweating, in spite of the brisk wind. The Avenger private who'd wanted to allow the evacuation of Nordshaven stood like a temple image.

Perhaps he has the cleanest conscience.

"In the Lord's name—load!"

Rounds snapped into chambers with a convincing rattle. At least it convinced the Proctor. Hiko would have wagered that some of the rifles remained unloaded.

"In the Lord's name—aim!"

Twelve rifles were leveled. Some of them were definitely shaking. The Proctor either didn't see it or chose not to notice.

A faint sigh from the audience, who represented every major unit of the Brotherhood's army. Hiko wondered how much staff work, vehicle time, and fuel had been used to bring them all. He also considered what might happen if any enemy air strike came in.

A ragged crash. The condemned stood free, hands tied and eyes blindfolded. The bullets hurled them back against the wall. Two lay still. Ryan kicked and writhed, blood running out of her gagged mouth.

So quietly that Hiko only noticed it when she'd finished, Ruth knelt and vomited. So did two of the firing squad.

The Proctor officer had some of both courage and compassion. He walked in front of the still-leveled rifles, drew his pistol, and gave Ryan the *coup de grace*.

She died in silence. Hiko realized that one scream or even moan might have snapped the control everyone was so carefully maintaining.

One of the Avengers had gone beyond the limit, anyway. At the command "Firing squad—about face!" he dropped his rifle and sprinted for the gate of the school yard.

He was five meters from the gate, directly in line with the towering gray-black cloud on the northwestern horizon, when the Proctor's pistol cracked three times. The man threw up his arms and crashed to the ground.

"Mutiny is punishable by instant death," the Proctor said. "Let that be remembered, in the Lord's name."

"The Lord's will be done," came a ragged chorus.

Ruth was pale and sweating as hard as Ryan, but Hiko didn't dare touch her, even to guide her around the body of the Avenger. The Proctor couldn't be watching everybody at once, with no more than the normal number of eyes. He might have seen Ruth vomiting, though, and he still had his pistol drawn.

It was two days after the execution before Hiko and Ruth found a safe place to talk. Hiko shut out of his mind what Ruth must be enduring, alone and doubtless watched. He also knew that she would regard it as another burden to bear in the name of the Lord, and draw real strength from that idea. Probably more than he could have lent her, when keeping discipline among his own Teams was a sufficiently demanding job.

Fortunately the Teams would probably be on their way back into action before anyone drew the Proctors' attention. Rumor said that the P.F. had largely completed its redeployment, and would attack from the Kocher Pass perimeter as soon as it finished the ammunition resupply. Meanwhile, the Federal forces to the east were only skirmishing against the Brotherhood's supply lines. The Saints holding that area were not the Lions, but it would take more than skirmishing to force them away.

The Brotherhood's ammunition was flowing freely. So far the Proctors had continued reasonably fair about issuing it. They might know that this not only maintained strength and morale but dispersed targets for the enemy air force. If it turned from precision strikes against the Protectorate back to tactical operations—

Hiko settled himself into the dry grass and waited for Ruth.

She was an uneasy half hour late. The volcano's plume had merged with the darkness in the west when she finally climbed down the last stretch of scree and sat down beside him.

Without apology or invitation, he put an arm around her shoulder. He had never seen anyone so badly in need of the human touch. Her stiffening was so brief it hardly deserved the name. Then she put her hand in his, and twined her fingers around his.

"I thank you, whether in the Lord's name or not."

"For what?"

"Osgood has found a place among the Lions."

"They sent word to you and not to me?"

"Pride is not Godly, Brother Hiko. Also, they may have thought that the less you knew, the less you could tell."

"The Lord has sharpened your wits, Sister. Not that they were dull before, but—"

"The Lord has worked through the Proctors, which is indeed working in mysterious ways. Truly, my friend. Are you offended? The Lions trust you, I am sure, but hardly the Proctors."

It would have been useful to be at the center of everybody's secrets, but hardly necessary for him or safe for others.

"You spoke of a new ammunition depot, Ruth. Where is it?"

She gave coordinates and a terrain description and he recited them back until she was sure he'd memorized them. They couldn't risk showing a light, still less being caught with any written material.

Hiko placed the new dump on his mental map and considered its implications. It seemed likely to be intended for the supply of the guerrillas facing Nordshaven as well as the main force facing the Kocher Pass offensive.

Most of the guerrillas in the west were actually operating against the land routes out of Nordshaven. They were the principal barrier to the city's evacuation. Facing the Peace Force and the Jaegers, they were taking heavy casualties; one P.F.'er or Jaeger was equal to five guerrillas.

The guerrillas could be in five places at once, however. That advantage might prolong their blockade of Nordshaven until the threat from the Teuffelberg brought the enemy to the truce table on the Brotherhood's terms.

Or at least that seemed to be the War Council's hope.

Suppose that the guerrillas could no longer hope for ammunition? Five disarmed men could do nobody any harm, no matter how mobile they were. If they also faced suspicion or even hostility from the Proctors—which would be an easy thing to generate, for one man prepared to die in the process . . .

If the Peace Force knew of the Teams' presence on Zauberberg, the Master would be associated with anything that happened there. If that turned out to be the Teuffelberg's burying fifty thousand Nordshaveners in the ruins of their city, the Planetary Union might consider action against the Master. Even if they had to act through Terran governments, they would not lack allies.

So what could be done to save Nordshaven had to be done. That would also turn the Brotherhood's defeat from a probability into a certainty. The Representative, associated with failure, would not appear in the field again. The next Teams to travel to the stars might be led by someone with a broader vision of how to achieve the Master's goals.

Hiko knew that men he'd served with would suffer from his success. Yet they would suffer still more if the enemy was driven to wage war to the death. As for the outcome of the war—when the Kocher Pass offensive failed to break through and turn half a million more Federal citizens into hostages, that outcome had been determined. Anything Hiko did would change no more than the schedule.

Hiko put his arm back around Ruth's shoulders. This might be their last meeting. He could not even leave a last message for her. The Proctors would too easily believe that she had known of his plans.

"Sister Ruth, how fast are they filling the new dump? It makes some difference to what I should suggest about ways to defend it."

"The low casualties from the eruption so far are the result of several factors," Professor Bahr continued.

Someone in the audience coughed. Parona wondered if that was a comment on Bahr's lecture style or a stronger-than-usual whiff of fumes. The medical school auditorium's air filters kept out the dust but not the smell. Living in Nordshaven this past week was like living downwind from a busy recycling plant with a faulty exhaust scrubber.

"First, the predominance of heavy matter in the volcanic ejecta, which has reduced its fall in the populated area.

"Second, the architecture of Nordshaven. Buildings intended

to be earthquake-resistant and energy-conserving are well equipped to shelter their inhabitants from even the worst the Teuffelberg is likely to do.''

''What would that be?'' Major Abrams asked.

''I will come to that in a minute,'' Bahr said relentlessly. ''Third, the fact that the eruption began after the opening of the war. The military and civilian disaster-relief organizations were already fully mobilized, and the civilian population alert and organized for self-help. I cannot escape the feeling that it would have been desirable to immediately evacuate a large part of the city's population, or at least the refugees. That this did not take place, I feel—''

The cough this time was unmistakably a comment, since it came from Carlo Biancheri. Bahr frowned, then shrugged and went on:

''—was due to the logistical difficulties it would have presented, and the fact that the violence of the eruption was not anticipated.

''Fourth, the activity of the Federal military and police forces and the Peace Force in organizing the evacuation of the city, once it became necessary. I have nothing but praise for their work.''

Parona joined vigorously in the round of applause from the civilians. He'd seen a few of the evacuation troops in church or heard their confessions; one and all they seemed to be working hours that would have caused mutiny among galley slaves.

''Exhibit Two, please,'' Bahr said.

The screen behind the lectern displayed a map of the Teuffelberg Peninsula and the Nordshaven area, with all the volcanic activity marked in red. In moments Parona had totally lost the thread of Bahr's lecture. The bombardment of technical terms might be essential. It might also be Bahr showing off his knowledge. It achieved less than clear communication either way.

The audience's collective impatience finally reached critical mass and emitted a question from Major Abrams.

''Are you trying to tell us that the Teuffelberg might just blow up like a bomb?''

''That's oversimplifying, but—''

''Yes or no?''

''I can't say yes or no.''

''Then give odds.''

''This is not a card game, Major.''

''I know. It isn't a class in vulcanology, either.''

Bahr looked sulky for a moment. The self-confidence he'd gained from his field work clearly didn't go too deep yet. Well, he was young and gifted; there was hope for him if he lived to grow older.

"I would say that there is about a seventy-percent chance of an explosive eruption of one or more cones. There is a roughly even chance of that explosion being violent enough to devastate the Nordshaven area."

He turned back to the map. "Much depends on what kind of explosion from which cone. If the main cone simply blows apart like Mount Saint Helens or Mount Djamba, the explosion could be violent enough to level Nordshaven. If one of the secondary cones erupted in a Peléean manner, the fire cloud could also reach the city."

"What about a Peléean eruption of the main cone?" asked a thin dark woman in naval uniform.

"That might actually be less dangerous. The fire cloud would have a long way to travel, not all of it downhill. Much of its heat and velocity would be dissipated. A Peléean fire cloud is a devastating weapon, but short-ranged.

"Also, it would be more directional than a simple explosion. Its chosen direction might take it away from the city."

"What about fire storms?" Dr. Laughton asked.

"Except for the parks and the industrial enclaves, Nordshaven isn't particularly inflammable. I understand our military and police colleagues are prepared to evacuate civilians from around those areas."

Abrams nodded.

"Good. Otherwise the intense heat won't last long enough to use up the oxygen in the city."

"What's your estimate of the maximum distance for lethal effects?" General Van Doorn asked.

"If you want to make sure that nobody in the open suffers more than a bad scare and a large cleaning bill for their clothes—everybody should be at least seventy kilometers from the main cone."

The radius sprang onto the map, in the form of a red circle. On the average, the red circle ran fifteen kilometers deep in enemy-held territory.

"Thank you, Professor Bahr," Biancheri said. He let the applause run on until Bahr was grinning, then cut it off with a wave.

"Now, Commander Marie Dubignon, Executive Officer of Peace Cruiser *Ark Royal*, representing the Navy."

The thin dark woman stepped up to the lectern. "Our contribution comes in two forms. One is supporting our comrades in the ground forces against the Brotherhood.

"The other is using fusion charges against the Teuffelberg. We are hardening some of our tactical warheads and adjusting them for sub-kiloton yields. If possible they will be placed by ground teams and detonated by radio command from the air, with timer backups. We hope to open additional vents in the active areas, to release pressures in safe directions."

"What about your ship-mounted beam weapons?" someone asked.

"Particle and microwave weapons aren't effective against this kind of target. To use our lasers, we'd have to use them at high intensity and short range. That will shorten their usable life and force us to keep a ship at low altitude within slant range of Brotherhood ASAT weapons. The enemy may have none left, but we'd rather not lose a ship finding out otherwise.

"Also, we'd be operating against our targets through dust and ash clouds, dust and ash deposits, and whatever outgassing we'd have from our lasers. How much good our lasers would do before they burned out is questionable, and the Thorshammer Shower isn't over yet."

Commander Dubignon's brevity produced a round of applause that made Bahr look sulky again.

General Van Doorn was the last speaker. He gave a summary of the Peace Force strategy that was a masterpiece of reticence, then added:

"If luck is on our side, it may be possible to evacuate people on foot into what is now enemy territory. The Joint Command is drawing up a set of amendments to the civil-defense regulations. Basically, everybody should have on hand at all times heavy shoes, a liter of water, and warm clothing. We'll try to provide these for anyone who doesn't have them, out of military or commandeered civilian stocks."

"What about shelter?" Biancheri asked. "That's been the biggest problem."

"It's still going to be a big one," Van Doorn said. "However, between existing buildings and tents, we should be able to take care of the sick, elderly, and children. For everybody else—well, a couple of nights in the open won't be comfortable. Staying in Nordshaven could be just plain dangerous."

With that blatant understatement, the briefing ended.

• • •

Marian Laughton met Parona on the way out of the hall. He took one look at her and smiled.

"Would it help if I suggested, as your confessor, that you might be guilty of the sin of suicide if you don't get more sleep?"

"Only God can make the day longer, Your Eminence. When the work I have to do in that day grows shorter . . ."

"As you wish."

"I would like to ask a favor from you, not as my confessor but as a—person with influence on Zauberberg."

"What is it?"

"I think that I would like to settle here after my term is up. I have two more years on my obligation, but after that—I think the Peace Force is not the place for me. Neither is New Frontier. I joined the Peace Force to get away from it."

Parona had learned those reasons from her confession. She'd been obliged to inform on a drug ring operating out of her hospital, a ring that turned out to include the surgeon who'd been her teacher, mentor, and lover. Legal immunity and even the respect of law-abiding colleagues hadn't eased the pain of this miscarriage of good intentions.

"Running away is only wise if one knows what one runs *to* as well as *from*. Unless, of course, one is running from a volcano . . ."

"Even then, one is running to a safer place. I thought the Peace Force would be one. I don't mean physically, I mean—fewer hard decisions."

"You will not find that safety on Zauberberg, not for many years. This planet will take a great deal of healing after the war, not all of it the kind you do so well."

"I'd still feel that I was doing something—closer to what I felt called to do when I applied for medical school."

"The Security Police may have long memories, you know."

"That's a risk I'd have to take."

It wouldn't be much of a risk if the old professionals continued to reassert themselves. Parona had heard rumors that this reassertion was approaching the dimensions of a purge.

It also helped that most of the young hooligans had been concentrated in the two battalions on the north shore. Few of them had reached safety. How did God judge a man who died bravely and honorably in a war he'd helped to bring about? Two millennia of exegeses on "Thou shalt not kill" and the Just War gave Parona little help and hardly more confidence in theologians.

"I must confess that I asked that question more as a test."

Laughton looked half indignant, half relieved. "Then you will help?"

"Zauberberg will certainly need people who aren't looking for easy solutions. But wouldn't it be simpler to just stay here with the Peace Force garrison, and take your discharge when your term runs out? I'm sure a civilian hospital would have an opening for you."

"That would mean transferring out of Fourteen. I'd rather stay with them, if I can."

"They won't be part of the garrison? If that's asking about a military secret—"

"No. It's just that Peace Force doctrine is to take a unit that's suffered heavy casualties out of the field. We'll go home to New Frontier for at least a year, train, get back up to strength—unless there's a real emergency. Either way, they'll need me. It's another kind of healing."

Parona thought Laughton might need her battalion as much as it needed her. *Soldiers, priests, doctors—if we are to be truly worthy, we need a vocation. We go where God and that vocation call us. We still need something to call home.*

The first thing Parkes saw as he left the hovertruck was a column of smoke to the west. The second thing was the Amazon, standing at the edge of the parking lot.

Parkes was sure neither of them ran, but they were still shaking hands and gripping shoulders almost at once. Even through the battledress, Parkes could feel how Kat had lost weight.

"How about some cold chicken? A farmer on the road broiled up fifty and sent them down to our fuel stop."

"Bless you. I missed breakfast, orienting the new naval liaison people who came in with the resupply aboard *Von Lettow-Vorbeck*. I tried to make up for it with an early lunch, but that was eight hours ago."

Parkes returned to the truck and brought back a sack of chicken and three beers. He found Kat examining the markings painted on the truck's right side, toward the rear.

"The top ones I recognize—that's trips completed and people carried. What's the bottom?"

"Those are storks."

"Storks, as in the kind who bring babies?"

"Exactly. This is the maternity ward that Mr. Fuchs gave the furs for."

"His name really is Fuchs?"

"Yes. He said that if there was anything called a fox on Zauberberg, he'd have to change his name, his profession, or his planet."

"I suppose each stork represents a baby born on the road?"

"Right. I think it's going to stop at six, because the really critical near-terms are now being airlifted out. They've put the vertis that came with the resupply in service."

Parkes wanted to ask about the smoke on the horizon, but Kat was looking too yearningly at the bag. The way she tore into the chicken hinted that she hadn't told the truth about lunch, but he held his peace. They were all driving themselves to the limit and beyond, because they didn't have any choice. Kuroki's brigade was in-system and coming as fast as the G-loads and ships' tankage would allow, but that might not be fast enough for the people of Nordshaven.

Kat finished the second chicken, washed down the last mouthful with the second beer, and sighed comfortably.

"I want that farmer's recipe."

"What I want is to know what that smoke cloud is."

"You didn't get the word?"

"If it came through in the last half hour, no. We're not on the satellite network while we're on the move. The hills cut us off from the short-range stuff."

"The Brotherbuggers hit the fuel dump at the mouth of the Roccanegra. A one-plane strike, and I don't think the pilot planned to get away. He bombed the dump, then strafed until one of the A.D. mounts got on to him."

"Casualties?"

"Light. Even the civilians are getting shrewd about taking cover. Also, the last big batch ferried across had hit the road before the strike came in. He didn't follow them, thank God.

"So we lost mostly just fuel and a couple of unfinished shelters. Council or Leihno's got a big labor gang organized, though. He had them hauling new stone for rebuilding before the plane stopped burning!"

That almost made Parkes feel better. "Thank the Wise One for friends who don't give up easily. I only wish the Brotherhood didn't have the same habit."

"No, you don't, John. We're professional soldiers, not professional exterminators."

He tried to make his embrace professional. He didn't succeed.

"John. I'm off duty. What about you?"

"Technically, I'm on duty. But it's just watching this truck until the drivers get back. The number two got the runs and the number one wanted to see her to the medics. I volunteered to watch the truck until number one either comes back or sends somebody to take her into the depot. I have some paperwork to finish."

"Can the paperwork wait?"

"I suppose—" he began, then stopped at the look on her face. Desire, love, sense of duty, respect for the Articles, discipline, and loneliness threw themselves into an all-out fight for control. The knowledge that he or Kat might be dead tomorrow joined the battle. In the face of these reinforcements, duty, respect for the Articles, and discipline yielded the field.

"Yes."

The embrace ceased to be remotely professional.

"We'd better get inside."

"Do you still have the furs?"

"They've even been sterilized."

It was too cold to remove more than the necessary minimum of clothing, even if they hadn't been in a hurry.

"Having to stay dressed spoils the sensation of making love on fur," Kat said meditatively. "I'll see if Herr Fuchs will sell me a few pieces."

"How about a joint purchase? You'd be surprised what a sergeant major with few vices can save."

"I'm glad you weren't a sergeant major with *no* vices." Her hands moved with assurance. "And I'm glad I'm a woman."

"So am I, but . . . ?"

"Women are at an advantage, in telling if a man's ready."

"They're also at a disadvantage in necrophilia."

"You're a remarkably lively corpse."

"Maybe it's the inspiring environment. I haven't made love in the back of a truck since I was twenty." He kissed her on each eye. "More likely, it's the inspiring company."

"Flattery will get you quite a few places."

"Let's limit it to the obvious ones, then get out of this truck and back on the job. Not everyone's as discreet as Dietsch."

20

"THAT SHOULD BE it," Ruth said.

Hiko nodded. The IR emissions were too strong for an uninhabited cave and it was the only one close to the right coordinates.

Hiko pulled out his scan-sensor. The warning light glowed immediately; he shielded it with one hand as he read type and strength.

"Our bafflers can handle this." He drew a plastic-wrapped bundle from his pack and unwrapped a metal-free crossbow. It could shoot a microbaffler close enough to scramble the cave's sensors from well beyond their effective range.

When the bow was assembled, he used the night glasses again. More than the cave mouth was glowing. The ground was distinctly warmer in front of it. Geothermal heat? Too faint for that. It looked more like the residual heat from ground heavily traveled recently.

"They must brush out the wheel traces."

"They would be wise to do so."

"You're sure they don't have anyone regularly inside the cave? The Q.R. post hardly holds enough men—"

"Remember that the Proctors do not do the work themselves. With five hundred hostages camped within four kilometers, they have enough able-bodied men and women to labor in the Lord's cause." The last phrase held no irony that Hiko could detect.

Hiko loaded the first baffler into the bow and cocked it. This moment had been inevitable since yesterday, when a coded message left at Team HQ led him to Ruth's hiding place in the bush. She had fled to avoid arrest for concealing Ryan's Godless ways.

"Of course, it will not take long for them to decide that I have shared her unnatural lust myself. In their zeal, the Proctors now think all they arrest are not merely criminals but monsters."

He'd offered her supplies to escape, but she'd refused. "The

Lord commanded me to help others flee from the zeal of the Proctors. He has now commanded me to strike a blow against them. I cannot imagine a better way than helping you."

Hiko knew that if she'd seen his shifting loyalties that clearly, he'd been living on borrowed time for weeks. Well, the loyalties *had* shifted, and now he would probably not have to kill Ruth, a task he would have found distasteful, dishonorable, and painful.

Hiko set down the loaded crossbow and laid out the other three bafflers. He could hardly shoot all four so fast that the guards would suspect nothing. While they were only suspicious, he would still have time to act.

Did Ruth realize how small the chances of escape were? Or did she accept her death as the price for setting her judgment against those who spoke in the name of the Lord, even those with such a dubious claim as the Proctors?

As Hiko picked up the crossbow, a soft voice spoke from behind:

"Team Leader, wait. Please."

It was Jamshir Singh.

A hundred kilometers to the northwest, Nordshaven was dying slowly under the rain of ash. The airport lay under thirty centimeters of ejecta; fixed-wing airlift was a thing of the past. Most of the newly landed vertis in the area were hauling newly landed ammunition to the allied forces before Nordshaven. They would need all they could get, or else claw the enemy out of his positions around the city with blood and bare hands.

A hundred kilometers to the east, the offensive from the Kocher Pass was grinding forward. Tomorrow night the Jaegers would leave Fourteen's southern flank and be airlifted into that battle. The battered battalion would be stretched even thinner, more dependent on orbital fire support against the still-active guerrillas.

Katherine Forbes-Brandon expected a busy few days for both herself and the battalion.

She stretched, yawned, looked around the C.P. for anything wrong, and yawned again. Half an hour until she turned the duty over to Magnusson. Then nothing to do except sleep—alone—for a whole six hours until morning stand-to.

Cold air trickled through the camouflage shrouding as the door opened. Dallin came in, lay down on the pallet by the desk, and crossed her hands on her breast with elaborate care.

"That bad?"

"I'm beginning to think there's something to be said for medical limits on flying time. I feel about eighty."

"Brandy?"

"Parkes has a better claim."

Dallin must really be tired, to be that—no, not rude. Blunt, as she always was even with her friends. Concerned, too.

"I restocked from the reinforcements." She poured a canteen cup full and held it out.

"*L'chayim.* If you ever run for empress of the galaxy, I'll vote for you. Ahhhh. Lovely stuff." Dallin closed her eyes. "By the way, how are you and Parkes getting on?"

"Meaning how many times could we be court-martialed?"

"You know I don't mean that."

Forbes-Brandon looked at the bottle and decided that she couldn't make herself unfit for duty on what was left in it. She poured herself a cup, then brought Dallin's up to full strength.

"Cheers. I don't think either of us has an easy answer for that. Let's say—I think we've each found in the other something we didn't know we were looking for until we found it. The next job is to figure out what it is."

"And then again, maybe that'll be a waste of time?"

Hiko allowed himself a whole second for surprise, then said: "I will not ask how you tracked us." In training, Jamshir Singh had broken several records for night movement. Whatever he had done before he joined the Game Master must have involved a fair amount of night work.

"I will, however, ask why."

"For the same purpose as you."

Hiko slipped a *shuriken* from his wrist sheath into his hand. He had Singh located well enough for a disabling throw. Ruth had already drawn her pistol.

"Yes?"

"To weaken the Proctors so that they cannot enforce their will on the honorable warriors of the Brotherhood," Jamshir replied. "What else?"

"If you are correct—"

"Team Leader, do we have time to question each other's faith and judgment?" The polite request came in the tones of an order.

"Probably not." Ruth was as alert as he to the danger of treachery. If they made sure that one of them was watching Jamshir at all times, the worst that could happen was their chances of survival returning to their original low level. With Jamshir's aid, on the other hand . . .

"Did you bring your crossbow?"

Jamshir stepped forward, a bundle under his arm. "Also some bafflers."

"Did you steal them?"

"I also knocked the guard senseless. I wanted to make it seem that they had been stolen by someone outside the Teams. The man should survive, although I lack your skill at striking precisely."

"You lack few others." Most people had to learn *ninjitsu*; a fortunate few had it born in them. Jamshir seemed one of those, further refined by training.

"We have no time for praise, either, although it is more pleasant to hear than suspicion."

"True." Hiko pointed to the left. "Move about a hundred meters that way and shoot on my signal." Eight bafflers instead of four would do more than double their chances of success and even give them a hope of escape.

Jamshir Singh vanished into the darkness. "Ruth, keep down. If he plans treachery, he should not have two easy targets."

"As you wish, Hiko." It was the first time she'd called him by his name, without "Brother" added.

Hiko waited a reasonable time, then signaled with his scanner set for IR. The silence was broken by the faint *chunk* of Jamshir's bow.

Dallin lay on the pallet. Fatigue and brandy hadn't brought sleep.

So Kat and Parkes think they're on to something good? Please God it's true. Both of them have earned some good luck ten times over.

But they don't know what that something is? I wonder if that's what keeps Vela at arm's length—not knowing what basis we'd have for being more than friends? God knows he wouldn't mind taking that extra step. That wasn't a brother watching my legs when we undressed for our naps in Duchamp's bedroom.

Odd if that's the way it is with Jesús. You'd think anyone who'd spent fifteen years soldiering among the Hrothmi would be a little more comfortable with mysteries. But maybe he wants more than a Forty-six affair or a term marriage? He's Old Hispanic; they often want a life term or nothing.

"E.T.A. of 2nd Brigade, seventy-four hours twenty-two minutes," intoned a voice in a foggy distance. Dallin cursed the voice and wished for something, anything, that would bring Kuroki's people in faster and down into the rear of the Brotherrammers trapping the people of Nordshaven . . .

"Five and a half minutes, Team Leader," Jamshir whispered.

Hiko stifled annoyance. "Don't honk, I'm setting the fuses as fast as I can." He fused a sentinel mine and adjusted its sensors. "Here." He pushed it across the slick stone floor toward Jamshir. "Lay that in the corridor and anybody coming in will set it off. The blast wave will trigger the pressure fuses."

"I will go as soon as Ruth returns. I did not think that anyone could become a soldier without a concept of field modesty."

"Consider it an addition to your education, my friend."

Jamshir's reply was an expressive grunt. Hiko himself would have felt better if Ruth hadn't insisted on retiring to change into Proctor uniform. He trusted her to find a place where she could watch the rear without being seen, but still—

He heard the footsteps behind him at the same moment as Jamshir's warning hiss. He finished setting another fuse, then slid *shurikens* into both hands before turning around.

"Greetings, in the name of the Lord," he said blandly. "The sentries reported unauthorized people in sight from the perimeter. They could not leave their posts, and I am only halfway through—"

"What Lordless villains would—?" began one of the three Proctors. His leader waved him to silence and drew his pistol.

The pistol left Hiko with little hope of surviving the encounter, although the Proctors would not have long to rejoice. The two rear men were also drawing when Ruth stepped out of the niche she'd been using as a dressing room.

She carried her trousers in her hand. Below the waist she wore nothing except socks.

The rear man had the best view, judging from the way his eyes widened. His gasp made the second man turn. Two opponents off their guard neatly reversed the odds.

Hiko's *shurikens* tore into the leader's face, drawing a scream and a blind shot. Hiko pivoted on his hands and slammed his boots into the man's chest, crushing ribs. The leader flew backward, knocking the second man off his feet. Jamshir put a bullet through the second man's head. The third man was trying to look in all directions at once without taking his eyes off Ruth when she pulled her own pistol out of her trouser pocket and shot him in the chest.

As he hit the floor, she sank to hands and knees, dropping her pistol though not quite vomiting.

Hiko knelt by her and put an arm around her. He spoke to her in a wordless murmuring, as he might have talked to a wounded animal. It seemed to work; she stopped shaking, then sat down, turned fiery red as the cold floor reminded her of her exposed condition, and hastily jerked on underwear and trousers.

As she pulled on her boots, she found her voice. Eyes still on the floor, she said, "I did not have a clear shot where I was. If I had to move, I thought it might distract them if I—was seen as I was."

"It certainly did. It nearly distracted me, too," Jamshir said.

Ruth smiled. "Have you been so chaste all your life that you have never seen a woman as the Lord made her?"

"No, but—well, when you use a diversionary tactic, it helps to divert only the enemy."

"I shall remember that the next time."

"The chance of there being a next time will increase if we save the tactics lecture until after we leave the cave," Hiko said, adjusting another fuse. "Ruth, have you unpacked that launcher?"

"Yes. How many rounds did you want?"

"As many as you can carry and still run."

Ruth popped back into her niche. As she reappeared with the rocket launcher and four rockets, Hiko set the last fuse.

"There. Between the booby traps, sensors, and timers, *something* is going to happen. At worst, the Proctors will have several days of digging dead comrades and ammunition out from under the rocks. At worst—I suspect the enemy will detect the explosion on their seismographs."

He looked at his watch. Nine minutes since they ran into the cave, leaving the two sentries stunned behind them. The Q.R. force might be only two minutes away, if they had somehow been alerted by the sentries' fall. They also might not have left their post.

Either way, they could make little difference now. Hiko and his comrades had done their work, and surviving beyond that had never been essential, as long as they could face their ancestors (or their Lord, or Kali, if Jamshir truly believed in the Lady of Destruction).

Hiko rose. "Let's be on our way, my friends."

• • •

A flight of vertis droned overhead, low enough to be audible within the C.P. They were probably on their way south to pick up the Jaegers.

Hope somebody remembered to load them with refugees before sending them out.

Bleeeeeemmmmmmmm!

The seismic-event alarm brought Forbes-Brandon up out of her chair so fast it fell over. The clatter was lost in the scream of the alarm.

Colonel Vela was closest to the seismograph. He slapped the alarm cutoff, restoring silence and sanity, then stared at the dial. ''Low force—three or under. Something funny, though—it doesn't look like another volcanic shock.''

''Want me to get a triangulation on it, Colonel?'' said Sergeant Gorres, at the master communications console.

''Good idea.''

And one I should have had myself, Forbes-Brandon thought. *We are all too tired.*

Gorres didn't need to work for the triangulation data. It flowed in within five minutes; he plotted it on the map display and punched it up.

''There. Way inside enemy territory. Not even on any known fault line, or so they say.''

''Maybe it's not seismic after all,'' Vela said.

''Or maybe the Brotherhood has decided to start their own volcano,'' Forbes-Brandon put in. Vela's look told her what he thought of that joke.

Forbes-Brandon sat down and noticed that Dallin had slept through everything without even turning over. Vela knelt beside her and spread a blanket over her. For a moment his hand rested on her cheek. Then he stood.

''Heads up, people. I'm going to remind HQ to cut us in on any E.I. intelligence they get. I do *not* like unexplained bangs in my A.O., even if they're on the bad guys' side.''

The guard set on the cave had been inexcusably light, even for a force spread as thin as the Proctors. The Q.R. force couldn't compensate. At least it lived up to its name, with three all-wheelers dashing up to the cave mouth only a minute later than Hiko's predicted minimum.

That was thirty-two seconds before the time fuses did their work.

Hiko had just replied to the challenge of the first man out of the first truck when the ground heaved. A horizontal jet of flame thundered out of the cave mouth, catching the first truck like an insect in a blowtorch. Its men were dead even before its fuel exploded.

The second truck rolled over, catching one man underneath. The third was unscathed. Its four Proctors piled out and ran toward Hiko.

"The Lord be thanked!" he shouted. "From what we saw in the cave, there must have been ten of them."

"Them?" a Proctor said.

"The guerrillas, curse them! Do you think this was an accident? The Lord would not allow—"

"The Lord will know what to allow better than you," someone said in clipped tones. "You are under arrest, in the Lord's name."

Hiko fired from the hip, cutting down half the squad at one burst. Jamshir Singh sniped the gunner on top of the third truck. Ruth put a rocket into the overturned second truck, then picked off the two survivors crawling away from the flames. Hiko finished off the squad facing him, then led his companions at a trot toward the intact truck.

"Do we want to visit the hostage camp before we leave the area?" Ruth asked.

"What do you think?" Hiko replied as he fed power to all six wheels. The truck rocked, then bounced out of a rut and swung toward the road.

"It would be a service to the Lord. But we do not know how many Proctors are yet at the camp. Also, the time we spent might give the Proctors and other zealous people the time to rally. The Lord has sown confusion among our enemies. Let us not spurn His gift."

Jamshir nodded silently, bracing himself with a grip on the door handle as they rattled off into the night.

"How do you feel, Sonny?" Vela asked, bending over her.

Dallen looked at her watch. "Like I've had a lot more than two hours' sleep."

"Good. Because I've just received a digest of the E.I.'s since that bang." He handed her a three-page printout.

Dallin scanned it, and suddenly felt even more awake. She told herself not to waste adrenaline hoping.

"Looks as if somebody blew up a major ammunition dump, and the Proctors are trying to find somebody to blame for it."

"That's the way it looks to me," Vela said. "Duchamp and MacLean, too. I don't suppose the guerrillas really were stupid enough to cut their own throats. We've had some indications, though, of the Proctors being rather tight with the guerrillas' ammunition. If some of the guerrillas tried a moonlight requisition and somebody got a little trigger-happy . . ."

"The Proctors were *born* trigger-happy," Forbes-Brandon said. "But what good is all this . . . ?" Her voice trailed off and her mouth stayed open.

"I didn't think you were *that* tired," Vela said.

"No. If the Proctors start a real witch-hunt among the guerrillas, those poor bastards are going to have to fight facing both ways. I wonder if they'll have the heart for it."

"Or the stomach, or the liver, or the spleen," Dallin put in.

"I'd better go wake up Parkes," Forbes-Brandon said.

Vela shook his head. "That's being taken care of. MacLean's calling a Command Group meeting for 0230. We want to rough out contingency plans and issue preliminary orders. Then everybody who absolutely doesn't have to be awake is going back to bed. We don't know what's going to happen, but we're putting our money on its happening *fast* when it does."

Hiko flipped the night vision goggles up onto his forehead and pressed the door opener. Jamshir Singh slung his rifle and hooked his canteen to his belt.

"You will not change your mind, Brother Jamshir?" Ruth asked.

"I have explained why I must go back and keep watch over the Representative."

"True. You do the Lord's work as well there as you would with us."

"Better, perhaps. Unless the Proctors run completely amok, they will have to deal with the Teams through the Representative. If he does not cooperate or is not there to cooperate, that will at least buy our comrades time to escape. The more of them who escape, the better informed the Master will be about what has happened on Zauberberg."

"I hope you will try to be one of those who escape," Hiko said.

"If I did not, I would be such a fool that you would owe me no vengeance."

"You are no fool," Ruth said.

Hiko nodded. "I also wonder how devoted to the Lady of Destruction you are. One would think that the chance of sending so many to her—" Hiko knew the answer well enough; what he didn't know was how Jamshir would tell the tale.

"If the Teuffelberg erupted?" Jamshir frowned. "It—I would rather not speak of this, if I had a choice. But I owe you so much—by way of paying part of the debt, then . . .

"It is simple enough. The people of Nordshaven were not dedicated. An undedicated sacrifice is not pleasing to Kali. To displease the Lady, when one needs her favor to continue one's own work—did you think me such a fool?"

"No." *Nor do I think you any more a worshipper of Kali than I did before. What else you may be, I doubt that I shall ever know. I do not doubt that I was wise, to assume that hostile ears might hear if the Teams were associated with the slaughter of Nordshaven's people.*

"Indeed, there are some of us who will not deal with nuclear or chemical weapons. They take undedicated victims by the thousands. This is a secret we prefer not to be known, you understand. Much of the power of Kali depends on her sworn worshippers being thought *worse* than they truly are."

They gripped shoulders awkwardly, on the narrow front seat, then Jamshir Singh slipped out the door and vanished into the night. Hiko sat looking after him long enough for Ruth to reload her launcher.

"Hiko," she said gently. "Where now?"

"As close to enemy lines as we can take the truck, then the rest of the way on foot. I think our best chance is to merge with the refugees, then disappear into Nuovo Milano before they start checking identification."

"And then?"

Did he hear a hint of desire to stay with him? Certainly they might have a better chance together than separately, if only because Ruth would need to learn the ways of a secular city.

"Then we shall look for the best way of surviving, until we know what we want to do."

"May the Lord grant us that knowledge."

"John! John, wake up!"

It was Kat's voice, but the Command Group meeting had been over for hours. He couldn't have fallen asleep at it.

"John, we're alerted."

Parkes swam up out of sleep, reaching for the lovely long-nosed face floating just above him. She caught his hand and held it against her cheek, with a smile that sent warmth washing through him. He wanted to float away on that warmth, back into sleep.

Instead he forced consciousness if not coherence into himself and sat up. A cup of coffee appeared miraculously under his nose, and disappeared almost as fast.

"You make a good ministering angel, among other things."

"Angels are supposed to be sexless."

"I said 'among other things.' " He shook the fog out of his head. "What are we alerted for?"

"Anything and everything. A whole platoon of guerrilla deserters just came into our line. They said the Proctors tried to arrest several key guerrilla leaders. The leaders resisted, and the Proctors are supposed to be rounding up the guerrillas' families as hostages."

"What the—?" He stared as if Kat had just grown a second nose.

"Exactly. The platoon put their heads together, and decided that maybe it was rumor, and maybe it wasn't. Either way, they decided that the war was lost and they didn't want to be killed in its last battle."

"Any confirmation from other sources?"

"The E.I. intelligence doesn't confirm or deny anything except a lot of confusion. Most of the prisoners tell the same story, though."

"It's been—how long since the explosion?"

"Eight hours."

"God, I've been a sluggard."

"You needed that sleep."

"So did you."

"I went down right after you did, and stop being solicitous. This big girl can take care of herself."

"Sorry, Kat. I was just thinking. Eight hours. Say, four or five hours before the arrests. They couldn't have rehearsed the story. So the guerrillas could be falling apart."

" 'Could be' is right. They could also be massing for a last desperate offensive, to prove their loyalty to the Proctors."

"I know what they say about optimism in the tactics courses. But damn it, I *want* to be optimistic for once!"

21

THE CELLAR BARELY held the Command Group of Task Force Vela. When Colonel MacLean rose to conclude the briefing, he had to stand sideways to avoid obscuring half the map.

"Any questions? Captain Parkes?"

"More of an opinion, Colonel. I thought you were giving us a fragmentary order, the first time I saw it. This is all we're going to get, isn't it?"

"Yes. We thought of letting the situation develop for another day. We finally decided that might give the Proctors time to respond."

"Not to mention the Avengers," Vela put in.

"They'd have to move from the Kocher Pass perimeter," MacLean said.

"True. But even a company of the Brotherhood's bitter-enders in the wrong place could wreck us. We're not being sent out to fight our way through organized opposition."

"No, you're not. Damn! I wish I was going with you."

"Never mind that, Colonel," Vela said. "We'll see you outside Nordshaven." He came to attention and led the rest of the Command Group in a salute.

As they filed out, Parkes let himself fall behind. He had gained new respect for the ancient Chinese proverb "Be careful what you wish for. You may get it."

He'd all but prayed for command of a rifle company in this campaign, just in case something went wrong with his permanent commission. Now he was going to race through guerrilla territory in a hover as X.O. of a two-company task force, one Peace Force and one Federal Jaeger. Their mission: to swing north and take the Brotherhood perimeter around Nordshaven in the rear.

Once there, they were supposed to imitate a brigade, ready to play hammer and crush the Brotherhood on the anvil of Nordshaven's defenders. If their imitation wasn't good enough, they were to secure and hold an airhead until a real brigade could be flown in.

Three hundred people, nine hovers, ten A.P.C.'s and scout cars, four all-wheel tankers to be ditched once empty. Plenty of automatic weapons, four launchers, and dedicated air support. Fourteen's Mediator Goff and the Feds' Councilor Leihno, in case talking turned out to be more effective than shooting.

It might be enough, *if* the guerrillas really weren't fighting seriously except in self-defense. The task force's mapped route led it clear of known guerrilla positions, and orders were not to fire on guerrillas unless fired upon.

If the guerrillas weren't making a separate peace—was Task Force Vela too many people to lose? Setting aside the fact that he was one of them, probably not. Certainly not with Kuroki's brigade only four days from on-planet deployment and the Brotherhood incapable of a serious offensive.

Was Duchamp racing Kuroki, trying to win the war before anybody else could claim a share of the credit? Unlikely. Duchamp's principles were as well known as his ambition.

It was the fifty thousand people still in Nordshaven on Duchamp's mind. Fifty thousand people watching the ash from the Teuffelberg pile deeper in their streets each hour, smelling the fumes, feeling every shock and jar in the ground under their feet. Fifty thousand people who only need to walk twenty kilometers east or south to be safe—

Someone bumped into him.

"Hello, John. Was the briefing that dull?" It was Kat, in full field kit, with a slung carbine.

"Just thinking. This is going to be a hairy one. Worth it, though."

"Damned right. We may even win those medals Duchamp couldn't give us for Hill 1242. This time there's no question about our—"

"What do you mean *we*, lady?"

She indicated her kit. "I'm naval liaison for the task force. You'll need the best." She frowned. "Didn't you see me?"

"You were at the back of a dark room. Besides, I was concentrating on the map." He forced a smile. "I already know what you look like."

"John, does it bother you that—?"

"Kat, it's not going to work if I have to pass the test over and over again."

"What test?"

"You know. Does he react as lover or soldier? The soldier's going to lead, but the other's going to be there."

"This is a hell of a time for our first quarrel."

"It would be our second, but I agree. So let's not have it."

Her face set into its glacial mask for a moment, then softened into an unsteady smile. "Sorry. You don't know how hard it is to find somebody like you. All those centuries of what we call equality and mixed units—it doesn't seem to have done the job. When a woman finds someone like you, he seems too good to be true."

"I thought I was the one who was supposed to go around feeling unworthy to have this or do that."

"We'll take turns. Now let's mount up, before Vela starts comparing our ancestors to goats."

Hiko finished the inventory of their gear and contemplated the total without enthusiasm but without complaint, either.

In every war, every soldier from recruit to general wanted more of something. He and Ruth would also have been limited in what they could carry over this kind of terrain. The truck might have taken them farther without the undetected fuel leak, but they could never have driven all the way to safety. The truck would have been too visible.

They could not really have managed more than larger medical kit, more water purification tablets, a snare trap, three more rifle magazines apiece, and another dozen *shurikens*. Hiko thought with brief yearning of his *nunchaku*, and swore never to fight again where he could not carry it.

Dry grass and stones crunched. Ruth came around a stand of frog's tongue, rifle in one hand and fastening her belt with the other. Her notions of field modesty didn't let her relieve herself in his presence.

"Any sign of the enemy?" He wondered whom she meant by that, but they agreed on avoiding all contact.

"Just a pair of attackers. Probably Federals, but too high for a ground-attack mission."

"May the Lord keep us free of—"

"Wait. Listen."

They heard the distant drone and rumble swell, then fade into silence. Hiko looked at his watch and map.

"Hovers and heavy wheelers, going over the track on Giambattista Hill or somewhere near it."

"Whose?"

"It sounded like company strength, at least. The guerrillas don't have that kind of transport. The Proctors and the regulars wouldn't be moving by daylight this far west. Besides, that column was heading east."

"The Peace Force and the Federals, then."

Hiko nodded. "Probably a local offensive, to take advantage of the guerrillas' disorganization, or maybe establish an airhead."

A look at Ruth's face kept Hiko's pleasure silent. He had betrayed only an unworthy Representative of the Master and a dishonorable faction among the Brotherhood. By all she had been taught, Ruth had betrayed God.

The Avia attacked while Parkes was supervising the last stage of the refueling. Two hundred meters above the crew unloading the portable pump, it salvoed its rockets at the hovers two kilometers ahead.

By the time the rockets hit, every automatic weapon in the task force was shooting back. The launcher crews started to unlimber and break out boosted AA rounds. The Avia's pilot turned sharply to make a strafing run. This slowed him down, well inside the range of the hovers' and A.P.C.'s ring mounts. A dozen lines of tracer converged on him, shells punched through armor, and the fuel tanks exploded.

"The pump is loaded," said the Jaeger sergeant in charge of the refueling party. "Permission to search the crash site?"

Parkes shook his head. "There won't be any survivors and we're not after intelligence data. At least not about the Saint Michael Wing."

"Yes, sir."

I'm getting used to being called "sir." Maybe someday I'll be able to see a column of smoke rising from where Kat is without thinking about her.

They had to take to the fields to catch up with the main column; the plane's burning wreckage blocked the road. None of it would have told them more than they'd learned from the attack itself, that the Saint Michael Wing was going to fight to the last plane and maybe to the last man.

As they drove into the laager, Parkes saw Kat sitting on the rear ramp of a hover, one foot bare, a medic kneeling in front of her. Fifty meters away, the column of smoke rose from a burning hover.

Vela met Parkes as he dismounted. "I want you to take point from here on in. That hard case in the Avia was broadcasting a warning to somebody he thought was around here. We jammed as soon as he started, and we haven't heard any acknowledgments. I'd still rather have you on the spot if we need to fight off an ambush."

"Okay." Parkes scanned the laager. A lot of grass was burning, as well as the hover. A second hover had part of its skirt lying on the ground, and several people burrowing under it.

"Private McKee's dead. Four litter cases, five walking wounded. One hover needs a new fan. It could have been a lot worse."

"It probably will be, from here on in."

"Maybe. But we've covered eighty-five kilometers. Only forty to go. They won't ask us to turn back east and join the Kocher Pass fight now."

Both Parkes and Vela had dreaded meeting heavy opposition before they turned northwest. The contingency plan then was for the task force to strike the Brotherhood perimeter around the Kocher Pass from the rear, or at least divert strength from it.

That would probably break the pass fight wide open. It would also pit the task force against the Brotherhood's best troops, including the Lions. This might win the battle but it would probably destroy the task force, a long way from a still-blockaded Nordshaven.

"Parkes, I may be stepping out of line, but could you persuade your—the Amazon to be a little more careful? She picked up a splinter in her foot trying to salvage the ring M.G. from the burning hover. Almost got another in her—where she sits down."

"She probably said we're not too fat on M.G.'s."

"She did. Want to guess what I said?"

"That we're even shorter of Naval Liaison officers."

"So you can read both our minds. Well?"

"Well what?"

"Are you going to talk to her?"

"Is it an order, Colonel?"

"Would you obey it if it was?"

"No, Colonel. It's not a lawful order. You'd be asking me to use a personal relationship to bypass official channels. Besides, you've said the same thing I would, and she's more likely to take it from you than from me."

"That makes a weird kind of sense, but . . ." Vela shook his head.

"Chalk it up to our all being really too tired for this sort of mission. When Kat gets tired, she gets careless of her own safety. When I get tired, I get depressed and guilty. When you get tired, you start minding other people's business."

"Parkes, don't push your luck."

"Sir, I don't think I have any left." *Not after finding Kat.*

"All right. *Both* of you be careful. Dismissed."

Two of the guerrillas seemed to rise from the ground, the other two from behind a boulder. Their tactics were acceptable. Their noise discipline was as wretched as it had been a month ago on the north shore, and their speed was lamentable.

Three were easy kills. The fourth had to be slowed by a *shuriken* before Ruth could shoot him. Hiko contemplated the corpses with a distaste that memory of their ineptness did nothing to ease.

"I was hoping the guerrillas had given up the fight. Everything we've seen says so."

"Against the enemy, perhaps," Ruth said. "But against the Proctors?"

Hiko frowned. "That might explain why they came in close. They wanted to capture us . . ." He didn't like where that line of thought led him.

"Yes. They are at war with the Proctors. In Proctor uniforms, how could they take us for anything else?"

"Ruth, apart from offending your principles, it's too cold to climb these hills naked."

She didn't even try to smile. "We could have sought other clothing. Innocent blood is on our hands."

"I doubt if these guerrillas are so—" Hiko began. He broke off as he saw Ruth's face twist in pain. As she went to her knees, he saw the dark stain on her inner left thigh.

"Ruth. Let me see that."

She pulled her pants down, unslung her pack, and pillowed her head on it as he probed the wound. Her only sound was a faint hiss, but he saw her sweating.

"It looks worse than it is. Bleeding freely, no bullet or bullet fragments, and no damage to the bone—I think. If I remember my first aid, you should have no more than a scar.''

''Will I be able to walk?''

''That depends on the muscle damage. I'll cut you a staff, and you'd better leave the rockets behind—''

''It would be simpler to leave me here. Is this not the Lord's judgment?''

She was not talking to him. He doubted that she even saw him. He hoped desperately she could hear him, as he tried to find words to bring her through this crisis.

''It would be strange if the Lord passed His judgment on you for my mistake. It was my mistake, not to think of packing extra clothing and changing once we were in guerrilla territory.''

He hoped her convictions wouldn't keep her from listening. It really had been his mistake, and if he'd made a similar one at the head of his Team he would be having more than one thought about requesting demotion. Ruth seemed to be proposing the equivalent of *seppuku*, which had barely crossed Hiko's mind since he was twenty.

Was his determination to save her a selfish one? Did she need to be reconciled to her God as much as his ancestors had needed to be reconciled to theirs, and by the same method? Or was this a simple moment of doubt, which she could survive if she knew she was not alone?

Hiko locked away his own doubts and focused his powers of persuasion on Ruth. He not only had to talk her out of dying, he had to do it quickly.

Other guerrillas might have heard the shots. If so, they might stand off and shoot from ambush. Hiko had always loathed the idea of death with no chance to strike back.

He forgot what he was saying when he finally saw Ruth smile. He now understood why people sang hymns of praise. If he'd known any, he would have sung them, ignoring the presence of guerrillas or the absence of any Higher Power to hear him.

Her smile widened. ''It is said that overscrupulousness can be a sin. This never seemed to stop people like the Proctors and my uncles. Perhaps that proves there is some wisdom in it.''

Hiko looked at Ruth's wound and realized that he'd been cleaning, dressing, and freezing it while he talked. His hands seemed to have worked well enough without any direction from his brain, and it seemed likely that he'd been right about the muscle damage.

''We certainly need have no scruples about robbing corpses.''

Stripping the bodies was a grisly job that produced enough wearable clothing to make Hiko and Ruth look like something other than Proctors. Demons from a child's nightmare, perhaps, but not something likely to be shot on sight.

As the freeze dose took effect, Ruth stopped sweating. With the aid of a staff and Hiko's shoulder, she even managed to hobble.

They left the Proctor uniforms and the rockets scattered among the rocks. "With luck, nobody will be able to figure out who did what to whom until we are well clear of the area," Hiko said. "After that, we look for a good place to hide until we find that safe route into Federal lines."

We also hope we can find that hiding place before our last dose of freeze wears off. How long will four doses last?

For the third time in two hours and fourteen kilometers, the order to halt and deploy had gone out. Parkes jumped from the command hover and trotted toward the brush north of the road.

Probably another false alarm. Wish Dallin would finish tanking up and get back on station as F.A.C. She doesn't see things.

A Brotherhood armored car popped over the brow of the hill.

Parkes's belief in a false alarm lasted two seconds more—a full second longer than Dietsch's. The sergeant snap-shot a burst at the car's front tires; both run-flats quivered and sagged. As the car roared down the hill, Dietsch sprayed the automatic turret on top with a second burst.

That delayed the car's return fire long enough for the top gunners on every hover and A.P.C. within range to let fly. A burst of 25-mm fire crippled the turret; a rocket gutted the engine compartment. The deploying point platoon hit the dirt, all in more danger from friendly ricochets than from the armored car.

Parkes looked up long enough to see that the car carried Proctor insignia, then flattened again as its ammunition exploded. Fragments scoured the ground; one clipped his helmet and another drew a scream from somebody. "Deploy along the crest!" Dubnick shouted. His platoon swarmed up the hill. Parkes waited just long enough to praise Dietsch's shooting, then joined the rush. He was supposed to supervise his platoon commanders, not do their job for them, but to supervise you had to see what was going on.

Two minutes on the hilltop showed Parkes mostly more hills covered with boulders and patches of scrub bloodthorn. Beyond the farthest hill was a hint of woodland, with a verti hovering over it. Green and yellow marker smoke rose from the woods, and from somewhere beyond them.

In the two minutes, Dubnick had deployed his platoon in fine style. A month of fighting had knocked slowness out of him more thoroughly than Podgrebin could have done in a year.

"Fire in the hole!" came from right and left.

Demo charges cracked, toppling trees and gouging the ground. Parkes's ears rang and gravel pattered down around him. Automatically he checked his rifle. Troopers rushed about, looking like fidget-fever victims but actually doing a first-class job of setting up a defensive position.

"Enemy infantry!" someone shouted. Six Proctors ran out of the rocks to the right of the position. For two seconds they had perfect enfilade fire and made the most of it. Then a stocky corporal turned one of the L.M.G.'s 90 degrees and caught the Proctors before they could take cover. He finished the shooting one-handed; one of the wounded who had two good hands helped him load.

Dubnick got his platoon repositioned with three orders and two hand signals, then ordered grenade fire into the boulders. Eight grenades produced two secondary explosions, several flying bodies, and a lot of screaming and calling on the Lord.

Reinforcements arrived in the form of Colonel Vela.

"Looks like a force of Proctors drawn from several different units," Parkes said. "If we'd faced one coordinated attack instead of three separate ones, we'd be in trouble."

"Nobody ever said the Proctors were good field troops," Vela said. "Okay, John. You block here. I'm going to leapfrog 4 Platoon ahead and around the left. The Jaegers'll go in on the right."

"What's out there?"

"Air says a lot of vehicles and people, some of them in uniform. Could be anything from an ambulance train to the landing of the Grand Galactics. Dallin's coming on F.A.C. station and there's a Tollhouse strike about ten minutes away. The launchers are deployed and loaded."

"What about orbital fire?"

"We're holding off on that until we know a little more who's out there. *Bruce* is on five-minute call, and the Amazon's linked up to Dallin."

"Sounds good."

"Could be worse, could be worse." Vela turned and charged down the slope, his nuggety body almost bouncing from boulder to boulder. The left-flank platoon tramped past with more concern for speed than for dispersal or silence.

The uncoordinated Proctor attack was the last sign of the enemy Parkes had for nearly two hours. The infantry attacks went in on the flanks; firefights boiled up in both places, and the launchers went into action. Two of the Tollhouses expended their loads in close support; one went down to a shoulder-fired missile.

A second platoon passed through Dubnick's lines and tied in with the left-flank attack. It broke things loose temporarily, then got sucked into an even bigger firefight a few hundred meters farther on. Parkes waited for orders to go forward and take over, releasing Vela to return to the C.P. Instead the company C.O. came up. Parkes turned to passing ammunition forward and casualties back.

Eventually even this required no more than occasional supervision. Parkes knew that the Wise One couldn't be expected to conjure up a platoon of Proctors just because he wanted to take a personal bash at the enemy. He still needed to find ways of staying out of Dubnick's hair.

Part of the time he spent examining the dead Proctors. Part he spent helping the medics, when they needed a spare pair of hands. The rest he spent listening in on the supporting-fires network. Kat and Dallin seemed to have everything nicely under control there.

They also apparently had enough identified targets to let *Bruce* open up. Salvoes of cluster bombs and slugheads were hitting the enemy left about every ten minutes. Gray and white smoke rose steadily higher, whipped about by the hypersonic shock waves of the slugheads.

In between the sonic booms, Parkes listened to Kat's incisive orders and comments. Apart from the accent and a certain extra grace of language, the Naval Liaison Officer on the radio had very little in common with the woman he knew.

She's right. Women don't have as much experience balancing the human and the warrior as men do. The best thing to do for her is not to joggle her elbow while she's doing it.

"Captain, a stretcher party just brought in a civilian casualty." It was Dietsch. "An escaped hostage, she says."

"Damn." Anybody who'd spent the past month in the hands of the Brotherhood deserved better than to be hit in the moment of liberation.

"She's not hurt that bad. She wants to talk to the S.O.P., though. I guess that means you."

"I guess it does."

• • •

The third freeze dose wore off as Hiko and Ruth covered the last half kilometer to the shepherd's hut. Once he was sure it was deserted, Hiko pushed forward as fast as Ruth could manage. They still covered the last hundred meters with her on his back. Hiko staggered through the door, hoping the hut would offer more than a few hours' shelter.

While the last freeze dose took effect, Hiko searched the single room. The water tank was empty and the power pack gone, but a hidden shelf under the bed still held bottled water and a few cans of food. The bedding was gone, but a battered mattress remained, at least more comfortable than bare floor or bare ground.

Hiko piled all the spare clothing over Ruth, then filled their pot with bottled water and slapped a heat tab under it. When the water boiled, he added freeze-dried cereal and soy cubes.

He wasn't surprised when Ruth refused to eat, not after tasting it himself. He forced down a few mouthfuls, set the rest aside, and sat down on the bed. If Ruth needed more than his presence and rest, they were in trouble, but she would have that.

She was sleeping and didn't seem to be feverish, but from time to time she twisted and moaned. The crisis of conscience might be past but the nightmares were still with her.

The escaped hostage was a gray-haired woman who introduced herself as Theresa Duran, a professor of classical literature at the University of Nordshaven.

"I was visiting my family in Beppe when the war started," she said. "If I'd known as much about walking as I do now, I wouldn't have stayed around to be captured."

Professor Duran had learned the hard way, judging from the mass of blisters on her feet. She also showed signs of at least one beating, apart from her arm and calf wounds. She still told her story concisely.

Facing Task Force Vela was a column of Proctors and supporting troops from the Good Shepherds. They were escorting five hundred hostages and a few prisoners. The prisoners included the commanding officer of the Sentinels, one of the battalions holding the Nordshaven line. The Proctors were spread too thin to notice that the Shepherds were trying to sit out the battle and the hostages trying to escape.

"If you hit them just a little bit harder—on the ground, please, not from the air—the Proctors will break."

"They'll break, anyway."

"What if they slaughter the hostages? My grandchildren are in there!"

"If they—" Parkes began, then stopped. Nuclear weapons on Protectorate bases wouldn't bring the dead back to life. They also might kill even more children, no matter how precisely aimed.

Saving kids was one of the things you signed up for, Fruit Merchant.

"Dietsch, get Vela. Goff, too."

"Radio's faster."

"You're not being paid to tell me things I already know. This is too hot for the radio."

"On my way."

Dietsch returned with Goff ten minutes later. The Mediator wore a bush hat and battledress without insignia. His goggles were pushed up onto his forehead, leaving dark circles in an otherwise dust-pale face.

Parkes started to explain, then had to start over again when Vela arrived with Leihno. Finally they all listened to Duran while Parkes tried not to fidget at the number of key people one sniper could take out.

"We'll push," Vela said finally. "Parkes, you take Dubnick's platoon forward. If anything else is needed, Professor, we'll have to do it with air support." He didn't add that the task force would be without a reserve once the platoon went in. They all trusted Duran, but she might be recaptured.

"I'm going up, too," Goff said.

"No, I'm going," Leihno replied.

"Why the devil should either of you go?" Vela snarled.

"We need to talk to the Sentinels' C.O. as soon as possible. The Proctors may try to kill him."

"They'll surely try to kill you if you're within range. You're a lot less expendable than any Brotherhood officer."

"Got a coin?" Goff said.

Leihno shrugged and reached into his pocket. "Call it."

"Heads."

The coin sparkled, then rolled on the gravel. Parkes picked it up. "You want a gun, Art?"

"I suppose I'd better," Goff said. "Now let's see—which end does the bullet come out of?"

22

THE ROOM QUIVERED. Dust rose as the shelf of printed books on the rear wall gave up the ghost and crashed to the floor.

"The Teuffelberg is becoming quiescent, so there is no danger in your staying," Bishop Heinreid said. The sarcasm was so delicate that nobody but Parona could have recognized it.

"Quiescent hardly means quiet," the cardinal said. "But the mountain seems to be less dangerous now. Why would the Peace Force have ended their work with stress-releasing charges?"

"I have heard that this is because there were no longer any safe places to put the charges," Maria Biancheri said. "Also, I believe they want to use all their airlift for either the evacuation or supporting attack on the Nordshaven perimeter. I heard that a Peace Force column passed through guerrilla lines this morning and is now operating in the enemy's rear."

"Your sources in the Army grow no less cooperative," Heinreid said. "His Eminence grows no more so." Suddenly the lightness vanished from his voice and face.

"Your Eminence—we beg you. If you cannot be persuaded to leave Nordshaven, can we at least persuade you to tell the truth? It would be hard for our last memories of you to be—other then the truth."

In another moment he and Maria would be on their knees. Parona felt shame wash over him. Heinreid was right.

"The truth is, nobody knows how much danger is left. The ashes and fumes have diminished. The unreleased stresses and pressures have also diminished, but I admit not as much. The volcano may explode before the soldiers clear the way for a final evacuation of Nordshaven. It may explode after. It may not explode at all.

"Ignorance always forces compromise. The best compromise

seems to be you two leaving the city and me staying. That will prevent a panic, and put you two where you can do the most for the refugees.

"All of us staying will do nothing for anybody if the volcano does not explode. If it does, it will add slightly to the death toll and vastly to the ensuing chaos. We have fought chaos side by side for thirty years. Let us continue the fight to the end, even if we must part to do so.

"Besides, I think I have some claim to be a captain, or at least a chief officer, of this sinking ship. It is my privilege to go down with it, if I wish."

Maria smiled, and Parona knew he'd won. She added, "It is my recollection that the custom was for the captain to be the last man off. He did not have to go down with the ship unless he felt some responsibility for the sinking."

"Pedant," Heinreid muttered, but he was smiling, too.

A sonic boom loud enough to make the dust dance hammered the building. Heinreid hurried to the window and cranked open the blast shutters. The automatic closer was long since useless.

To the east, lightning in colors no thunderstorm ever spawned danced along the horizon. Streaks of it seemed to leap up to heaven and down to earth again.

At the heavenward end of the lightning chain, blue-white fire blazed, brighter than any star if not as bright as the lightning.

"The Navy's gone into action," Parona said. "That could mean reinforcements, or the end of the Thorshammer Shower." Heinreid and Biancheri coughed almost in chorus. "It could also mean the Peace Force is in a hurry, or needs to protect their raiding column," he added hastily.

Then they were silent, because men wielding thunderbolts were not a topic for light chatter.

Hiko had expected to sleep almost at once. He could not remember ever having been so tired, not even in the early days of his *ninja* training.

Instead his thoughts turned to his own motives and Jamshir Singh's. His own now seemed clear. Whatever he might have told himself about duty to the Master (and not denying that it might be the truth), he had done what he had simply because he could not do otherwise. There were things he would not stand by and allow to happen, if he could prevent them. And if he could do anything to prevent them, his life had to be dedicated to that purpose and not cast away by *seppuku*.

Jamshir Singh remained a mystery. The man was both more and less than he'd seemed; did the details matter? Yes and no—and Hiko's frustration lasted until he remembered a *sensei*'s words:

"Ambiguity is at the heart of life. The better you endure it, the better you will live until it is time to die. Only death lacks ambiguity."

Jamshir Singh's mature years, his obscure background, his skill at night work, his pretended reluctance to reveal the so-called secrets of the New Thugs—these marked a man who served something or someone besides the Game Master. Certainly himself, and probably some third party, or even more than one. The number of people who might have some interest in knowing the secrets of the New Thugs and the Game Master could not be counted on fingers and toes combined.

That was one fact. Another was Hiko's debt to Jamshir Singh—his and Ruth's. They probably owed him their success, certainly their lives.

Hiko had never wished to shake off the Japanese concern for discharging debts. So he owed Jamshir Singh a larger debt than he was ever likely to have a chance to repay.

Of course, Jamshir Singh might go on to betray the rest of the Teams, men whom Hiko had led. Then the debt would turn into one of vengeance.

Hiko went to the hut's small window and stood where he could see out without being seen. He wore only his shorts, in spite of the chill.

One problem and one solution at a time. None of his *senseis* had ever taught that, probably because they thought anyone too stupid to know it had no business learning *ninjitsu*.

Lasers seared the northern sky.

His exclamation brought Ruth awake. She lurched to the window and stood beside him, hastily hanging various items of clothing around her. When she spoke, her voice was like the scratching of mice in the wall.

"The Peace Force is on the march. May the Lord have mercy on those facing them."

Then she was the professional again. "Hiko, I thought we had agreed not to keep watch. There is no danger greater than that of exhausting ourselves."

"You were in no condition to keep watch. I—" He put aside reluctance to admit weakness. "I could not sleep."

She muttered something that sounded like a prayer. Then she said, "Hiko—I woke cold. I—we would be warmer if we slept under the clothes. Together, for the warmth. I—I am not abandoning my chastity. I trust you."

Hiko was not sure the trust was wholly justified when he curled up against Ruth and discovered she was naked. In spite of his exhaustion, his body stirred. This time his exclamation didn't wake her, muffled as it was in her hair. Presently the warmth did what Ruth had predicted and he fell asleep.

Parkes woke to a catalog of aches and pains. He read it back to himself, remembering each of yesterday's incidents by its lingering trace of discomfort.

The grit in his mouth was dust from shellbursts. The raw throat was from H.E. fumes and thirst. The sore thumb was from hitting the dirt when the last Proctor armored car opened up. (Several troopers had worse than sore thumbs, but their diversion had kept the car from firing into the hostages.) The sore left buttock was a nearly spent fragment from a "friendly" cluster bomb. The tight belly was being too tired to eat before falling asleep—

Someone was singing close by. The voice was familiar but ragged with fatigue.

Parkes wriggled out of his sleeping bag, added a tingling crazy bone to his list of discomforts, and stood up. Dietsch nodded.

"Morning, Sergeant. Leihno and Goff back yet?"

The two negotiators had taken off at sunset, with Colonel Kean of the Sentinels. Under a flag of truce, they were flying into the Nordshaven perimeter, to propose a cease-fire.

Dietsch shook his head.

"Any more reinforcements?"

"A sort of company of Security Police—"

"What?" Bad news, Parkes reflected, was becoming a sure cure for drowsiness.

"Take it easy. They were handpicked from the Old Guard and wearing Fed uniforms. Besides, they're mostly guarding the Proctor prisoners from the hostages."

"MacLean in yet?" The C.O. was supposed to bring in Second Company. That would give the blocking force extra muscle in case the negotiations broke down.

"No."

"You're full of—good news—this morning."

"I do my best."

"Your best had better include some coffee."

"Your wish is my command. Shall I bring it down there?" Dietsch pointed downhill, to where the Amazon sat on a boulder, her wounded foot bare and being dressed by a medic. She was surrounded by a circle of wide-eyed hostage children, and was singing "Once I Had a Comrade."

"Ten minutes ago." Parkes started downhill.

As he reached Kat, she stopped singing. "All right, children," she said. "Run along now. I'll give you some more songs this afternoon."

The children and medic retreated far enough to let Parkes hug Kat. "Mmmmm," she said. "Highly nonregulation and badly needed."

"Have you been up all night?"

"I had to stay up long enough to transfer all the target data to *Warspite*'s team."

"*Warspite*? Did she put on the fireworks display? I thought she was back with Kuroki."

"She was. They brought her in at full acceleration, and ran her just about dry putting on the show. Now she's refueling from *Von Lettow-Vorbeck* and *Yanagida* and taking off their crews. Empty, they're expendable, while we get some more muscle in orbit two days early."

"Hallelujah, I think. Hey, is that MacLean coming in?"

A verti was droning toward the L.Z. just downhill.

"No, that's the one that took Leihno and Goff in last—"

She broke off. One thought shouted in both minds. *To hell with setting a good example. We've* got *to find out what happened.*

They sprinted downhill, Kat carrying her boot in her hand. They reached the L.Z. just as the verti landed. Goff came out first, a huge grin on his face. Leihno followed, saw Forbes-Brandon's bare foot, and tried to frown.

"Shameless woman, immodestly exposing your sinful—"

"Bugger off," the Amazon said. "Did we win?"

"We did," a third voice said. General Lindholm scrambled out of the verti, staggered, and would have fallen if Leihno's hard muscle hadn't supported her. *Drunk on duty?* A second look showed red eyes, cracked lips, and round cheeks fallen in. *Even generals can work hard enough to wear themselves down.*

"MacLean's not in yet," Parkes said. "Vela's off placing the security reinforcements, and I think the Jaeger C.O.'s asleep."

"Never mind," Lindholm said. She slumped onto a convenient boulder as Dietsch ran up with the coffee. Fortunately he'd brought a whole pot, so there was enough to go around. Goff and Leihno drank theirs, then vanished into the radio shack like fluffaces into an untended vegetable garden.

Lindholm drained her coffee, let out an ecstatic sigh, and said, "We have a cease-fire in place everywhere except around Nordshaven. There they have to pull back twenty-five kilometers, stay within five kilometers of the coast, and leave all permanent shelter to us."

She waved her cup at Dietsch, who refilled it. "My guess is, it's going to turn into the end of the war. The Proctors really declared war on the guerrillas over the ammo dump explosion. Except for a few real hard-cases, the guerrillas declared peace on everybody. That put the wind up the Proctors.

"They started rounding up all the hostages and pulling them back. I can guess why. *This* in turn put the wind up the C.O. of the Lions, who's the son of Joshua Strong-for-Truth, the Principal of the Council of Elders. That's like being royalty, in the Protectorate.

"Anyway, the Proctors found themselves *being* arrested instead of arresting somebody else. The Lions sprang all the hostages in their area, shot any Proctors who objected too strenuously, and invited us to airlift the hostages out. That's why MacLean isn't here. His airlift is hauling hostages."

The landscape did a slow dance around Parkes.

"When word of that went around, the Brotherhood's Nordshaven Area C.O. asked for a high-ranking military representative to join the cease-fire negotiations. That was me.

"I suspect that the Elders are going to take about a day to realize that they have to make peace, or lose their whole army. Not to mention a civil war, that would give the Feds a chance to invade.

"Of course, they can't hope to invade without P.F. support, which they won't have. That's top secret, by the way."

Lindholm yawned, displaying a phalanx of flawless white teeth. "I've got orders for you people, too. Because *Warspite*'s taken over—'' another yawn ''—and Parkes's experience with evacuation—evacuation—''

Her head sagged sideways. Parkes caught her in time to keep her from falling off the boulder. As he struggled to support her eighty kilos, she began to snore.

It took a regular stretcher party to stow Lindholm in a tent. Parkes zipped the flap and said to Forbes-Brandon, ''I'm going to get on the horn and find out what those orders were.''

''You may have to wait. Our diplomats are going to be bringing the good news not only from Ghent to Aix but to everybody who will listen.''

''Yeah.'' Suddenly they were hugging each other. ''Damn! It's over. All but the shouting.''

''And our walking mountain,'' she said, disengaging a hand to point west.

23

Squorrrkkkk!

THE VITAL-SIGNS alarm produced a flurry of movement in the cabin of the medevac verti. Cardinal Parona craned his neck, trying to make sense of the medical attendants' high-tech ballet.

"Spleen's packing up."

"Laughton's got a spare support pack. Get on the horn."

The copilot slapped radio switches. "Medevac Blue Four, we need a 234 support pack."

Laughton's voice, distorted by static:

"On the way. How many attendants?"

"Two."

"You'll need a third, with a 234 pack."

"Now, just a goddamned minute—" howled the pilot and copilot in chorus.

"Got a problem, people?"

"We're at max overload right now, Major. One more body aboard and I don't think we're going to get off the ground."

"We can cut corners, can't we?"

"It's not cutting corners we're afraid of, Major. It's wracking up this bird and everybody aboard her."

Parona tapped the pilot on the shoulder. "Would it help if someone already aboard got off?"

The pilot started to glare, then realized who'd tapped him and what Parona was hinting at.

"Your Eminence, we have orders—"

"I doubt if you have orders to physically restrain me. That is the only way you can keep me aboard while a casualty is left behind." Parona levered himself out of the seat and braced himself against the fuselage while he sought firm footing.

"My bag, please." The copilot obeyed as if hypnotized. The shoulder bag weighed less than six kilos, but every bit of weight removed from the verti would help. Parona had heard the pilots saying what eating volcanic ash was doing to their engines.

A medical attendant stood between Parona and the door, apparently reluctant to move. Parona raised his right hand.

"God bless you, my daughter. Now, if you'll excuse me—"

She still didn't move, but she didn't resist when Parona sidled past her. Two more steps and he was at the door. He resisted the temptation to jump down—Dr. Laughton hardly needed another patient now!—and used the ladder.

A light truck pulled up and disgorged a medical technician carrying the self-contained life-support pack. Parona waved at the driver.

"Can you take me back to the aid station, please?"

Surprise kept the driver silent until Parona had climbed in and closed the door. Then conversation became impossible as the verti ran up its engines and lurched into the air. A blizzard of ashes and dead leaves swept over the truck. The verti barely cleared the bare trees at the southern end of Hansa Park, then slowly climbed away to the south.

The driver found his voice. He was a Federal militiaman, not much younger than Parona himself. "Your Eminence, I thought you were supposed to be—"

"They had a medical emergency," Parona replied, in a tone that discouraged conversation. "I'm sure Major Laughton can find me a corner until the next flight comes in."

The driver fed power. As the truck turned, Parona had a good view of the Teuffelberg. It seemed to be waking again, after being quiescent all night and half the morning. Red smoke swirled above the main cone and one of the secondaries. And was it just a trick played by old eyes, or was the side of that secondary cone beginning to glow?

The field shelter shook and a corner joint popped. Dr. Laughton looked up from the smashed knee she was debriding, swore, and shouted for a repair crew.

The corporal in charge of the crew studied the joint dubiously. "We're nearly out of bonder-sealer—"

"Then stuff something in the crack. Anything, as long as it won't burn or melt!"

"Okay, Doctor."

Laughton had finished the knee and the repair crew had contrived to use surgical epoxy and a strip of aluminum sheeting when someone knocked on the door.

"Sorry to bother you, Major, but the satellite's down!"

Laughton swept the back of her hand across her face and bit her lip. "How many inside?"

"Twelve, fifteen. About half the staff. A crew's already mounted up."

"Line up a second vehicle. Dickson, load it for major trauma."

"Yes, ma'am."

Laughton slumped into a chair by the end of the empty gurney. "Just when I thought we were getting on top of everything . . ." Tears made tracks in the dust on her face.

"I assume this satellite is not the orbital kind, but a building," Parona said.

She nodded. "It's one of the park admin buildings. Very solid, very heavy, very roomy. We used it for storage of potentially inflammable or explosive supplies. Then we used them up and the patients overflowed the field shelters, so we set up a satellite hospital in the building. It's about three hundred meters north of here."

"Will it help if I join you?"

"We're going to be out of reach of shelter if something does blow. These field buildings are designed to take some overpressure and heat. Out in the open—"

"If that's where people need us, why not? If you think I would be in the way—"

"No, no. You've been as good at practical nursing as you are at confessing."

"Thank you. I'm not a licensed paramedic like Heinreid, but the Niebuhr Seminary did insist on first-aid training for all candidates."

"I wondered. Well, let's go."

The glow on the side of the secondary cone was distinctly brighter when they reached the collapsed building. Parona took one look at it, then turned his attention to the people who needed all the help they could get. When a heavily constructed "earthquake-proof" building didn't live up to its name, the weight of falling material inflicted truly ghastly injuries.

Two vertis came and went while Parona heard confessions, gave the last rites, held hands, washed faces, and helped splint, seal, pack, and freeze. A third verti arrived and began disgorging people into a truck. Laughton straightened up from a depressed skull fracture to announce that some Federal engineers had arrived with heavy-rescue equipment.

As she bent over her patient, the ground heaved. Parona's grip on her shoulder kept her from falling. She put her arm around his waist, and they stared at the secondary cone.

A ball of raw orange-red fire was growing out of the side of the cone, with an insensate roar. It was already a kilometer in diameter. As they watched, it grew still more and rose until only a slender stem tied it to the ground.

Then it began to move. Parona watched for lateral movement and saw none.

"I think the mountain is walking our way," he said quietly. His knees wanted to knock together and his bowels wanted to empty themselves. He wanted dignity in his last moments too badly to give way to either.

The Twenty-third Psalm came to mind.

"The Lord is my shepherd. I shall not want—" Laughton joined him at, "Yea, though I walk through the valley of the shadow of death, I shall fear no evil—"

This was not the shadow of death, but death itself coming at him.

They finished together and Laughton smiled. "Don't forget the soldier's version—yea, though I walk through the valley of the shadow of death, I shall fear no evil, for I am the meanest bastard in the valley."

Parona smiled back. He felt both more peace than he had expected and a very real presence. God, human companionship, or both, and where did one begin and the other—

This time the heaving of the ground knocked them both off their feet. Sitting, they saw the rest of the building collapse, heard the screams, saw the truck with the engineers overturn, and watched the main cone of the Teuffelberg explode into a monstrous gray-black cloud.

"Both kinds of eruptions," Parona murmured. "I hope Professor Bahr has a good place to watch." Did he just imagine that he could feel the heat of the deathcloud now? How long would the blast wave from the main cone take to reach them?

He rose to his feet and helped Laughton up. Otherwise neither of them moved, except to slip arms around each other's waist.

• • •

Dallin kept her eyes firmly on the horizon as the verti cruised toward Nordshaven. The dead city on top of her half-dead Transportation Company might be a little too much. She would *not* let herself cry or get the shakes in the air, even with a first-class copilot like Gallagher. Not with General Kuroki aboard.

They passed over what was left of Nordshaven. More than anybody except maybe Bahr the Omniscient had expected, but the rebuilding would be a long slow matter. There were two meters of ash to clear away in some places, a shroud for the city's four thousand dead. That really was better than forty thousand, and Dallin wasn't too worn to know it. It helped, too, that a lot of them were people who'd stayed because it was their job and died at their posts, like Marian Laughton and the little cardinal.

It wasn't just the Peace Force who knew the Birkenhead Drill.

In another minute the horizon offered an almost equally dismal spectacle. The eruption was over and the cubic kilometers of matter blasted into the sky by the main cone was mostly on its way to other destinations. It would ruin crops and maybe cropland. It would probably put Zauberberg on the edge of famine unless out-system supplies or synthetics appeared in large quantities. It no longer obscured the view of what had been the Teuffelberg.

The main cone had collapsed in on itself and was now a sprawling pyramid some two thousand meters lower than before. The secondary cone that had spewed the deathcloud had lost its entire western face; the rest jutted up from a cloud of steam and vapor like a solitary black tooth. Steam vents and still-cooling lava flows in a dozen other places added to the murk.

"Is this as close as you would like to go?" Kuroki's voice came from the back seat.

"Frankly it's about five kilometers closer except in an emergency. Our own vertis have been eating ash and cinders for too long. The resupply ones and yours are still fresh, but I don't know how long they'll need to operate."

"Neither do I," Kuroki said. "It seems likely that we can meet the needs of operations in the eruption area by ground and water transportation. You may return to base."

He sounded disgruntled, and in fact his broad face had worn a discontented look ever since he landed. He was too honorable to regret that a war was over, but he would have been superhuman not to wish that he and his brigade faced more challenging work.

According to Duchamp's original plan, Kuroki's 8th Brigade

would have lined up from Nordshaven down to the Kocher Pass, then wheeled toward the northeast. As it wheeled, it would have pushed Brotherhood forces into retreat or stamped them flat if they fought. With a line of retreat open to the east, Duchamp had expected that most of the Brotherhood's troops would take it.

Instead a truce that looked like becoming permanent had ended the fighting. The Brotherhood was evacuating by sea, the guerrillas were being offered amnesty, and there hadn't been as much as a platoon-sized action since two days before the eruption. Kuroki's people would be busy with disaster relief, resettling refugees, guarding prisoners, finding guerrilla arms caches, and a dozen other jobs. The painstaking Kuroki and his well-trained brigade would do a fine job, but two Security Battalions who hadn't expected a good fight against first-class opponents could have done as well.

Dallin tapped Gallagher and he took the controls; the verti banked and headed toward the coast.

Ten minutes later and four kilometers out to sea, they were passing a hundred meters above a shoal of dead fish. The radio came to life.

"All aircraft, all aircraft. Investigate unidentified ferry-type ship at—" A pause, then a set of coordinates not more than twenty kilometers from Dallin.

"Are we the closest?" Kuroki asked.

"Possibly, sir."

"Then we can join the investigation."

"Is that an order, sir?"

"Why do you ask?"

"An unidentified ship could be a load of wounded going home or hostages being returned. It could also be a load of fanatics—Proctors or Angels or Saint Michael ground crew, with plenty of weapons and a big grudge. Gallagher and I and this verti are expendable. With all due respect, sir, you are not."

"Very well. I withdraw the suggestion. Where are we going now?"

"I'd like to refuel before taking you back to your HQ. What about Camp McKee?"

"Which one is that?"

"It keeps an eye on the remaining Brotherhood units in the Nordshaven area. Its people are a company of my own Fourteen and a company of Federal Jaegers."

"I have no objections."

Dallin took the controls with an easier mind and a steadier hand. It would be about time for lunch when they landed, so with luck they could stretch the stop to an hour or more.

With even more luck, Kat and even the Fruit Merchant would be there and they could let their hair down. Kat had said something about two kids Parkes had thought dead turning up as live hostages, and how he looked five years younger. That Dallin wanted to see, even for a few minutes.

When so many of your friends were dead or in the hospital, you savored the live and whole ones more than ever.

Ruth handed the leaflet back to Hiko. "If we want the amnesty, we shall have to go in as surrendering guerrillas. What if no one will vouch for us? Worse, what if someone suspects us in the deaths of the four we killed?"

Hiko unfolded from the lotus position and began to pace up and down the tiny hut. "I doubt if any of the guerrilla bands had complete records of their members. As for the other—we met no one after leaving the bodies. How could anyone associate us with their deaths?"

He was more patient with her objections than he might have been otherwise, because they showed she was thinking clearly again. Even more, they showed that she wanted to survive. That hadn't been so certain the day the Teuffelberg erupted, when the nightmares came back and with them the certainty of the Lord's wrath.

Turning themselves in at one of the amnesty stations had another advantage, one that he didn't want to wound Ruth's pride by mentioning. Her thigh wound was healing normally, but she was hardly fit for a long hike.

"It certainly seems to be the best way out of this war," Ruth said at last. "The Lord willing, we shall have more time to decide where to go from there."

" 'We,' Ruth?" Hiko stopped his pacing abruptly.

"You do not think I have any more of a home to return to than you?"

"The Proctors are going to be—"

"*Rumors* say that the Protectorate will abolish the Proctors. But they may not, and even if they do, there will be former Proctors. My uncles, for one. What welcome would they give to someone who fled from the Proctors' judgment *and* the field of battle alike?"

"I did not plan on casting you adrift, Ruth. I only assumed—"

"Is such an assumption worthy of a seasoned combat leader as yourself? Rather, assume that I join my namesake in the Bible in saying, 'Where you go, I shall go also. Your people shall be my people, and your God my God.' "

Hiko had started pacing again. Now he nearly walked into the wall. When he had gathered both wits and words, he said slowly, "Ruth, I have no people. The best I am likely to find is a mercenary unit. And—I think you should know that I have no God."

The second silence was even longer than the first. It would have plucked on Hiko's tight nerves like torture if he hadn't realized that Ruth was trying not to laugh. Finally she managed to stop at a smile.

"Hiko. I have seen those vowed to the Lord. I have seen you. Whatever you have that is not the Lord seems to serve you well. I have no fear that you will go astray, or corrupt our children."

Hiko did not walk into the wall, because he was standing still. He did not fall silent, either; he had the feeling that he had been a big enough fool already.

"I think it would be well if you—we—remained chaste for some time. Perhaps until we are in a place where the children can grow safely. Unless you—you are of an age—where children are soon or never?" He decided that silence made him seem less of a fool than babbling.

Ruth put her arms around him in an embrace that held all the calm in the world, and rested her cheek against his. He was tall for one of Home Islands descent, but Ruth was some four centimeters taller.

He would not fight her now. Indeed, the more he thought about the matter, the more he felt inclined to let it work out as she so clearly wished. True, he had never contemplated entering into a permanent and monogamous relationship with a woman who clearly knew little about pleasing a man. What he wished her to know he would have to teach her.

A year ago, the idea would have been ludicrous. That was not work for a man, nor work at which he would have much skill. Yet there were few limits on what one might properly do for someone to whom one owed a debt. If he was not in debt to Ruth, then no one could be in debt to another and the world was without honor and obligation.

That thought made him shiver, in spite of Ruth's warmth and closeness. She felt the shiver and tightened her embrace.

24

THE BAR OF Nuovo Milano's Hotel Sforza was as quiet as expensive bars usually were. It was an oasis of peace after the crowded suite upstairs, where Captain Cooper was holding his promotion party.

Parkes knew that Cooper had earned his stars. He also knew that he himself really wasn't in a mood to party tonight, at least no longer than duty required. That wasn't long at all, for a Ground Forces captain at a Navy affair.

Cooper's departure for a flag-level post would also be one more departure from the *Ark Royal*/Battalion Fourteen team. This outward flow was beginning to feel to Parkes more like the breakup of a family, less like a normal change of unit.

"*Signore Comandante*, I really urge you to try the amaretto—"

It was the bartender's third try. Parkes glowered. "I'm a captain, not a major. You can't flatter me into drinking that strangler piss." The bartender retreated.

Maybe it was leaving his enlisted career behind that weighed him down, not just leaving Fourteen. Or maybe it was leaving—

"Hello, John. Partied out?"

"Hi, Kat. Out of that party upstairs, anyway."

"Same here. I paid my respects to all the right people, then tried to set up a bridge game. Cognac, please," as the bartender caught her eye.

"Anyway, I thought I was lucky. I had Magnusson as my partner, and Dallin had one of her old transport people. Magnusson's damned good, and we were skinning them alive when Dallin's partner started on the shakes. He was a P.O.W. for the whole war and had a rough time with the Proctors."

The cognac arrived. She inhaled luxuriously. "Cheers."

"To us."

"So that was the end of the bridge game. We found a medic for Dallin's partner, then Magnusson went back to barracks and Dallin left with Vela."

"Think she's out to trip him?'"

"More like she didn't want to be alone."

Her tone said she wasn't the only one. Parkes put his arms around her.

"Lovely. Where do you have to go now, if anywhere?"

"Dietsch's wetting down his stripes, and I really have to hit that one. Otherwise, I'm free."

"No, you're not. You're about to be carried off to the Ryki Hotel. I wangled a room with a private sauna."

Parkes felt his body responding. To Katherine or to the sauna? Probably both.

"Dietsch first, Kat."

"Mind if I join you?"

"No problem, as long as you don't mind coming as the captain's lady—"

"In what sense were you using the word 'come'?"

Parkes looked at his glass and said in aggrieved tones, "You're neither explanation nor excuse." Then he grinned and kissed Kat. "The party's going to be incredibly decorous. Dietsch wants to keep his stripes this time."

"Wanting and having aren't the same."

"Don't I know it, though. I'm lucky. What I want, I have."

For tonight, and maybe for a few more nights after that before one of us gets our shipping-out orders.

"Want an escort?" Dietsch asked as Parkes and Forbes-Brandon approached the door of the bar.

Forbes-Brandon shook her head. "We've both got our side-arms." She peered through the star-shaped window in the center of the door. "Besides, it's started to snow."

"Then good luck, and—thanks to both of you. I wasn't sure I'd have another shot at these"—Dietsch touched his stripes—"and maybe I wouldn't, except for you two."

"Call it betting on an outsider," the Amazon said. She gave Dietsch a peck on the cheek. "It's still up to you to finish in the money."

"Yes, ma'am," Dietsch said, saluting and opening the door with his free hand.

Outside, the snow was beyond the flurries of the past three

weeks. It was a heavy fall that had already turned the streets white and muffled their footsteps as they descended the steps to the sidewalk.

Parkes kept a lookout for suspicious characters as they headed up Freni Street, but didn't expect to find any. Brotherhood or Game Master terrorists in Nuovo Milano had been few and far between. Their toll for the whole war was half a dozen incidents and fewer than fifty casualties. Their already slim pickings vanished entirely when the city was flooded with refugees from the north. None had any love for the Brotherhood and most were willing to cooperate with police and military intelligence against anyone who blew their nose suspiciously. This didn't always make Nuovo Milano pleasant; it did make it safe.

The biggest threat to public order in the city after three months of peace was clashes between the paroled Chosen and the Federally hired Flannigan's Own. Wanting to do something on its own, the Federal Chamber of Delegates went out and hired Flannigan's Own without checking with their own military on that mercenary unit's record. The battalion that landed two days after the war was the leavings of half the mercenary outfits that Parkes had ever heard of and a number he was glad he hadn't.

The simplest solution—ship the battalion straight home—would have forced a hundred-odd politicians to publicly admit that they were wrong. So Flannigan's Own was still sucking off the Federal Treasury, promising to be fit for the field real soon now, and brawling with the paroled Chosen, who quite justifiably despised it.

Halfway to the hotel, it struck Parkes that Kat had been unusually silent since they left Dietsch's party. "Anything wrong, Katy Kat?"

"Not wrong, no. My new assignment has come through."

"A stinker?"

"Quite the contrary. I'm assigned to a special board reviewing security for planetary satellite-control computers. I think I'm supposed to be the resident generalist, to keep all the mad scientists in or out of uniform on the track. The head's got three stars—Admiral Friesner—and one of the members is the former Deputy Chief of Staff for Liaison."

"That sounds like a plum. It also sounds like you have a problem with it."

Don't ask if it's going to separate us. Assume that it will. Also assume that she won't forget it if you ask.

"I'm still going to be a bloody harumphrodite. Not 'soldier and sailor, too,' but *neither* soldier *nor* sailor. John, even with that commission your life is so damned simple. All you want is a rifle company in combat."

"And a battalion, and—no, I suspect field grade is the limit for me, if I'm lucky. I'd have to take off too much time to catch up on my education for anything above light colonel. I suppose I'll pull the plug at thirty and put my feet up."

"And I'll become the chief concubine of the Rajah of Uparas."

"Right. Actually, what I'd like to do is lead out a pioneering party. We don't need more planets or even more room on the planets we already have. What we do need is getting the idea back into people's heads that you don't have to shoot your neighbor if he misbehaves. One of you can move."

"Solving problems like the Brotherhood that way means pioneering on the grand scale. That probably means getting the governments in on it. Couldn't that be using a cleaver for brain surgery?"

"Cleavers have saved lives, by relieving pressure on the brain. I'm not sure a series of wars like this one wouldn't be about as bad.

"Besides, I'm not going to wait around for the governments to act. Kat—if I headed out at the right time, would you come with me?"

"John, what's the right time, for something like that?"

"I don't know, Kat. It's not now, for either of us. Beyond that—we'll have to sit down and sort it out."

Her embrace drove the breath out of him and he was sure her kiss was going to melt the snow off his coat. Finally she relaxed enough so that he could kiss her on both eyes.

At least we're saying good-bye with no more loose ends dangling than necessary. That's pretty good for any relationship. For a couple of professional soldiers, it's a damned miracle!

The snow grew heavier as they turned the corner.